Meadowlark

Other Lark Dodge Mysteries by Sheila Simonson

Larkspur
Skylark
Mudlark

Historical novels by the same author

Love and Folly
The Bar Sinister
Lady Elizabeth's Comet
A Cousinly Connexion

Meadowlark

SHEILA SIMONSON

St. Martin's Press
New York

A THOMAS DUNNE BOOK.
AN IMPRINT OF ST. MARTIN'S PRESS.

MEADOWLARK. Copyright © 1996 by Sheila Simonson. All rights reserved.
Printed in the United States of America. No part of this book may be used
or reproduced in any manner whatsoever without written permission except
in the case of brief quotations embodied in critical articles or reviews. For
information, address St. Martin's Press, 175 Fifth Avenue, New York, N.Y.
10010.

Design by Nancy Resnick

Library of Congress Cataloging-in-Publication Data

Simonson, Sheila
      Meadowlark / by Sheila Simonson.
          p.   cm.
      "A Thomas Dunne book."
      ISBN 0-312-14013-4
      I. Title.
   PS3569.I48766M4   1996   95-45194
   813'.54—dc20   CIP

First edition: February 1996

10 9 8 7 6 5 4 3 2 1

This novel is dedicated to my son, Eric—who has a degree in sustainable agriculture from the Evergreen State College—with thanks and love.

Prologue ~

Western Meadowlark
(Sturnella neglecta)
Orioles *(Icteridae)*

Description: 8½"–11" (22–28 cm). Robin-sized. *Mottled brown above, bright yellow below, with V-shaped black bib; top of head has black-and-white stripes.* Sexes look alike. Yellow on throat extends farther onto cheek (malar area) than in Eastern Meadowlark; mottled back and tail are lighter brown than Eastern. White tail margins are prominent in flight, and tail flicks open and shut when bird is walking.

Voice: This popular bird has a large repertoire of songs very different from the Eastern Meadowlark. It may utter its loud, melodious flutelike phrases one at a time or repeatedly. The male sings even when migrating or wintering, and at the height of the breeding season may rise in air while singing *hip, hip, hurrah! boys; three cheers!; oh, yes, I am a pretty little bird;* or *U-tah's a pretty place.* Call notes include a harsh *chuck.* Its bright colors, fearless behavior, abundance, and above all its loud, cheerful song make the Western Meadowlark perhaps the most popular of western birds.

. . . Meadowlarks are shaped like starlings. In flight they keep their wings stiff, typically fluttering them a few times and then sailing.

Source: Miklos D.F. Udvardy, *The Audubon Society Field Guide to North American Birds,* Western Region, New York: Knopf, 1987.

1 ☙

I HAD MY new bookstore going before Christmas. That surprised me. I recycled the name, Larkspur Books, from my place in California. I also recycled the capital, almost a windfall, from the advantageous sale of the other store.

It was strange the way the money rolled over. The pleasant couple who bought the old store had sold a home in L.A. just before the bottom dropped out of that real estate market, so they weren't haggling. I recouped my family's original investment with a tidy profit and we moved north. Because my husband, Jay, had also sold his house for very good bucks, I hadn't had to touch "my" money to buy our house in Shoalwater. So there was all that cash sitting in the bank, attracting IRS agents like mako sharks around a dying tuna. In the nick of time, the Robinson Building came up for sale.

The Robinson Building was a narrow, two story Victorian property, brick-fronted and loaded with atmosphere. Wonder of wonders, it had new wiring and plumbing. It sat smack on the main street of Kayport, which was then gentrifying by fits and starts. Because the decline of fishing on the Columbia River had thrown the local business scene into disarray, the price was right. More than right—a steal.

I called my parents. They flew out and fell in love with the *fin de siècle* charm of the old riverport, as I had hoped they would. They were ready to invest. They suggested we buy the building, and lease out the smaller of the two commercial spaces and the two apartments overhead to cover the mortgage payments. That left me a large area for my bookstore, rent free.

The woman who ran the doodad shop in the smaller space wanted to stay and the used furniture business in the larger part had died the year before, so there was nothing to slow me down. Thanks to remodeling experiences with our house in Shoalwater, I knew which carpenters and electricians to call and which not. October is downtime for builders in a beach town. We had the interior fitted and a dedicated line run in for my computer by Thanksgiving—only two thousand dollars over and two weeks later than what the contractor promised. A miracle.

I held a reception in the spruced-up shop on Thanksgiving weekend for Jay's colleagues at the community college. Everyone seemed enthusiastic about having a real bookstore in town. Apart from two used paperback outfits and the college bookstore, which specialized in textbooks and sweatshirts, I had no competition on the Peninsula. I liked that.

My stock began coming in that week. My friend and neighbor, Bonnie Bell, helped me inventory and shelve books. Out of sheer exuberance, I held another reception the next weekend, a tea, with a tantalizing display of books but nothing for sale yet, for grade- and high school teachers and librarians.

Some book dealers think of librarians as the natural enemy. I don't. Apart from being nice people, librarians create a huge appetite for books, especially hardcovers. I've known patrons to develop a passion for a given author at the public library, then move over to collecting hardcover first editions. True, many people use libraries because they can't afford to buy books or don't have the space to shelve them. If they can't afford hardcover prices, killing the libraries isn't going to change that. I like libraries.

So I had a tea for the teachers and librarians, two men and eighteen women, and I was able to announce my grand opening, ten days before Christmas. Just right for desperate last-minute shoppers. Also, my mother was coming. My guests at the tea were mildly interested in that, and the reporter for the Shoalwater *Gazette* even picked up on it as worthy of mention in the Calendar of Coming Events. I didn't care a lot whether the local paper carried the story. I was aiming higher—or, rather, farther.

My mother, Mary Wandworth Daily, is a major minor poet. The Borden Press had just brought out her *Collected Poems,* and Ma decided she would do her first West Coast signing, not in L.A. or San Francisco or Seattle or at Powell's in Portland, but at little old Larkspur Books. Between us, we conveyed this fact to the Seattle, Portland, and Astoria newspapers. Since Ma was set to do a short course at a prestigious Portland liberal arts college in January, the Portland press gave us space. One local TV station even sent out a camera crew and interviewed me standing in front of my spiffy display window. For Ma's signing I pulled out all the stops, even the weather cooperated, and we had quite a large turnout, as signings of poetry collections go.

About halfway through the evening, a chic woman with a cap of gleaming mahogany hair and intense brown eyes came up to me. I was standing with Bonnie trying to decide whether the canapés were going to last the evening. The woman caught Bonnie in midsentence. I gave the stranger an automatic smile.

She waited until Bonnie drew breath, then thrust a square, beringed hand at me. "You're Lark Dodge."

I admitted I was.

"I'm Bianca Fiedler. You know my husband. He teaches at the college."

I drew a blank.

"Keith McDonald."

"Uh, yes. I've met Dr. McDonald." McDonald, then head of the English department, had led the opposition to Jay's police training program. He and my husband were not friends

3

and McDonald had not showed up at the first soirée.

She said, "Keith couldn't make it tonight but I came anyway. I wanted to meet you."

"It's a pleasure."

She was ignoring Bonnie, the intense eyes boring into mine. "I need you. I've set up a writers' workshop for the first week in March and I'd like you to help me run it."

I cleared my throat to utter a polite refusal but she continued, "I believe you plan to close the store for six weeks."

"February first to March fifteenth," I conceded. She must have seen the TV segment. I had told the interviewer I was going to enjoy this store, not enslave myself to it. It would be closed Mondays and Tuesdays, and for six weeks every year, like one of the successful upscale restaurants in Kayport. The Peninsula was touristless by February and didn't revive until the schools let out for spring break.

". . . so you'll be free," she was saying. "And it's a worthy cause."

My feeling about worthy causes is that they are indeed worthy, and can blot up your life, especially in a small town.

"The Environment." She pronounced the word with reverent exactness.

My eyes began to glaze over and I glanced at Bonnie to see if she was going to rescue me. She was staring at Ms. Fiedler, poker-faced. No help there.

"I really don't think—"

"I'm bringing in first-class speakers." She named two nationally known science writers. "And the students are all journalists and magazine writers. We have to educate the public. . . ."

Memory stirred. Some joke about Old McDonald. Didn't McDonald and his wife run an organic farm? "Meadowlark Farm," I said.

"Yes." She gave a brisk nod, like a bird after a juicy bug. "It'll be at the farm. I'm opening a study center. Everything's

4

set up, but I do need a coordinator for the event because that's tilth time, you know."

"Tilth?"

"Soil preparation. I want somebody literate and well-organized. I've been watching you set this operation up and I'm impressed."

"I'm not a writer," I protested. The woman's intense focus was flattering because I was the object. It was also very rude to Bonnie, and I needed to turn my attention to my other guests.

I said, "It sounds interesting, Ms. Fiedler. Why don't you call me at home tomorrow . . . no, Tuesday. My parents leave tomorrow. We can talk it over Tuesday. Have you met my friend, Bonnie Bell? Bonnie's a novelist." An unpublished novelist. "Bonnie, Bianca Fiedler."

Bonnie said hello and Fiedler gave her a brief smile and nod, then homed in on me again. "I'll pay you a thousand for five days of workshop and the opening day—reception, general mingling. I'll do the paperwork. Okay?"

"I'll think about it. Nice to meet you." I went off to rescue my mother from the Poet Laureate of Shoalwater County. Several people, books in hand, were waiting for Ma to sign them. Jay and Tom Lindquist, also our neighbor, were working the crowd under my father's experienced eye. Bonnie headed for the caterers' station in the back room. Fiedler melted into a clump of chattering guests.

That was my first encounter with the owner of Meadowlark Farm.

Later that evening, when Jay had taken my parents home for a drink before bed, Tom and Bonnie and I started the inevitable cleanup.

Bonnie said, "Guess who offered Lark a job?"

Tom was hauling an armload of folding chairs to the back room. "Hillary Clinton?"

She grinned. "Bianca Fiedler."

He shifted the load. "The same job she offered me?" Tom

was a novelist, too. Unlike Bonnie, he was published.

I was stuffing napkins and other food debris into a plastic garbage sack. The caterers had taken their glassware and china and left me with the junk. "She wants me to coordinate a writers' workshop. I take it you turned her down."

"Flat. The book's due the end of March." Tom was finishing his third novel and what with one thing and another was running behind schedule. He chunked the chairs into the back room and returned, dusting off his hands. "Don't tell me you suckered?"

"I told her to call me later. 'Suckered?' "

"It's a tax write-off."

"Oh." A worthy cause indeed.

Bonnie was straightening the poetry shelves. "You know who she is, don't you?"

"Keith McDonald's wife."

Bonnie chortled.

Tom shoved at his forelock, which was inclined to droop. "There are those who say he is Bianca Fiedler's husband."

Bonnie clucked her tongue. "Men are so catty. She's Eli Fiedler's long lost heir, Lark. Don't tell me you missed out on that story. It grabbed Hollywood by the ears, I can tell you." Bonnie was raised in Santa Monica and regarded the film industry as her turf.

I had dim recollections of a tabloid sensation several years back. "Eli's son was into drugs so Fiedler left the bulk of his estate to a daughter living in a commune. . . . Holy cow, the farm?"

Tom said, "She's Maria Canelli's daughter, as well as Fiedler's, so little Bianca wasn't exactly a barefoot flower child."

"She has Canelli's red hair." I didn't know much about Maria Canelli except that she hit the screen around the time Sophia Loren showed up. Unlike Loren, Canelli had disappeared before I got around to watching films.

Eli Fiedler was among the first generation of directors to break away from the studios and set up as an independent producer-director. He was much married. He had also made two of my favorite films, but the bulk of his fortune had come, after a series of flops, from the sale of videotape rights to his creations. He had been shrewd enough to recognize the importance of that market, and he had cashed in not only on the two hits but on the box office flops, too, some of which made pretty good movies on the small screen.

Tom was watching me. "Are you going to do it?"

I said, "If Bonnie would mind the shop I might."

Bonnie restored the last copy of *The Collected Poems of Mary Wandworth Dailey* to the poetry shelf. "You'll be closed."

"Yes, but I'll have stock coming in."

She cocked her blond head to one side, considering. "You're on, but I want a daily bulletin."

That was easy. I had this tendency to tell Bonnie everything anyway.

"What about *your* novel?" Tom's tone was stern. He and Bonnie may or may not have become one another's all at that point but he was definitely mentoring her career.

She said airily, "No problem. It's coming in huge hunks. I'll be done with the first draft by then."

He looked skeptical but raised no further objections.

I wasn't sure I was going to take the job on and told them so.

Tuesday Bianca Fiedler showed up on my doorstep in Shoalwater at ten in the morning. The store was closed. There I was in sweats with my fences down.

She peered up at me intently from the intense brown eyes. "Have you thought it over? I brought a brochure."

"Good heavens, come in." I led her through the hall past our redecorated living room and unregenerate dining room to the kitchen, all cream and yellow tile, and offered her a cup of coffee.

When she ascertained that it was freshly ground she accepted. She sat in my nook and looked around her. "I like this

7

house. It reminds me of the place Keith and I rented in Eugene while he was doing his doctorate."

I sat and stirred creamer into my cup. "He's a folklorist, isn't he?"

"Folktales and ballads." She seemed oblivious to my lack of enthusiasm for her husband, perhaps because she sounded less than enthusiastic herself.

"I understand he's also a guitarist."

Bianca snorted. "Not really. Keith has a great voice for ballads and back then a good folksinger could get by with four chords and a Dobro. Times have changed but Keith hasn't—much. He does strum away at the twelve-string now, but it's the same old song." Her mouth gave a wry twist.

I hoped I was not going to be treated to a husband-bashing. I didn't know her well enough for that.

After a long sip, she shrugged and took another tack. "My mother decided to underwrite her grandchildren when Fiona was born. Keith and I moved out of the commune and into the Eugene house. He went to work on the doctorate and I took business classes between gestations."

I raised an eyebrow, indicating, I hoped, polite interest.

She gave a sudden, thoroughly disarming smile. "We'd bought the whole hippy scene, you know—somewhat after the fact. It was the seventies by then. I got interested in organic farming on the commune. College was just an interruption. I was raised in a hotel."

Both my eyebrows went up.

The smile softened. "My stepfather owned and managed the Bon Chance in San Francisco."

The Bon Chance was a small, exceedingly expensive San Francisco hotel, very classy then and now. I nodded and got up to freshen her coffee.

She held out her cup. "I was a city kid, but I loved plants— flowers and potted trees and fresh veggies. Papa—that's what I always called my stepfather—virtually invented California cuisine when he called in Carlo Forte to run the hotel restaurant. That was exciting to watch, and I heard all about the problems Carlo had getting good produce. He used to take me with him when he dealt with the market gardeners. I was supposed to be his daughter." She sighed. "Poor dear Carlo. He died of AIDS seven years ago, one of the first. He was a sweet man. Between Carlo and Papa I never missed my father. So it was a shock when Eli Fiedler left me all that money."

I said, "You hadn't had any contact?"

Bianca shrugged again. "Not much. He made a settlement when he divorced Mama, of course, and he sent checks on my birthday, but I'd seen him maybe half a dozen times before he died. He never met my kids."

That was sad. I was still trying to have a child. My gynecologist said women athletes sometimes have problems conceiving, but I'd given up basketball five years before, so I wasn't sure I bought the diagnosis. "How many children do you have?"

"Three." Bianca made a rueful face. " 'Children.' Fee is twenty-two—that's Fiona, our first. The twins are twenty and coming home from Pepperdine next week. So they're not exactly babies. I was twenty when Fee was born and too damned young to be a mother. Anyway, five years ago my father left me most of his money. It's a hairy responsibility."

Possibly she saw my skepticism, for she added, "Mind you, I'm not griping. Mama had been helping us buy Meadowlark Farm, and I'd already got the Organic rating for our meat and produce. I'm proud of that. When I inherited my father's estate, though, I could think about using the farm as an educational center for People who Care about the Earth."

Anyone who speaks in capitals makes me uneasy. Bianca Fiedler was making me uneasy, partly because I'd begun to like her. "You've built a convention center?"

She dimpled. "Not exactly. It's more like a small hotel. Papa's influence. He's retired now but he helped with the design. We have room for twelve to fifteen students in residence plus adjunct classes through the college. Maybe your husband told you about them."

He hadn't. It was finals week and I'd barely had a chance to explain Bianca's offer. Jay had driven my parents to the airport in Portland the day before and got home late.

Bianca looked a little disappointed when I shook my head no. "Shoalwater Community College didn't even have an ag program, would you believe it? This is one of the most rural counties in the state. So I underwrote a certificate in sustainable agriculture and set up six internships at the farm. The graduates can transfer to WSU or the Evergreen State College for their bachelor's degrees. The program's working pretty well. Three of our former interns have already entered graduate school, so I thought it was time to set up a series of workshops. This one's the first, and I didn't realize the work it would entail. I do need help, Lark."

What could I say? I read her brochure. It sounded as if she knew what writers would want. The first expert would give a talk followed by open discussion, writing sessions, and another solid day of workshopping the results. The second would deal with a different topic and follow the same pattern. Part of the early morning was to be devoted to a short excursion—to Shoalwater Bay, up the Coho River, over to the port. Evening would be social, though it was clear Bianca intended to propagandize a bit. The two speakers had already sent her extensive bibliographies.

She said her staff could handle meals and housekeeping. She was doing all the registration and speaker arrangements. She wanted me on the spot to see that everything went smoothly because she intended to be out with her tractor spreading lime and compost. It was that time of year. Also, the sheep would probably start lambing—they tended to do that whenever you scheduled something important in springtime, she said. I took her word for it.

The setup seemed workable. The fee for six days' labor

wasn't splendid, but neither were my credentials.

I said, "It's a shame you couldn't get Tom Lindquist."

She had the grace to blush but she made a quick recovery. "Was he at the signing? I've never met him in person."

"Yes."

"He sounds like an interesting man and I love his books, but I think you may be able to deal with the organizational side of things better than he could."

"Tom's an old hand at workshops."

She smiled. "Like your mother?"

"Ma invented workshops. I don't think it's hereditary, though."

Bianca laughed. Then she pleaded some more and I waffled. I had meant to strip the floor in my dining room and redo the room, floor to ceiling, during my vacation. The truth was, though, that my six weeks off didn't coincide with any of Jay's academic holidays, and the joys of remodeling are overrated. In the end I caved in and agreed to run Bianca Fiedler's workshop.

That evening I confessed what I'd done over dinner.

"Sucker." Jay lifted a forkful of canneloni and chewed with evident pleasure. I was learning to cook.

"Tom's exact word."

"Tom is a shaman."

I toyed with my pasta. "If you have serious objections, Jay, I'll call Bianca and tell her no. It's not too late."

He set his fork on the plate. "Do you want to do this?"

I cut a bite of canneloni. Stuffed with spinach and ricotta, it was. "I don't know. It sounds interesting. She's invited Eric Spielman and Francis Hrubek." I shot him a glance. He was frowning, but the frown was thoughtful. "I'll make them autograph all their books for the store."

"Shrewd move." The scowl lightened. "Is the workshop a tax scam? The classes and internships are kosher. I asked the Dean." That was quick. I'd told him Tom's reaction Sunday evening.

"Bianca may get a write-off, probably does, but she's genuinely interested in educating farmers and writers."

He sighed and took a sip of wine. "Okay, but watch out for Keith McDonald. He stepped down as department head because of student complaints."

"Sexual harassment?"

"I don't think he's ever done anything that would provoke a successful harassment suit, but he's pushing the limits. Secretaries avoid him and the women in the English department are pretty frank. They don't like him."

Somehow I wasn't surprised and I began to understand Bianca's lack of enthusiasm for the father of her three children.

Jay polished off his canneloni. "Maybe I'm just jealous."

"I trust not," I said austerely.

The next day Bianca called me at the store. I had a customer so I put her on hold while I showed the women where my children's books were.

When I came back on the line Bianca thanked me again for agreeing to supervise the workshop, then said, "Are those apartments above your store vacant?"

"One is." A longtime tenant occupied the other. The old gentleman, a widower, had been mayor of Kayport for many years. He said he like living in the center of his town. I liked him. So he stayed.

"One of my managers, Hugo Groth, is looking for a place starting January first." She cleared her throat. "Hugo's a little odd. He rides a bicycle and dresses like a case for the Salvation Army, but he's solvent, believe me, and quiet. Lives alone." She hesitated again. "He's one of our old friends from the commune. I like him." Be kind, she was saying.

What was I letting myself in for? I told her to send him in around closing time and I'd take him up to look at the apartment.

"What was his name again?" I got out a pen.

"Hugo Groth. He's a master gardener. Grows all my field veggies."

I sighed. "Okay. Look, I have to go." The customer was moving purposefully toward me with three very expensive picture books in hand.

"Thanks, Lark." Bianca hung up.

Hugo Groth. I stared at the name for a moment. Then I complimented my customer on her choices and rang up the sale.

2 ⤳

HUGO GROTH WAS a small man. I didn't expect that. I was closing when I saw him ride up through a zesty December rain on his sturdy mountain bike. I watched him lock the bike to a parking meter. My last customer had left at six-thirty—so much for the Christmas rush—and it was five of eight. The wind drove the rain through the dark in gray curtains. Spooky.

Groth peered in the window, checked his watch, and huddled under the overhang. I set the book I was shelving in place and strode to the door. "Mr. Groth?"

He looked up at me like Jack at the giant. I am six feet tall and he was probably five-five. "Yes?"

"I'm Lark Dodge. Please come in."

"I'll drip on your carpet." He had a deep voice for a small man, deep and calm.

"It's been dripped on all day." I backed away from the open door so he could enter. "Come in."

He stood in the doorway a moment, blinking at me and letting his eyes adjust to the light. When he removed the hood of his rain jacket I saw that his hair was receding and pulled back in a stringy ponytail. I thought he was in his mid-forties.

His eyes were light gray and rather beautiful, wide-set and thickly lashed, but he suffered from an active case of what looked like cystic acne. The boils distorted otherwise regular features. His mouth was thin, his nose indeterminate. He was short, skinny, and ugly.

The silence got to me. "Ms. Fiedler said you were interested in renting my apartment. Why don't you come into the back room and take off your rain gear? Would you like a cup of hot coffee? You must be cold."

"I don't drink coffee." His voice was deep and calm, unchallenging.

My irritation eased. "Herb tea?"

He nodded.

I gave up the effort at conversation, set the CLOSED sign out, and led him to the back room. I fixed him a mug of Celestial Seasonings Sleepytime while he got out of the rain suit. It was Goretex, not exactly Salvation Army fabric, but he was wearing faded jeans, a ratty plaid shirt, also faded, and a boring gray sweatshirt beneath the jacket. His sneakers looked third-hand. They were wet.

He hung the rain gear on my coatrack and accepted the mug with a nod, warming his hands before he sipped. The hands looked hard-used, as if he didn't bother with gloves much.

He looked around my office and the piles of boxed books, taking everything in.

Nervous, I made a final entry on my computer and used the mouse to back out of the system. The screen blanked.

"I like books."

The comment was so unexpected I jumped. "I have to check the display room and turn the lights off. Would you like to see the store?"

He nodded.

I gave him a tour. His silence made me want to babble. I told myself I didn't have to and kept my remarks brief.

He lingered over the small gardening section but what seemed to interest him most was the reading nook I'd made out of the side window that overlooked the garbage cans.

Like all the windows in the Robinson building, the side

window had a wide sill, wide enough to sit on. I'd blanked the panes with rice paper and put a pad on the narrow ledge. A small person—I had children in mind—could curl up there and read. There was a larger sitting area with easy chairs and a rug by a Franklin stove, but he just gave that a glance. The window seat seemed to fascinate him. He stood by it a good minute and even touched the pad.

At last I dimmed the lights and led him to the back, grabbing my keys.

"You don't have much on gardening." His tone wasn't accusatory. He was making an observation.

I bit back a defensive reply. "I don't know enough to know what to order." I unlocked the interior door that led to the hallway. The original shopkeeper must have lived over the shop. "Why don't you give me a list of titles? I'll order them."

"All right."

My other tenant was watching TV. I could hear the sound in the hall, but when I switched the light on in the apartment and closed the door behind us the noise went away. There was no street noise either. The building was *solid*.

I decided to let him look without a tour guide. The place had high ceilings and big rooms, and the carpets and fixtures were plain but new. I'd had my crew repaint the walls. The apartment reminded me of the flat I'd had over the Calfirst Bank when I first moved west.

I stood by the windows that overlooked Main Street and watched the wind and rain whip at the city's gaudy Christmas decorations. There wasn't much traffic at that hour. I could see straight down the street to the boat harbor. Lights danced in the rain and the wind rattled the windowpanes.

I couldn't hear Groth. He moved quietly but lights in the other rooms flashed on and off. The refrigerator door closed. Eventually he came to stand beside me. We looked at the street.

He touched the wide sill of one of the three sash windows. "I could sit here."

16

"Yes."

"And see the river."

"Yes. In daylight. Except when it's foggy." I told him the rent and the rules. "Do you smoke?"

"Sometimes I smoke dope, but outdoors."

I looked at him. He didn't smile and his tone was calm and unapologetic. Good thing Jay isn't here, I thought. Jay was inclined to the letter of the law. "Well, er, I asked because I'd prefer not to rent to a smoker. Mr. Williams next door smokes, but he's lived here for years and he's pushing eighty, so I didn't feel right asking him not to. Cigarette smoke clings to the paint and drapes." I was babbling. I drew a breath. "Do you want to rent it, Mr. Groth?"

"You should call me Hugo." He peered through the blown rain at a passing car. "Yes. I like it. Can I move in on the twentieth?"

"Of December?"

He nodded. "I live at the farm. It gets crowded during the holidays."

"Uh, I don't see why you can't." I was feeling pressured again. Shouldn't I check him out or something? Maybe he had lousy credit or a long string of pot busts. I thought back to my conversation with Bianca. She liked him. But did I like Bianca?

He pulled a checkbook from the breast pocket of his shirt. "Got a pen?"

"Downstairs."

We traipsed down and I showed him the street entrance. "I don't have the keys here tonight. I'll bring them tomorrow and you can pick them up here when you're ready to move in."

"Okay."

He wrote out his check for first and last month's rent plus damage deposit, shook my hand, and wriggled into his damp rain gear. I watched him unlock his bike and head off into the storm. Did he have to ride all the way back to Meadowlark

17

Farm? I thought about racing out and offering him a ride home, but he was already out of sight.

I went back for my handbag and coat, locked up, and drove home, feeling edgy. At no point during the brief meeting had Hugo Groth smiled, or said please or thank you. He hadn't praised the store layout or the apartment or explained himself. Bianca had said he was odd. He was very odd. I hoped I hadn't rented the apartment to a serial killer.

I went about the business of selling books and getting ready for Christmas. When my brother-in-law came home from Portland, I put him to work in the store and got some of my own shopping done. Christmas, complete with long-distance phone calls to Jay's mother and my parents, came and went. Some time in all that, Hugo Groth moved in above the store, but he was so quiet I half-forgot him.

One night around closing time he came into the store. I was trying to hustle three impatient customers through the ringing up process, so I gave him a smile and went on verifying credit cards.

He disappeared into the shelves. When I could set the CLOSED sign up at last, I remembered him and walked to the gardening shelf. He wasn't there, but I caught a glimpse of movement on the other side of the store. He was sitting in the window seat reading a paperback.

"Hello, Hugo."

He looked up, blinking as if I had startled him.

"Do you want me to ring that up? I'm closing."

"Oh. No, it's just Wendell Berry. I have this one." He stood up and shut the book. "I brought the list."

List? My turn to blink.

He looked mildly disappointed. "The list of horticulture books you wanted." He handed me a sheaf of neatly stapled papers.

I glanced through it. A printout ten pages long, with full information on the titles including ISBN numbers and publishers. "That's very thoughtful." Also impossible. I had shelf room for perhaps ten more books in that section.

He stood up. "Those are the best. I coded them. The starred ones would be good for beginners and amateurs. You don't want too many in a store this size."

At least he was tracking. I saw only a few asterisks. I relaxed a little and I hope my voice warmed. "Thanks. I'll do an order tomorrow."

He strolled to the personal essay shelf and put Berry in his place.

"Is the apartment working out for you?"

"Yes. I've been taking my bike upstairs and leaving it at the landing. Mr. Williams said he didn't mind."

"Good." I hoped the bicycle wasn't a hazard, but the landing at the top of the stairs was large and well-lit.

"Can I leave through your side door?"

"Sure. I'll get the key."

He followed me as I tidied things and dimmed the lights. I set the list of books on my desk. "Have you read all these?"

"Except for the last six. Those I got off the Internet forum. They sounded good."

I flipped to the last page. Small presses, two university presses. I got my keys and purse, and took my coat from the rack. "Well, thanks again. The list will be a useful reference. Customers are always asking for recommendations."

He ducked out with a flip of his hand and I locked up and went home. I ordered the five books he had starred by regular mail and had two of the ones he hadn't read sent by Federal Express. When they arrived I left him a note.

He came down around seven looking freshly scrubbed. The acne glowed purple-red.

For once I wasn't in the throes of a sale, though another customer was browsing, so I greeted Hugo and pulled the two books, one a cheap paperback, almost a pamphlet, and the other a beautiful hardcover dealing with the horticultural philosophy of a famous Zen master. The photography in that one was dazzling but it was pretty expensive.

I handed them to him. "Here. I know you didn't order the books, so don't feel you have to buy them."

He had the dazed look of a child with a birthday surprise. He took the books off to the window seat without a word.

The other customer bought a Stephen King and left. I pottered around, dusting, dealt with another customer who came in to pick up a cookbook, and began to think about closing up. It was almost New Year's and dark. I was thinking of closing earlier in January. I drifted, tidying books, wondering what Jay had in mind for dinner. It was his turn to cook.

"Lark?" Hugo stood by the cash register holding the two books.

I came over. It was the first time he'd said my name.

"I want both of them."

"Great." I started to ring up.

"Check okay?"

I smiled. "Yours are."

He nodded, serious, and wrote out a check. "How'd you get them so soon?"

"Federal Express."

His pen hovered. "That's expensive. Shouldn't I pay for shipping?"

I said, "I owe you. Your list is going to be very useful this spring."

"Okay." He flushed. "Do you mind if I drop in once in a while? I don't want to be a nuisance but I like to browse."

My heart sank but I said, "Feel free, Hugo, and if I can get you anything else let me know. I guessed on those two." I told him about the starred books I'd ordered and he seemed interested. Finally he left via the front door.

I was half afraid he would haunt me, hanging out every night, because he was clearly a solitary man, but it was a week before he came in again. And he did browse, taking his finds to the window seat for a good long look. He bought a paperback and ordered another of the books from his list. When he came in a couple of days later and just browsed and left, I decided he

20

wasn't going to be a pest. I half wished he'd talk a little. It was January by then, the weather was wet and turbulent, and business was slow. I could have used a little companionship. However, Hugo was not a talker. He never smiled and he never thanked me, but he was slowly becoming a presence in my life.

Still, I didn't get to know him. We weren't friends. The relationship was like an object in a Zen painting—defined by the blankness around it.

Bianca Fiedler invited Jay and me to dinner at the farm for the first Sunday of February. She and I had had phone conversations in the interim, and she had sent me more information on her workshop. Now she wanted me to see the facilities firsthand.

Larkspur Books was closed by then. We drove out to the farm around five-thirty. After a warmish week in which crocuses bloomed and daffodils sprang, the weather had turned nasty. It was sleeting.

When Jay drives in the rain, he switches the windshield wipers off and on. He has some theory that he's saving wear and tear on the little engine that runs them. In my opinion, a wreck would cost a lot more than replacing the wiper engine, but some folks don't listen to reason. I gritted my teeth whenever my window went blank with accumulated sleet.

Meadowlark Farm lay on the east side of Shoalwater Bay, about half an hour out of Kayport, so it was a good hour's drive for us from Shoalwater. By the time we reached the open gate, my jaw muscles were cramping.

Partly to ease them, I said, "You don't like Keith McDonald but you're going to keep the peace, right?"

The windshield went blank. Jay turned the wipers on and swerved, skidding a little, to avoid a fallen branch. "I promise I'll keep my satires to myself, even when Keith sings 'Sir Patrick Spens' in fake Scots."

"Lord, will he do that?"

"He has been known to do worse." The wipers stilled

21

again. Sleet thudded on the windshield. "So watch his hands. When he starts comparing you to a long-stemmed American rose . . ."

"He's more likely to compare me to a crane." Jay is subject to the husbandly delusion that all men find his wife irresistible. Flattering but unrealistic.

"You're hypersensitive." Jay turned the blades on again. Lo, there were lights. We slid across a cattle guard and sloshed up a hill to the house. It was indeed large. I could form no other judgment about it because of the darkness and sleet.

As we scuttled for the front entry, the door opened.

Bianca hurried us inside. "Leave the car there. Nobody else is going to drive in tonight. God, what weather. Makes me homesick for California." She took our coats.

"Me, too," Jay said. "Malibu at sunset, to be exact."

Bianca made the rude noise San Franciscans emit when anyone confesses an attachment to the L.A. area, but this time her rudeness was friendly. She was an odd woman and I'd half-expected her to ignore Jay the way she'd ignored Bonnie.

I introduced them, in case she hadn't focused on him at the signing, and she murmured pleasantries. She was wearing a pink, orange, and purple print tunic over orange stirrups and gold flats. Bright. I was glad I hadn't decided on jeans and an anorak.

She led us down a modern oak-trimmed hall that was covered with elegant but practical Berber carpet. Good watercolors of local flora had been hung to advantage. An arch led to carpeted steps and a sunken living room with a cathedral ceiling. The room was big enough to hold a small convention, so the workshop would be no problem. It was furnished in good modern pieces, in native woods and earth-tone fabrics, with a huge stone fireplace dominating one wall. Bianca plunked us down by the fire and went to a portable bar. I was still taking in the room. The far wall consisted of a rank of what looked like custom-built French doors. Clearly they were intended to give a view of something. At that moment the view was of driven sleet.

She served us our wine and perched on a persimmon hassock that faced the couch we sat on, beaming at us. "The others will be showing up soon. Del and Angie are just getting off work, and Michael's with his dad. Keith's in the shower, and Marianne's in the kitchen, of course."

The only name that rang a bell was Keith. Jay looked blank but polite. I sipped the wine, a chardonnay. Sleet rattled the wall of glass. It was hot buttered rum weather. I shivered, though the room, despite its acreage, was warm. "Do they all live here?"

"Yes. So did Hugo, before he took your apartment." That seemed to rankle, for her face darkened. She gave herself a small shake and gestured with her left hand. "That wing is the kids' rooms when they're here, plus guest rooms downstairs. The Wallaces live upstairs—Del, Marianne, and their son, Michael. Del oversees the livestock and pasturage. Marianne is my cook-slash-housekeeper." She waved the other way. "That door leads to the kitchen and two small apartments. Angie, my greenhouse manager, lives in one, and Hugo used to live in the other. The master suite and Keith's library are upstairs. Would you like to see where I'm putting the workshop?"

"Good idea," I said. I thought that was the reason for the invitation. Something was strange.

"Do finish your wine first. Those little crackers are homemade. Marianne's a great cook."

We nibbled and sipped while Bianca rattled on about the workshop. The walls were hung with oils on a scale to suit the room, tasteful and interesting but slightly intimidating. A sound system played something soft and baroque. The lighting was skillful—it broke the huge space into conversation areas. All in all, a qualified triumph of modern architecture. Given Bianca's personality I hadn't expected *Country Living*

23

kitsch. The room felt more hotel than farmhouse, though.

When we finished our wine, Bianca rose and led us through an arch on the far side of the fireplace. There the floors were ceramic tile in warm shades and the scale more human.

"We have six bedrooms off here," she said. "When the kids are home that leaves only three for guests, but the offspring won't be here when the workshop's on." She opened the first door on a large bedroom with twin beds and a wall with a built-in dressing table and closet. The room had Mediterranean colors and bits of what looked like Etruscan artifacts scattered around. A handsome painting of an Italian hill town, impressionistic rather than representational, hung on the wall opposite the dressing table. A chair and reading lamp sat beneath it.

"Fee's in Italy with her grandmother." Bianca turned to Jay. "Our daughter, Fiona. She's trying to make up her mind whether to be an archeologist or an art historian. She graduated from Mills last year." Bianca sounded indulgent but scornful, as if her daughter should have a clear goal in mind at twenty-two.

Bianca opened a door. "The baths are shared, or can be, between rooms. The boys' rooms across the hall share a bath. This one is Fee's but that"—she indicated a door—"can be unlocked. Papa suggested the arrangement. I don't like the modern fad for bathrooms every ten feet."

The bathroom was a bathroom. Well-engineered and tasteful but otherwise unremarkable, rather like what you'd expect in a good hotel.

Bianca opened the locked door and showed us the bedroom on the far side. It was pleasant, but more impersonal than her daughter's room. We followed Bianca down the hall. At the end she opened a door on a large room, rather chilly, that was furnished with a conference table and the usual amenities. It had a carpet for acoustic baffling and a service area for beverages. I could see it as a classroom. In fact, though the fixtures and furnishings were new, it had a used look. A spiral stair in one corner led up to the second story.

"I like this." She gave us a conspiratorial grin as she led us up. At the top, she said, "Oh, sorry, Mike. I thought you were out with your dad."

"He sent me in." The voice was sullen.

I poked my head up into what looked at first glance like an office. The speaker, a kid of eighteen or so, stared at me. He had sandy hair and glasses and wore a Shoalwater Community College sweatshirt over jeans.

I said, "Hi."

The kid mumbled a greeting but when he spotted Jay his face brightened. "Professor Dodge!"

Jay hauled himself up the last steps. "Hi, Mike. I haven't seen you around this quarter."

The kid gave a shamefaced grin. "I'm hitting the books for a change."

"About time," Jay said mildly. "This is my wife. Lark, Mike Wallace. He took the evidence class fall quarter."

Mike extended his hand and we shook. "I flunked it, too." He seemed to hold no grudge.

"Everybody's entitled to one goof-up," Jay murmured. "At least you figured out what was wrong."

Bianca was smiling in an unfocused way as if she wanted to get on with the tour.

I strolled to the window in the gable end. As in the conference room below, it had a state-of-the-art French door with an arc of glass above it. "Must be a great view." I could see nothing but wind-driven sleet and a small wet deck.

"Looks out at Bald Mountain. Not a mountain really, a big hill. We called it Bald Mountain because it was being clear-cut when we moved in twelve years ago. It looks less scabrous now but the scenery's better from the living room—the Coho River estuary."

I murmured approval.

25

"What do you think of our information center?"

I looked around. Four color monitors, computers with modems, and a big laser-jet printer dominated a well-arranged space. I spotted a fax machine, another smaller printer, and assorted gadgets. "Wow."

That was apparently the right response. One of the monitors showed a computer game, the kind where something zaps something, and the rest were blank. Mike doing homework? He and Jay were standing by that computer talking school.

Bianca said, "Our interns use both rooms. The workshop participants can write here or at least edit and print."

"And go back and forth to the classroom. I see." I was wondering if Hugo had accessed his electronic forum from this room.

She opened a cabinet. "I got laptops, too, in case they want to work in their rooms." Four sleek new laptops occupied slim shelves in the cabinet.

"I imagine some of the participants will bring their own laptops."

"If they don't they can take turns." She pulled a drawer. It was full of yellow legal tablets and number two pencils. "Or do it the old-fashioned way."

"What about reference books?"

She activated the nearest computer and loaded a Windows program. "Each of these has the usual dictionary and thesaurus plus Internet access." The screen showed many other options. She clicked the mouse and the monitor went blank. "That wall of shelves next to the wet-bar in the conference room . . ."

"The one with the louvered doors?"

"Yes. That's the periodical collection." She gestured toward one corner of the "office" where similar doors formed a reading nook with chairs and lamps near the French doors. "That's our library."

"May I see it?"

"Sure." She opened the fan-fold doors and disclosed floor-to-ceiling bookshelves. They were almost full. As far as I could see, all the titles dealt with ecology or agriculture.

I said, "That's impressive."

"It's Hugo's collection as well as mine." A cloud darkened the intense eyes. "Hugo wouldn't come to dinner. He's phobic about strangers, you know."

"I guessed."

"And he doesn't like large groups either."

"Is that why he moved to the apartment?"

She nodded. "I guess so. Too many people here. I was trying to recreate the commune."

"Commune? Oh, the one you joined in the seventies."

"Keith and I both joined the year we got out of high school. That's where we met each other—and where we met Hugo."

"Oh." I had never known anyone else who had actually lived in a commune.

Bianca was still brooding about Hugo. "I thought he'd like the new house, but it just made him edgy." She sighed.

I pointed to the door opposite the French doors. "Where does that lead?"

"The Wallaces' apartment."

"Handy for Mike."

"I had him and my kids in mind, as well as the education center, when I planned it."

I said, "I guess you won't suffer from empty nest syndrome when your kids leave home for good."

She laughed. "Papa says it's a hotel. Feels like home to me." The smile faded. "But I wish Hugo hadn't moved out."

Michael Wallace was showing Jay something on the monitor, other than the game. They laughed.

Bianca checked her watch. "Oops, time to go." She made for the stair. "Dinner at seven, Mike."

"Yeah. Mom says I have to help serve it."

Bianca was out of sight. I followed, with Jay just behind me, down the spiral stair. As we left the conference room downstairs, Bianca showed us a discreet restroom on one side of the hall and a kitchenette on the other. She'd thought of everything.

3 ❧

WE ZIPPED BACK down the hall. The ceramic tiles echoed a little. When we reached the living room, two men and a woman were waiting for us, munching crackers and sipping the chardonnay.

All three looked up as we rounded the corner near the fireplace. A handsome bearded man in a periwinkle pullover and jeans sat on the raised edge of the hearth strumming a guitar. I recognized Keith McDonald. The guitar helped. He stood up, laying his instrument on the flagstone surface. His eyes were the same blue as the sweater.

Bianca said, "Lark, I believe you've met my husband."

"Once, at the Dean's house." I extended my hand and McDonald shook it, letting his grasp linger. His eyes were remarkably blue.

"Hello again, Lark. 'Bird thou never wert.'"

I extracted my hand. "I believe you're thinking of nightingales, Professor McDonald."

"Keith, please." His smile widened and the eyes sparkled. "Nope—it's Shelley's ode. Welcome to Meadowlark Farm, Skylark." He turned to Jay. "Dodge."

"McDonald," Jay said. He didn't offer to shake hands but his tone was mild, all things considered.

Bianca said, "And these are my managers. They've been out in the sleet saving my bacon."

"Bacon?" The woman grimaced and extended her hand to me. "Please, Bianca, I'm a vegetarian."

"Angie Martini," Bianca murmured, smiling.

Martini shook hands with Jay, too, and went back to her wine. She was an angular, attractive woman, almost as tall as I. She looked sleek, as if she'd just stepped out of a shower into the flame-colored silk jumpsuit. Her blond hair was cut close to the skull and she wore dangly silver earrings with a petroglyph motif.

"And Del Wallace," Bianca said.

Wallace was a beefy, balding edition of his son. "Pleased to meet you," he said with no apparent interest, and shook our hands. He was drinking something in a squat highball glass. He went back to his armchair and took a hefty swig.

"More wine?" Bianca flitted to the drinks cart.

Jay passed but I said yes. It was good chardonnay.

McDonald had picked up the guitar again. He played a little riff. We made safe comments on the weather, and I said I was impressed by the study center facilities. Jay said something nice to Wallace about young Mike.

Wallace gave him a brief glance over the whiskey. "You're the one got him to change his major."

"Yes," Jay said, still pleasant. "Flunked him, too. We talked. He doesn't want to be a cop."

Wallace snorted.

Keith McDonald strummed a chord. "I thought you were recruiting police officers."

"Only willing ones." Jay tempered his tone. "Mike needs to explore the alternatives."

I hoped the two men were not going to duke it out over Mike Wallace. "Is Hugo Groth a manager, too? This must be a big operation." If Bianca could call my bookstore an operation I didn't see why I should hesitate to call her farm one.

"It's getting bigger," Angie Martini said. "Hugo's too much of a purist, though."

"He's a prick," Del Wallace muttered.

Bianca sighed. "He may be a purist and he may even be a prick, but he's an outstanding market gardener. To answer you, Lark, yes, Hugo manages the raised-bed, intensive cultivation we've been experimenting with since we first came here. More important, he raises our field vegetables. They're very profitable."

"He's a fanatic, Bianca." Angie looked flushed, or perhaps it was just the reflection of all that flame-colored silk.

Keith did a few bars of "Amazing Grace" and struck a sour note. "The interns hate his guts."

Wallace growled, "He gave Jason Thirkell a D, by God. My best worker. Kid understands sheep."

Although McDonald said nothing his eyes shone. Clearly he enjoyed discord, though Bianca was right—he stuck to three basic chords and a seventh.

By then Bianca was flushed. "Jason wouldn't follow Hugo's procedures, Del. A D was generous."

"By God, I work with Groth's damned greenies. I'm generous as hell with them. I finally get a kid in the program who understands real farming, a kid who works his butt off, and that spaced-out freak gives him a D. All I can say is Groth had better take care of his favorites from now on. Miss Sadsack Sadat, for instance. She doesn't pull her weight on the tractor. We'll see how he likes it when I flunk the little bitch."

Angie Martini jumped up. "Mary Sadat is not a bitch, Del. If you can't deal with women students . . ."

"*You* will, eh?" Del Wallace finished his whiskey and leered up at her. "Sadat's a cute little piece, all right."

Angie said through her teeth, "I make it a practice not to hit on my students, nor do I call them sexist names, not even the men." She shot us a half-defiant glance. "I'm gay. At least Hugo can deal with that without coming unglued. Del takes exception to any woman who doesn't . . ."

"Come on, you guys," Bianca interrupted. "Cool it. I want Lark and Jay to like the farm, remember? And I think Marianne's ready for us in the dining room."

31

A dark-haired, rather heavy woman was standing near the arch that led to the entry hall.

Bianca called the tune, or perhaps everyone was just hungry. The men stood up. Angie was still pink with indignation. She led the way out. Bianca and Jay and I followed the two men, I carrying my half-full wine glass.

At the arch, Bianca stopped to introduce us to Marianne Wallace. Del's wife, Mike's mother, the cook/housekeeper. Marianne gave us a small polite smile but said little.

Oddly enough, the dining room was the coziest room I'd seen so far in the house. The table was the right size, and the colors looked like honey and spice. Bianca seated us conventionally. I had thought she'd put me on her right, the better to talk shop, and Jay on Keith McDonald's right, but there I was, sitting next to the incendiary guitarist, he of the effulgent blue gaze. Across the table, Del Wallace gave me a morose leer and poured himself a slug of wine from a carafe in front of him.

Jay, Angie, and Bianca were chatting up a storm at the other end of the table with the two central places vacant. That gap explained itself as Mike entered bearing a tray of steaming soup bowls, followed closely by his mother carrying baskets of bread. They served us rapidly, then Marianne joined us. Mike took the empty tray off and returned to the spot on my right. I gave him a smile he was too shy or sullen to return.

When all the bread and butter and wine passing were over, I took a sip of soup. It was a light oyster stew, almost a contradiction in terms, but full of tiny succulent Shoalwater oysters. Luscious. Learning to cook was teaching me to appreciate other people's cooking—or not, in some cases. Marianne Wallace was not a cook, I decided as I sampled the bread. She was a chef. The wholemeal bread, faintly Tuscan, smelled of rosemary.

Someone was groping my knee. McDonald—not a difficult deduction. To all intents, he was listening to Del Wallace grouse about something agricultural, but the hand groped, warm through the crinkled fabric of my skirt. I edged my chair to the right.

Mike said something.

"I beg your pardon?"

"Please pass the jam."

I obliged and took a sip of wine. The groping hand made contact again. At the other end of the table Jay was chewing oblivious bread and looking happy. He bent to hear something Marianne said. I didn't catch his eye.

Wallace took a gulp of wine and began slathering a piece of bread with butter.

McDonald's hand was moving up my thigh.

I said, "Professor McDonald . . ."

"Keith."

"Keith, then, I'd like to share my thoughts with you."

The blue eyes beamed.

I kept my voice low. "I have a nice salad fork here which I am about to stab into my left thigh. The odds are good the tines will intersect the hand you finger things with." I picked up the fork in my left hand.

Face impassive, he withdrew his hand. Del Wallace gave a small snort and caught my eye. He winked.

I gritted my teeth and turned to Mike. "So. Michael. Taking any interesting classes this term?"

Mike's mouth was full. He chewed and thought. "Yeah. Anthropology. I like it but it's hard."

"Cultural or physical?"

McDonald and Wallace were talking. Wallace kept watching me.

"Physical," Mike said. "You know, like skulls and stuff. Mrs. Horton, she's the teacher, brought in a real skull last week."

"Fun for you," I murmured.

"Well, it was. Prof . . . I mean, your husband says forensic anthropologists are real important in crime investigation these days." Clearly he thought Jay was terrific. I could deal with that.

Marianne said something and Mike shoved his chair back. "Gotta go." Mother and son went off. I sipped wine and wished the meal was over.

"You read poetry," McDonald said, supercilious now that he couldn't play his little game. "I suppose you were an English major."

"I had a double major in English and P.E."

"P.E.?"

"I played basketball for Ohio State," I said coldly.

I think that did startle him. He blinked again. "Your mother's a poet."

"So I've heard. I'm a little surprised you have." He hadn't come to Ma's signing.

He gave me an earnest smile. "Lighten up, Lark. I can take no for an answer."

"What was the question?"

He looked away.

I said, "I understand you're a folklorist. Do you study Nekana myths and legends?" The Nekana were a local tribe, part of the great coastal civilization that once ranged from Alaska to the Columbia.

He shrugged. "What with Marianne here as resident informant, I'd be remiss not to have looked into Nekana stories. They're pretty derivative."

I thought he was pretty derivative, by Lord Byron out of the Kingston Trio, but I didn't say so. He was keeping his hand to himself.

Marianne's salads—westerners tend to serve salad as the second course—were as good as her bread, and when I complimented her on the variety of greens she seemed pleased. They came from the greenhouses at this season, she said, nodding toward Angie.

Mike said, "Hugo grows interesting stuff in the spring and summer."

Angie apparently heard us. She bent forward and began to tell me about her Belgian endive, a rarity in those parts. Jay and Bianca joined in after a moment and I had the leisure to take a look at Marianne Wallace. She had grayish eyes and brown, rather than black, hair, but her round-faced prettiness and wide frame seemed Nekana-like. They were a handsome people.

The entree was lambshanks and onions braised in beer, a James Beard recipe I thought I recognized. Marianne served Angie an omelet. I managed to keep a foodie conversation going with that end of the table until, thank God, Bianca announced we'd have coffee and dessert in the living room. I felt like flight but the impulse made me twice as angry with McDonald, so I took my time rising and leaving the room.

In the living room, however, I stationed myself near Bianca on the theory that her husband would probably not grope me under her direct gaze. He was looking a little surly and Del Wallace kept watching me with a lurking grin on his red face. I could cheerfully have jabbed him with a fork, too. I almost asked Bianca where she kept her swine.

She was eager to talk shop and did so, in great detail. I had trouble focusing on her words. Jay seemed to be making an effort, another effort, with Keith McDonald, who was back at the guitar but just fingering it. Got to keep that right hand limber. Del Wallace downed another whiskey.

Angie eavesdropped on our conversation, yawning from time to time. Outside, sleet beat on the windows.

". . . and all the students should reach the farm by half-past seven that Sunday," Bianca was sayinig.

I said okay and watched Jay's jaw muscle knot. Tension rising there.

Michael brought in another tray—apple crumble with rum sauce, and coffee—and excused himself to go study. Marianne joined us, though. Ordinarily I hate a gathering that separates the men and women but that night I didn't mind.

Angie was asking Bianca what kind of floral arrangements

35

she'd want for the reception before the workshop.

"Do you grow flowers, too?" I asked.

She nodded. "Yes, though the market for organic flowers is limited to edibles for upscale restaurants. People just don't think organic when they buy flowers."

Bianca said, "All the same, you'll stick with the guidelines, Angie. That label's important to me—to our profits, too." She turned to me. "Organic meat and vegetables can be sold at a higher price than food that's full of pesticides and chemical fertilizers."

I swallowed coffee. "I imagine the market's limited, though."

She shrugged. "True. We've got about as many guaranteed sales to the specialized stores and restaurants as we're going to get, but supermarkets will buy limited quantities labelled 'organic' now, and they don't mind buying the surplus at the ordinary price either. They also take our excess flowers."

I said, "I buy organic tomatoes and lettuce when I can find them at Safeway, but I've never bothered with organic flowers."

Angie's face darkened. "Yeah, a few insect signs and people will go for a bunch of dusted roses instead."

"My friend Tom Lindquist grows an organic garden." I spooned the last drop of rum sauce. "I like his flowers just fine. I shake the bugs off and pop the blooms in a vase, but store-bought flowers are so expensive I want them perfect. . . ."

"Even if they're destroying the environment?"

Marianne said, "Tom Lindquist's grandmother was Madeline LaPorte. My mother always said Aunt Maddy's gardens were great."

"Are you related to Tom?"

She hesitated and glanced at her husband. "Sort of."

I said, "My brother-in-law is going to marry Tom's cousin."

Marianne smiled. "That'll be Darla. Everybody says she's real smart."

Darla Sweet was on the Nekana Tribal Council.

Angie had been brooding. "Hugo won't spray for anything, not if he loses his whole crop."

Bianca said, "He's too smart and too experienced to let that happen, Angie."

"And I'm not?"

"You're smart." Bianca smiled a conciliating smile.

Angie got up, restless. "But not as experienced as Hugo Bloody Groth. No, and not as hidebound either. The man's rigid."

Bianca sipped coffee. "What can I say? He sells everything he grows for top dollar. Focus on that. Your bulbs, and your statice and dry arrangements do very well. Forget roses. . . ."

And they were off on what was clearly an ongoing argument. I caught Jay's eye and raised one eyebrow. He nodded.

I said, "Jay has an eight o'clock meeting tomorrow, Bianca. We really ought to go. The dinner was superb and I think your center is exactly the way it should be."

We made our escape after reasonably brief ceremonies of disengagement. In the car, I said, "Keith McDonald groped my knee at dinner."

Jay's mouth twitched. "And . . . ?"

"What the hell do you mean, 'and?' I had a rotten time and I'm looking for a little husbandly support."

"The fact that I sat down at that man's table and broke bread is husbandly support, believe it." He started the engine. "Now tell me what you did to the bastard."

He laughed heartily when I told him, but I was still steamed. "I suppose he was using me to get at you."

"You betcha."

"I am not some goddamn trophy to be passed back and forth between rutting males."

"Yeah, and old Keith knows it." He was not going to be baited. I had to respect that.

"Turn on the windshield wipers," I muttered and sank down in my seat.

We drove homeward in silence, grim on my part, concentrated on Jay's. Sleet and rain pounded down on roads as slick as spit. The wipers swished away. I knew it was bad when Jay stopped turning them off.

We headed north on the Ridge Road, a narrow ribbon of highway with deep ditches on either side. The headlights probed absolute darkness, wind shook the car, and branches littered the asphalt. Jay was going thirty-five, but it felt like seventy.

Headlights and those nasty yellow fog lights loomed behind us and passed—a high-wheel pickup. Four-wheel-drive or no, its rear end fishtailed. A tall, chromed roll bar gleamed briefly.

"Damn fool." Jay hunched over the wheel. "Do you want me to tell McDonald to keep off, Lark?"

"No."

"Shall I tell him you're a black belt?"

"I told him I played for Ohio State. No need to lie."

"He'd believe me. He's a coward."

I stared at Jay's profile in the dim light of the dash. He does not make a habit of calling other men cowards, having been in too many tight situations himself.

He rounded a dark curve. "Uh-oh."

I peered ahead. The pickup that passed us had veered into the ditch. Its lights canted up into the evergreens on the left side of the road.

Jay was gearing down. I could see the driver standing by the vehicle now. Jay stopped the car and waited.

The driver walked to his side and Jay lowered the window.

"Give me a ride to Shoalwater?"

"I'll call the sheriff's office for you."

"It's fucking cold out here, man. I want a ride!"

I glimpsed a high-colored face, red with cold, and a pouty Elvis mouth.

Jay said, in his most peaceable voice, "Well, sure you can ride with us. I wouldn't leave an expensive rig like that unattended, though. Let me call in for you. I just live down the road here. Won't take long."

"Oh." The guy—a very young man—straightened to look at his sad pickup. "Oh, well, yeah. Thanks." He stumbled back to his truck and slid down into the driver's seat, though it was clear the door wouldn't close.

Jay engaged the gear and we eased away.

I said, "Liar." Nobody on the Peninsula was fool enough to stop in an ice storm to vandalize anything, not even the local vehicle of choice. I wondered if the pickup had a gun rack. Most did.

"The kid was drunk." Jay despises drunk drivers. They are lower on his personal totem pole than cowards.

"Plenty of antifreeze in his system."

"College student," Jay muttered. "I've seen him on campus." Jay drove on. He stopped in Shoalwater and talked to the deputy there. I had the feeling the pickup driver would be taking a Brethalyzer test soon.

We chugged on home. Later, as we twined warmly in bed, Jay murmured, "I'm sorry you had a rotten time, Lark."

"Me, too." I'd been thinking. "McDonald was pretty obvious and crude. You were right. He was using me, but not to get at you, or not exclusively."

"Who?"

"Bianca." I flopped back against my pillow.

" 'S possible."

"I won't say anything to her about it."

"And you're going through with the workshop?"

"Yes. That woman needs help." I thought of Keith and Del with their heads together, smirking and watching, and of the free-floating hostility in the air.

39

Hugo Groth had drawn most of the fire because he wasn't there. Bianca was probably partly to blame. She said she had been trying to re-create the commune—or the hotel she'd lived in as a child. If they'd all chosen to live together that would have been different. Bianca's wealth made her naive desire to create a community look a lot like coercion. At least Hugo had had the sense to move out.

Bianca called me ten days before the workshop was scheduled to begin.

I had gone in to the store to sort new stock and enter it into my inventory. "Is everything set?" I hoped neither of the speakers had backed out.

"I think so. Lark, have you seen Hugo?"

"He came in last week to pay the rent."

"He hasn't showed up at work for three days." She sounded tense.

"Has he gone off like this in the past?"

"Twice, but I traced him easily both times. Now I don't know what to do. Nobody knows where he is, not even his ex-wife. There's no sign of him here and he doesn't answer the phone, either."

"Better call the sheriff." The police would not be impressed. Hugo was a mature adult with a bank account. "Where's his bicycle?"

"I haven't seen it here. Do you have a key to his apartment?"

"Yes, but I'm not going to barge in on Hugo if he's taking a little vacation. I'll run up and knock, if you like, and look for the bike in the hall."

"Will you? I'd be grateful."

"I'll call you back," I said, resigned and not best pleased.

The bike wasn't on the landing and Hugo didn't respond to my knock. I tried Mr. Williams, too, but he must have been out. Downstairs, a utility bill addressed to Hugo and a couple of advertising circulars lay in the little basket below the mail slot. Mr. Williams' mail was gone.

I went back into the store to report my failure. "He hasn't picked his mail up recently."

At the other end of the line, Bianca heaved an exasperated sigh. "Damn Hugo. He went off before because he got restless, or so he claimed, but he never left me when there was anything crucial to do. I'm going nuts nursing this broccoli, getting his starts ready to set out, supervising the other digging—every one of those huge beds has to be composted and double dug before we can plant. I wish we'd never started that experiment."

I was trying to envisage Bianca in her vivid designer tunic digging up spadefuls of the Good Earth.

"It's almost the end of the term," Bianca wailed. "He has to evaluate the interns."

"Lawsy."

"What?"

"That must be difficult for you." I started to ask how I could help and bit back the words. I was already doing the woman a large favor by running the workshop.

I could hear Bianca gulping at the other end. She said in a muffled voice, "I'm sorry. If I come to town, will you at least let me into the apartment?"

That was doubtfully legal. I was not a cop, however, and landlords do have rights. I sighed. "Okay, Bianca, but make it snappy. I want to go home." I was fixing *boeuf en daube* with mixed veggies. The vegetables were organic, the beef just beef. Probably full of steroids.

"Half an hour?"

"Okay."

She showed up forty-five minutes later in jeans, a sweatshirt, anorak, and boots. She looked almost like a farmer—a morose farmer. A man's tweed cap hid the mahogany hair.

I led her upstairs and we knocked and called. No response. I unlocked the door.

By that time I was half-expecting a gory corpse in the bathroom. I was relieved not to find one. There was no trace of

Hugo, apart from his belongings. We took a good look around the living room and Bianca headed down the short hall.

I surveyed the living room with a landlady's eye and decided Hugo was a keeper, even if he was using the front room as a bedroom. A double futon lay flat on its frame, the bedcovers drawn up and the pillow plumped. There was no television but he had set up an expensive looking CD player and speakers. He had been reading the Zen master. The book lay on the arm of an easy chair. The furnishings had a second-hand look but they were reasonably tasteful and in good repair.

I strolled to the small dining table in the corner next to the utility kitchen. It held a placemat with a few crumbs, a salt and pepper shaker, and a bottle of vitamin C. In the kitchen, the counter was clean, but a bowl, a couple of spoons, and a paring knife lay in the sink. Nothing had molded in the clean, well-stocked refrigerator. Even the lettuce looked crisp. Staples—cereal, rice, soup, crackers—stocked the cupboard shelves. Hugo didn't have a lot of dinnerware but there was plenty for one, and he had stoneware of a good plain design. Altogether a decent bachelor establishment.

Bianca came out of the bedroom which he had apparently been using as an office. Her hair was ruffled and she clutched the tweed cap.

I said, "Everything looks normal to me. He told me he used dope sometimes. Maybe he just decided to hole up in a motel on the beach with a bong and a book. Don't pot smokers lose track of time?"

"Not that much time and not Hugo." She ran a hand through her hair. "Hell and damn." She glanced around the bedroom. "The plants look okay."

Trust a farmer. I hadn't even noticed the plants. Three neat houseplants, one hairy, two with shiny leaves, sat on one of the wide sills. I walked over and stuck a finger in the soil supporting the hairy plant. "Feels dry."

"That's a succulent," Bianca said crossly.

"Oh." I had so far avoided killing my Boston fern. Otherwise my relationships with plants had been fleeting. I looked at the other sill. "Oops."

"What?"

Hugo had placed a small cushion on the sill. It didn't cover the whole surface. A drinking glass sat in one corner. It held three cut daffodils. They had wilted.

Bianca expelled her breath with a whoosh that ruffled her bangs. "He wouldn't leave flowers to die like that. That means he hasn't been here in two or three days."

"No." I had a bad feeling about the daffodils, though Jay would probably have shrugged. Everything else looked cared for. "Hugo's missing, all right. Better notify the police."

Bianca groaned. "Why did it have to happen now?"

There was no answer.

She looked at me, eyes intent. "Will you come to the farm now?"

I started to say yes and caught myself. "What could I do?"

"Help me question the staff and the interns. Help me look for him. You're an outsider. You might spot something. Please."

I drew a breath. "No."

"Keith will be at work."

I stared. "I suppose he told you . . ."

Her cheeks were red. "He didn't have to. I know Keith. You were uncomfortable at dinner and you left as soon as you could afterwards."

I caught myself again. I had been about to apologize. I did feel sorry for Bianca, but she had chosen to seat me next to her husband.

My silence got to her. Her shoulders sagged. "Well, thanks."

"Hugo will turn up."

Tears welled. "If he doesn't I'm dead."

I sighed. "Look, I'll come out Saturday afternoon, if you

43

like, for a couple of hours. That's if he hasn't reappeared. Meanwhile, I'll ask Jay to do some checking through the sheriff's office."

Her face brightened. "Can he do that?"

"He's a reserve deputy and does consulting for their crime scene people."

"Oh. Okay. Thanks." She didn't sound hopeful.

I wasn't either. Tracing a man who didn't drive a car or use credit cards was going to be difficult. I called Jay to tell him we had a missing tenant.

4 ❧

I DROVE OUT to the farm Saturday afternoon around three. I wanted to see it in daytime anyway. Bianca had asked me to stay overnight, an offer I declined flat, with no qualms. Hugo's continued absence was worrying, but hardly an emergency. Bianca had admitted everything was set for the workshop.

The farm nestled in a meander of the Coho River. The tidal stream emptied into Shoalwater Bay three marshy miles west of the entrance gate. Above the open gate hung an arch of heavy timbers with the pokerwork legend MEADOWLARK FARM dangling on a slab of red cedar.

I drove straight up to the cattle guard, past a pasture full of ewes that looked as if they were about to produce quadruplets. A few spindly lambs, much whiter than their mamas, watched me chug uphill. At the cattleguard the graveled road dipped and rose in a wide curve toward the house. The exterior of the huge edifice was stained gray, an unfortunate effect. Bianca's house looked like a beached whale.

I parked in front of the main entrance and rang the bell. Nobody answered it. I turned around on the porch, a stylized veranda, and surveyed the countryside. It was at that stage when deciduous leaves are just beginning to show and sun-yellow forsythias and daffodils gild unexpected corners. A faint haze misted what looked like an apple orchard to my left and, to my right, as promised, the house gave on a spectacular view of the estuary. As was true everywhere in the region, the dominant winter color was the dark, dark green of conifers, fading to blue in the distance. Wintergreen.

"Lark?"

I started and turned.

Marianne Wallace stood in the doorway, looking anxious. "She's still out rounding up the kids."

I was supposed to help Bianca question the interns about Hugo. "Okay," I said. "My car . . . ?"

"You can leave it where it is today. The car barn's around back." She gestured to her left. "Come on in."

"Thanks." I stuffed my keys into my shoulder bag and followed her through the main hall. She waved at the coatrack and I shed my jacket and purse. "Where are we supposed to conduct the inquisition?"

She was moving at the unhurried pace that seemed typical of her. "Kitchen, we thought. I made coffee and spiced cider." She led me across the dining room and through the swinging door that opened on the kitchen.

I stopped on the threshold, one hand on the door. "Nice."

"It is nice," she agreed. "Coffee?"

"Cider sounds better." I sat on a blond chair by the big butcher-block table and admired a room that managed to be both high tech and friendly. The color scheme was blond and hunter green.

Marianne ladled a cup of cider for me and gave me a cinnamon stick as a swizzle.

I inhaled deeply. "I love cinnamon."

"It's cassia."

"Huh?"

"Most of the cinnamon used in this country is really cassia. Tastes the same. Much cheaper."

I hadn't the foggiest idea of the origin of spices and herbs other than garlic. I sipped.

"I'm worried about Hugo."

I stared at her, curious.

Marianne's round, pretty face drooped with distress. "Do you think you'll be able to find him soon?"

"I don't know. Not if he doesn't want to be found."

She poured herself a cup of black coffee and perched on a stool by the gleaming Jenn-Air range. "He should never have moved out. I told him so."

I said, "I think there are too many people for him here."

"Yes, some of the time, but it was Del, too."

I raised an encouraging brow.

She sighed. "Del's always riding Hugo 'bout one thing or another. Del don't know when to quit. I miss Hugo. And he's real . . ." She groped for words. "Real fragile. I worry about him not eating. He gets absentminded about it and then he has one of his stomach attacks. And riding the bike to town in the dark—that's dangerous."

I murmured agreement. "Have you known Hugo a long time?"

She considered. "Since we came six years ago. I can't say I know him. He's a quiet man. But I like him. He's got patience."

That observation startled me. Del and Angie had given me the opposite impression, of a man fanatical to the point of rigidity. My own impression of Hugo, though, was closer to Marianne's. Maybe he had a split personality. Maybe, like most people, he was just inconsistent.

A door opened and I heard scuffling and talking outside the room.

Marianne said, "That's Bianca and the kids in the mud-room. They'll wash up and come in in a minute." She rose and began filling mugs with cider.

"Can I help you?"

She flashed a smile over her shoulder. "It's no trouble."

Bianca burst in. "Del had them out with the sheep, Marianne. He wants Jason and Bill again in an hour, and Angie . . . Oh, hi, Lark. Sorry we're late." She wore her farmer getup and red plush booties instead of boots. I gathered she kept the slippers in the mudroom. "I hope the kitchen's okay. We have to keep the conference room clean for the workshop."

"Fine with me." I settled back to watch the first student enter, a bold-looking young man with brown hair and bright brown eyes. His color was high. Not, I thought, from shyness. He was followed by a smaller, slimmer boy with darker hair and eyes.

"Jason and Bill," Bianca said by way of introduction.

Jason, the one with lighter hair, stared at me, and I made a discovery. He was the driver of the pickup that had landed in the ditch the night of our dinner at the farm. I didn't think he recognized me. The other kid gave me a tentative grin.

Marianne set a huge platter of homemade scones in the center of the table then returned with a stack of ceramic plates in bright colors and matching cloth napkins. She set a big butter dish and a pot of what looked like blackberry jam in front of Jason, who did not hesitate to dive into the scones. Knives materialized. Marianne's sleight of hand fascinated me, and the other interns had entered before I registered their presence.

I nudged Bianca. "Where's Mike?"

Marianne said, "He drove to Astoria to pick up supplies for the workshop." She sounded defensive. Bianca said nothing.

Marianne handed mugs of spicy cider around, poured Bianca a cup of coffee, and retreated to her stool.

Bianca pulled a chair beside me. The rest had disposed themselves around the table, Jason and Bill on my right. The scones—I snagged one—vanished like snow in a chinook wind.

Bianca sipped coffee and murmured the others' names as they munched and chattered and eyed me curiously. On her left sat a small dark girl in a navy blue sweatshirt. Mary Sadat. Mary nibbled, ladylike, with downcast eyes, and said nothing. Beside her, two married students from the Evergreen State College, a couple of years older than the others, fed each other bits of scone. Adam and Letha Carlsen, he blond, she brunette, both ostentatiously grubby and rather plain.

The girl perched on the chair opposite me distinguished herself by ignoring the scones. I couldn't help staring at her. She wore cerise spandex leggings, a gray B.U.M. sweatshirt over a cerise turtleneck, and a lethal tangle of gold chains. Carol Bascombe, Bianca murmured, clucking a little.

Carol was using a white hair pick to fluff what I've always thought of as bordello hair. It was sunstreaked, though we hadn't seen the sun since February third, and each long tendril had been separately permed or tweaked with a curling iron into a riotous tumble. Carol looked as if she had just risen from the rank sweat of an enseamed bed. I'm sure her hair was clean but the illusion of steamy sex was impressive. I wondered if hair that long constituted a hazard in a farmer. Carol had pouty lips, capped teeth, a perfect nose, and luminous gray eyes just then clouded with anxiety.

She pricked at a clump of hair, it fell into place, and the anxiety vanished. She beamed at me. "Hi, I'm Carol. Are you going to find Hugo the Growth?"

Jason and Bill guffawed and the married couple smirked. Mary Sadat raised dark eyes from her cup.

Bianca said, "Kids, this is Lark Dodge. She'll be running the workshop. Meanwhile, we're trying to figure out what happened to Hugo. When did you see him last, Carol?"

Carol wriggled. "Saturday. I was, like, driving home to Kayport and I passed his grotty bike on the road. He was supposed to supervise the digging and composting Monday morning but he didn't show at eight, did he, Jase?"

"No, and we weren't going to hang around waiting for him, either." Jason was sitting a little too close to me. He sounded as righteous as a bank executive with a tardy loan applicant. I expected him to announce that he was a busy man but he just said, "I had a botany test at eleven so I sat in my rig and studied."

Bill said nothing. He was eating the last scone. I looked at the duo from TESC. "How about you two?"

The woman, Letha, said, "We thought about it when Bianca told us Hugo was missing. He supervised us Saturday morning, made me redig my bed. He seemed normal to me." She wrinkled her uninteresting nose. "As normal as Hugo gets. The man has no affect." She cast Carol a slightly scornful glance as if to say, "Read my thesaurus."

Carol was renewing her cerise lip gloss.

Adam, the husband, said with an air of conscious tolerance that was going to be annoying when he reached middle age, "Hugo's okay, honey. He's just real focused."

Bianca said, "Mary?"

Mary Sadat's olive skin flushed a darker shade. "Mr. Groth ate dinner at my parents' restaurant Saturday night. I was waiting tables. I saw him but we didn't talk. It was busy."

I smiled at her. "What time, Mary?"

She ducked her head and crumbled her scone. "Around eight, I think."

"Anybody see him Sunday?"

They exchanged glances but nobody said anything.

I was about to pursue the reasons for their silence when the door to the mudroom swung open and Angie burst in.

"Shoes!" Bianca shrieked.

"Oh, sorry." Angie stepped back to the open door. She yanked her wool beret off, running a long hand through hair too short to tousle. "I found Hugo's bike."

Bianca stood up. "Where?"

"Behind that stack of boxes by the flower house." She met my eyes. "That's one of the big greenhouses. The bike's just parked there, leaning against the framework of the building."

"Out of sight?" I asked.

Angie nodded. "The boxes hide it."

"You mean that humongous pile of flats?" Carol's voice rose. "Mary and I spent two hours stacking those grotty old things last Saturday. I broke a fingernail."

Mary said, "The bike wasn't there Saturday."

Everyone looked at her.

She blushed. "I guess that's obvious."

Bianca made a soothing noise. So did I. People would always soothe Mary.

"What time did you finish the crates?" I asked.

Carol twiddled her hair pick. "Around four."

"Hugo's rain pants are still wadded up in the saddlebag," Angie said. "I checked."

Bianca paled. Somebody shifted again. A chair creaked.

I was getting a bad feeling. Beside me, Jason and Bill sat quiet. I said, "Did anybody see Hugo Monday at all?"

Silence.

"What was he scheduled to do Monday?"

Bianca hunched on her chair. "He was supposed to show the interns how to prepare the raised beds for planting. We don't do much with that kind of cultivation because it's so labor intensive it doesn't pay. But it is interesting. We were doing heirloom beans there this year, among other things. Hugo intercrops beans with blue corn. . . ."

"Heirloom beans?" I drew a blank.

"Natural seed-stock." Angie scowled at me. "Is anybody besides me going to hunt for Hugo?"

Bianca stood up slowly, as if her bones ached.

I said, "You ought to call the sheriff."

"No!" Bianca swallowed hard and avoided my eyes. "I mean, not yet."

Angie said, "We could search the outbuildings."

Bianca nodded. "Marianne, will you call Del? Tell him I need Jason and Bill—and why."

Marianne lifted a cellular phone from the counter and left the room, extending the antenna as she passed through the swinging door.

The interns stared at Bianca, eyes wide. Mary Sadat teared up.

"Hugo may be with Trish. That's his ex-wife. She lives in Raymond." Bianca's voice lacked conviction.

I shoved my cider cup back and laid my napkin on the table. "I thought you called her."

"I did. Twice."

"Would she lie?"

Bianca threw up her hands. "No. I'm just looking for a comfortable solution. Something's wrong."

"The last time anyone saw Hugo was Saturday night at the restaurant," I mused. "If the bike's here, he made a trip out from town after that. Does he work on Sundays?"

"We all do if there's a crop to harvest or something else urgent. Otherwise we take Sundays off."

"So he probably rode out Monday morning."

"But why would he hide the bike behind the crates?" She shook her head. "Something's wrong." She looked around at the silent students. "Let's do this methodically. Pair up. Jason, you and Bill search the sheep sheds."

"We'll check the ice house, too," Jason said.

"Okay. Afterwards, go find Del. Tell him to poke around in the old barn. Angie, you and Mary can search the greenhouses. Carol . . ."

"I gotta leave at five, Mrs. McDonald."

Bianca's jaw muscle jumped. "Then go look in the car barn. Adam and Letha, you, too. Look around the machine sheds. I'll join you in a few minutes. And call. He may be hurt or sick. . . ."

"Or dead," Carol said, voicing everyone's thought. We all looked at her. She wriggled.

I said, "Since I don't know the place I won't be much use in a search."

Bianca nodded. "Go on, kids. I need to talk to Lark. Then I'll join Carol and the Carlsens. It's four. Come back here by dark—five-thirty, say—and report in."

I waited until they'd left, then I said, "You need the sheriff—and dogs, probably. This is a big place and Hugo could be anywhere."

Bianca shivered. "Anywhere or nowhere. It's been six, no . . . seven days."

"He could have parked the bike here and taken a local bus. You said he disappeared before."

Bianca hesitated, then nodded. "I hope that's what happened this time, too. He starts feeling hemmed in and just takes off. If so, he'll turn up at Trish's sooner or later. But the bike bothers me. Of course, the last time it happened he was living here, at the old house. . . ."

"Maybe he's there now."

"We tore it down."

I got up and walked over to look out the large window above the sink. I could see a field strewn with sheep. A couple of metal sheds lay beside it. Farther on lay another field with a small wood structure at its edge, possibly the ice house. Jason and Bill were already hiking toward the metal sheds, making good time. I supposed they were in a hurry to go home. As I watched they split up and each took one of the sheds. At that distance I couldn't distinguish which boy was which. "You really ought to call the sheriff now, Bianca."

"If Hugo's just done another walkabout I'll feel stupid and he'll be mad at me for making a fuss."

I tried to imagine Hugo red-faced and shouting.

Her shoulders slumped. "Okay. I'll call the cops when Marianne brings the phone back." She joined me at the counter and pulled a drawer open, fumbling the tiny telephone book from it. "What do I say?"

I repressed irritation. "Report a missing person. And you don't need the phone book. Dial 911."

The swinging door pushed in. "Hi. Seen Mom?" Mike Wallace was carrying an armload of cartons. He set them on the table and gave me a shy smile.

I smiled back.

Bianca said, "Angie found Hugo's bike near the greenhouses, Mike."

Mike's eyes widened. "But . . ."

"I sent the interns out to search."

"You think something happened to him, don't you?"

"I don't know."

"Did Mom . . ." His voice trailed and he flushed red. His glasses had steamed and he took them off. Without them he looked like a half-fledged owl.

Marianne reentered and set the phone on the table. "Del said he'd look in the old barn. The floor's rotting. Maybe Hugo fell and broke his leg." Marianne's eyes were pink as if she'd been crying. "Hugo used to climb up to the loft. He said it reminded him of home." She pulled a tissue from her pocket and blew her nose. "Mike, take those boxes to the conference room. I need to clear the table before dinner."

Mike said, "I'm going out to Dad."

"Put the boxes away first," Bianca said. "Then you can help me search the machine sheds."

He hefted the cartons. "Okay, but I bet Mom's right. Hugo's in the old barn." The door swung closed behind him.

Bianca picked up the phone and dialed 911. They put her on hold a couple of times. I watched her bridle her impatience. Eventually she explained the situation to somebody, listened, glum, to the response, and said, "Thanks." She set the device back in its cradle. "They'll send a car this evening." She looked from Marianne to me. "I'm going out. I have to do something."

I nodded. I was feeling edgy myself. "I'll wait here."

"Thanks." She headed out to the mudroom and I could hear her thumping around. Eventually the outer door slammed.

I took another look out the window. It was getting dark fast and I saw no sign of Jason and Bill. I drifted back to the table.

Marianne pulled a tray from a narrow cupboard near the sink and joined me. She began clearing the mugs onto the tray.

"Tell me about Hugo." I wadded a couple of napkins. "Where do you want these?"

"Hamper." She pointed and took her tray to the dishwasher.

I stuffed the napkins in the hamper. "Bianca says this isn't Hugo's first disappearance."

"Third." She ran a sponge under the hot water tap, squeezed it, and began wiping crumbs from the surface of the table. "People get to him. He can't stand being crowded."

"Do you mean literally?"

She stared at me and resumed wiping. "He don't like a lot of voices yammering, that's for sure. Neither do I. But I think what really pushes him is . . ." She broke off, shook her head, took the sponge to the sink and rinsed it. "It's hard to put into words. Bianca likes holidays. Christmas, Thanksgiving, Earth Day, the Fourth of July. She *gathers* everybody. It's nice. The kids—I mean Mike and her three and the interns, too—they like it a lot and the rest of us don't mind. Keith pulls out his guitar. There's lots of food and music and chatter."

"And it gets to Hugo?"

"Yes. He can't take it. It's like he can't breathe. Sometimes he goes out on the deck and just leans on the rail and inhales. I've seen him. The two times he disappeared were holidays."

That made sense. A holiday phobia is common enough. Sometimes enforced bonhomie bothers me, too. I relaxed a little. I wanted to believe Hugo had gone away of his own free will. "Do you think the upcoming workshop triggered him off?"

Marianne sighed. "I guess so, but I'm surprised."

"Surprised?"

"The feeling's different this time. Sure, there's that reception the first night, but Bianca told Hugo he didn't have to come to it. Apart from that there isn't any reason for him to tense up. He isn't living here now. Besides . . ." She opened the oven.

"Besides what?" I asked, distracted by the savory aroma.

"If he was going to bolt, he'd leave just before the conference starts." She put on a padded glove and pulled a vast casserole from the oven.

"What's that? It smells great."

"Shepherd's pie."

I watched as she glazed the surface with a smidgen of butter. The crust looked like mashed potatoes. She popped the ceramic dish back in the oven. I tried to imagine being organized enough to produce high tea for ten followed by a complete dinner for six a couple of hours later.

She glided to the refrigerator and began pulling vegetables out. Marianne never seemed hurried and, if she was harried, it was not because of her culinary responsibilities. She took a plastic salad spinner from a cupboard and began rinsing greens.

"May I help you?" I asked again.

"No, thanks. There's coffee if you want it."

I poured a mug of coffee.

"Cream's in the fridge."

"Thanks." I laced my cup with cholesterol. "You said Hugo was fragile."

"Did I?"

"Earlier. Did you mean physically or emotionally?"

"Physically, I guess." She twirled the spinner. "It was Agent Orange."

Something clicked. "The skin condition?"

"That and the stomach problems. His wife kept having miscarriages, too. That's why they split. She couldn't take it."

I set my coffee cup down. Marianne was hitting close to home. As far as I knew Jay hadn't been exposed to Agent Orange. Still, what if he had been and didn't know it? I lifted the cup and sipped. "That's so sad."

Marianne cocked her head. "Yes, it was. But Hugo's not sad, really. Just quiet. He likes his work."

"No chemicals."

"No pesticides and no chemical fertilizers." Marianne's air of precision reminded me of her comment about the cinnamon. She didn't sound belligerent or pedantic, just precise.

"Hugo's crew is boat people," she added, giving the greens a last critical twirl.

"What?"

"The crew for planting and harvest. Weeding, too. They're refugees. Bianca used to hire Mexicans." She took a huge ceramic salad bowl from the cupboard and began tearing lettuce into bite-sized pieces. "The year before Del started working for her, the Immigration people raided Bianca's crew. Most of 'em were illegals. She had to pay a big fine, and the story got into the paper. It was embarrassing. She decided to work with the Vietnamese after that. They have green cards."

"Boat people—that was a long time ago. They must be middle-aged."

"They are. Hugo says they were peasants, couldn't read and write their own language. There were classes for them at the college, but a lot of them dropped out of the program after a couple of years. They're women mostly, and they do what they've always done—farmwork."

I turned that over in my mind. "But Hugo . . ."

"Hugo gets along with them okay. He talks their language a little." She took out a French knife and began slicing a purple onion. She broke the slices into perfect rings.

Mike galloped through to the mudroom at that point without dallying for small talk. I heard the door slam as he went out.

Marianne finished her salad and carried the bowl to the dining room. Eventually she allowed me to help her set the table. I felt useless and resentful of Bianca for dragging me out to the farm. Why had she wanted me? As a witness? She must have known I would be of no practical help. Of course, she hadn't expected to find the bike. I pictured Hugo's sturdy mountain bike. He took good care of it. If he had meant to abandon it at the farm, wouldn't he have left it in the car barn? Not, I supposed, if he wanted to avoid pursuit. My mind made tight circles of speculation.

57

"You going to join us for dinner?" Marianne smoothed a napkin.

"No. My husband's taking me out on the town."

She sighed. "Lucky."

The telephone rang. I followed her back to the kitchen.

"Yes," she said into the receiver. "Yeah, she's still looking. Did you check the barn?"

I deduced she was talking to Del.

She made an affirmative noise. "Half an hour." She hung up. "Del and the boys are coming in. They didn't find nothing."

I didn't think they'd had enough time for a thorough search. Outside, a car started after two grinding whines and drove off. I checked my watch. Five-fifteen.

At five-thirty Bianca and Angie came in and other cars left. Bianca looked discouraged.

"No luck?"

She grimaced. "Zippo. It's awfully dark. I think you're right about needing bloodhounds. I keep imagining Hugo unconscious in a corner of the old barn."

Marianne turned the oven down. "Del said there was no sign of Hugo at the barn."

I stood up. "The deputy will probably wait until morning to do a police search. Do you want me tomorrow, Bianca?"

"I wish you'd stay now. . . ."

I shook my head. "No, Jay and I have a commitment. I will come out tomorrow, though, if you need moral support."

She nodded, drooping.

"I'll show myself out." I went home, feeling futile and obscurely used. I was sorry for Bianca, though. Her distress seemed genuine.

When I returned to the farm the next morning, a sheriff's deputy and a dozen volunteers from the Search and Rescue team had already set up a systematic search of the grounds.

I drove around to the back of the house and parked on the asphalt between a county van and a cop car. Marianne must have been watching for me because she was standing by the car, dressed for a hike, by the time I got out.

"Hi. Bianca and Angie are showing the deputy the bicycle. Do you want to come out to the old barn with me?"

I pulled on a pair of wool gloves. "Sure."

"I brought a flashlight." She showed me a small but powerful electric lantern. "Del says it was too dark in there yesterday to see much."

"Where are the interns?" I locked my door and stuffed the keys in my jacket pocket.

"Out with the rescue team. So are Del and Keith."

We began walking along the dirt track that led to the fields and sheds I had seen the day before from the kitchen window. "Where is the barn?"

" 'Bout half a mile—over the ridge, past the broccoli field and the ice house."

As we walked along I could see figures in the distance moving slowly, eyes to the ground. They were coming toward us, so I supposed they must have begun at the farthest field. They had probably already searched the barn.

Marianne was not in a talkative mood. Neither was I. It was misting out and the air carried eerie sounds—crows cawing, a log truck shifting gears on the highway, the occasional shout from one of the searchers. We passed the two metal sheds I had seen Jason and Bill enter the day before. My boots beaded water and the legs of my jeans were damp. I wished I'd worn a longer jacket. I stuffed my hands in my pockets and trudged along. Marianne set a good pace.

"That's broccoli," she announced as we approached a smallish shed. Behind and beside it, I could see rows of plants so heavy with moisture they looked gray in the dim sunlight.

59

They were well-grown. I had heard that some crops wintered over or were planted in January.

Like former President Bush, I am not a fan of broccoli, though I will eat a dutiful portion if necessary. The field looked as if it could supply the broccoli needs of a whole regiment of Republicans. The ice house, unstained cedar with a tarpaper roof, abutted the field.

"What's that?" Marianne stopped, head cocked.

"Sounds like an electric motor." The rain was coming down harder and I wanted to keep moving.

"Somebody must've turned on the ice machine." She strode to the ice house door. I followed.

The door was latched but not locked. She yanked the door open, switched a light on, and clucked. "Look at that. Knee-deep in ice. Bianca will have a fit."

I entered behind her, stepping into a puddle. There was a fug in the air, as in cold unlit spaces. Mold. Rotting plants. Something else. "A fit? Why?"

"We don't need ice until we cut the broccoli. It has to be iced before it's trucked out. But we won't start the first harvest until the end of the week."

The room was divided roughly in half, with a storage area, then empty, to the left and an icemaker with a catch-basin roughly the size and depth of a large hot tub on the right. The tub was heaped with fresh ice. A scatter of cubes so new they hadn't begun to melt strewed the wet floor. The walls and ceiling of the ice house showed foil-sheeted insulation. It was colder inside the building than outdoors.

A rough table of unfinished planks leaned against the near wall. A row of short-handled, wide-bladed knives gleamed above the table. Three scoop shovels rested in a neat line against the edge of the ice machine.

I walked over to the hill of glistening ice cubes. "Smells like my refrigerator."

"Yeah." Marianne wandered into the storage space and

looked around. "Wait till Bianca sees the electric bill. I'd better shut it off." She moved back toward the entrance.

I was looking at the ice. "Maybe somebody wanted to store something. . . ." Abruptly my heart slammed into distress mode. I picked up one of the shovels and began scraping ice off onto the floor.

"No, oh, no." I don't remember which of us said that.

We stood for a frozen moment staring at my excavation. The toe of a filthy sneaker showed through the ice. I had found Hugo Groth.

5 ~

THE SHOVEL I had used to clear away the ice clattered to the concrete floor. For perhaps half a minute Marianne and I stood staring into the bin. I thought I could see the distorted outline of Hugo's body, but that may have been imagination. The sneaker, however, definitely held a foot. I could see the sock and a bit of pale skin. I imagined I could smell death.

The ice machine whirred. Marianne breathed raggedly. I didn't breathe at all. Then, as we stared, the machine clacked. Fresh ice cubes cascaded down until they buried the shoe. The process must have been triggered by the level of ice in the bin.

I grabbed Marianne's arm. "We have to get out of here." I pulled her across to the door and out into the drizzle.

"Oh, God, he's . . . it's like a meat locker!" Marianne covered her mouth.

"Don't think. Don't even try to imagine what's in there. We have to get help."

Marianne turned away from me, gagging, and threw up on a clump of grass. I clenched my eyes shut, willed my stomach not to respond.

"I'm s-sorry." She had found a tissue and was wiping her mouth.

I took a gulp of air and counted to thirty, slowly clearing my mind. Across the open broccoli field the crows cawed. A truck rumbled on the state highway.

I exhaled on a slow count. "We have to get help. One of us

should stay here to be sure nobody else enters the building. The other will have to go find the deputy. You said Bianca was showing him Hugo's bike."

"Yes. They're at the flower house."

"Where are the greenhouses?"

"Over . . . never mind. I'll go. I don't want to stay here alone." She started off, wide shoulders hunched in her red jacket, tissue still pressed to her mouth. She had gone half a dozen paces when she stopped dead and turned around. "I'm an idiot. I can use this."

She pulled a portable phone from one pocket, extended the antenna, and punched in a number. Her hands shook so hard she almost dropped the phone, but I heard it buzz and a voice reply.

"It's Marianne. Lark is with me. We found Hugo." Quack, quack from the phone. "No. He's dead. In the ice house." Silence. Quack, quack. "I told you, in the ice house!" Marianne began to sob. "He's buried in ice. Somebody turned the machine on." Quack.

Marianne, still weeping, retracted the antenna. "That was Bianca," she choked. "They're coming."

"Was the deputy with her?"

"Yeah." She drew a quivering breath. "Dale Nelson."

I knew Dale. I had met him the previous summer under unpleasant circumstances. We got along. Jay had worked with him on that case and at least two others, and Dale was now a detective sergeant. He had been the senior patrol officer for the county when we met. If Dale had responded to Bianca's call, either she had pull or she was very persuasive.

She was very persuasive. I knew that.

"Give me the phone, please, Marianne. I need to call my husband."

Marianne handed me the transmitter. She didn't hesitate, but, even so, I felt defensive.

"Jay helps the sheriff's evidence team on difficult cases. This one will be a stinker because of the ice. How the hell does this work?" I had been avoiding cellular phones. I ripped off my woolly gloves and stuck them in my pocket.

Wordless, Marianne showed me the talk button. I tapped in our number. When the phone began to ring, I held it to my ear and looked around me. The Search and Rescue team would be approaching the broccoli field from the east. So far they were hidden behind the ridge at the far rim of the field.

After half a dozen rings Jay answered.

I said, "It's Lark. We found Hugo's body."

He cleared his throat.

"Dale Nelson's here—at the farm, I mean." I explained where I was and what I had found. I'm sure I was incoherent.

"Jesus. I'm coming out. Warn Dale." He paused. "Are you all right, Lark?"

"Physically unharmed and perfectly safe." But sick at heart.

"I'm sorry, darling." Jay almost always hears what I don't say.

My eyes teared and I broke the connection.

Marianne was crying hard, her hands covering her face.

I stuffed the phone into her jacket pocket and touched her shoulder. "Come on, Marianne. We should move out of this area."

I led her a few yards down the road and stood for awhile, patting her and making sympathetic sounds. I felt numb but little jolts of awareness warned me of the reaction that was bound to come. I was fiercely glad I had not got to know Hugo well.

The wait seemed interminable, but no more than ten minutes passed before I saw the revolving blue light of Dale's car. He was not using the siren. There was no real reason to use the light either. He pulled the car over and parked on the grassy shoulder a good distance from us. He and Bianca got out. So did Keith McDonald.

Bianca ran to us. She was crying, and she and Marianne clung to each other. McDonald and Dale moved at a less impetuous pace. They had the identical looks of men trapped in a female emotional display. The hell with them. The situation demanded emotion.

I went up to Dale and we shook hands.

"It's in the ice house?" Dale, improbably fair and pink-cheeked, always looked guileless. His eyes were worried, however.

I described what I had found, and he thanked me for not mucking up the crime scene, though we had trampled the area by the door and done God knew what damage inside. I told him Jay was coming.

He looked even more worried. He was carrying a battered 35 mm camera by the strap. The camera swung in a tiny arc. "I dunno, Lark. The county budget . . ."

"Think of him as my husband," I snarled. "He won't charge you." That was unfair. Dale thought of Jay as a mentor, and the sheriff's budget was in bad shape from the earlier investigations.

Dale flushed. "I always like to have Jay's opinion of these things. Speaking of which, I'd better have a look."

"Feel free." I wasn't going into the ice house again.

Keith McDonald started to follow Dale, but Dale waved him off. Keith looked at me. "You're sure it's Hugo?"

"How many of your people are missing?"

He chewed his lip.

I relented. "Yes, I'm sure. I recognized his sneaker. It was unmistakable."

Keith closed his eyes, opened them. "He always wore his clothes until they fell apart. It was a matter of principle."

"There are worse principles."

"Hey, I admired that. Hugo's a good guy. I mean, was." Mr. Profundity.

I was being unfair, probably because I was upset. By way of a peace token, I said, "I guess you've known him for a long time." I was watching Dale. He had taken a couple of snaps of the ice house and a close up of the lintel. He entered the building with exaggerated care, though Marianne and I had probably obliterated any clear sign of other pedestrians.

"I've known Hugo twenty years. Almost half my life," Keith added, sounding surprised. He ran a hand over his beard. "Christ. Old Hugo."

At that point Bianca pulled herself together. She gave Marianne a last pat, wiped her own eyes on the sleeve of her anorak, and came over to me. "He's under the ice?"

I nodded.

"You're sure he's dead?"

For a panicked moment I wondered. Maybe I should have dragged him from the bin and tried CPR. Sanity flooded back. "He's been missing a week, Bianca."

She gave a small, hiccuping sigh. "It's all my fault."

"What?"

"I knew something was wrong when he disappeared. I should have called in the cops then." She shot me a sad, reproachful look.

I almost bit. I almost said that was what I had told her to do, which was true. She was not making sense. People react to shock in strange ways. Bianca was like a black body, absorbing and radiating guilt.

I said, carefully, "You did what you could."

"If I'd only known . . ."

I waited. She was running through a list of standard responses, almost as if she had a script. That didn't necessarily mean her reaction was insincere.

Keith said, "You'll have to cancel the workshop."

"No!" She turned on him. "No, it's too late. I can't."

I said, "Those folks are journalists."

"They're science writers."

"They're would-be science writers." I had read the participants' bios. "Right now they're practicing newshawks and this is news."

Bianca pouted, avoiding my eyes.

Keith shoved his hands in the pockets of his jacket and

stared off in the direction of Shoalwater Bay. He had a noble profile.

"That boy, Jason," Marianne said.

Her entrance into the conversation startled me.

She blew her nose and tucked the tissue into her sleeve. "Jason said he was going to check out the ice house yesterday."

I stared at her. Keith had turned to stare, too.

"Jason!" Bianca sounded numb. "No, they wouldn't kill Hugo . . . not the interns . . ."

I was trying to visualize what Jason and Bill could have seen if they had just switched on the light and looked around without entering the ice house. "The body isn't visible from the door."

Marianne's jaw set. "Jason must have noticed there was ice in the bin. He should have said something about that."

I wondered why she was focusing on Jason. Bill had gone with him, after all. Of course, Jason was Del's protege—or so I had gathered the evening of the dinner. Perhaps Marianne was jealous of him—or jealous for Mike, more likely.

Dale emerged from the ice house looking green around the gills. "Okay, let's get started. Marianne, I want . . ."

"For God's sake, Nelson, tell us what happened to him!" Keith McDonald grabbed Dale by one arm. Bianca tugged at the other, gabbling questions.

Dale shook them off. When they fell silent, he said, "I need to call in again. The evidence van, an ambulance, and the M.E. are on their way. Ms. Fiedler, Dr. McDonald, you can go to the house and wait for me there, or you can stay where you are. I need to talk to both of you eventually."

"What happened to Hugo?" Bianca demanded.

Dale stared at her. His left hand clenched on the camera strap.

I said, "He can't give you that information now, Bianca. For one thing, he won't know for sure until the medical examiner has a look at the body. For another . . ."

"For another," Dale interrupted, unsmiling, "you're all suspects."

Bianca made an indignant protest.

Dale raised his hands chest high, as if he were fending her off. "I'm calling in. Then I want to talk to Marianne and Lark. I'll take their statements while I'm waiting for the technical crew."

Bianca yanked off her tweed cap and ran a hand through the mahogany hair. "I have a right to know what happened. I signed your damned permission to search forms. This is my property and Hugo is . . . was my employee."

If she'd said "my friend" I would have felt more sympathy for her. Any moment now she was going to announce that she was a taxpayer. It was in the script.

"I pay a lot of property taxes," she said on cue. "I pay your salary, Dale. I'm entitled."

Dale looked at her. He forebore to mention that he and I and Marianne and Keith were taxpayers, too, and that his salary wasn't all that wonderful.

Bianca burst into tears. Keith put his arm around her. "C'mon, old girl. The man's just doing his job."

She made a muffled noise of protest.

"I'm calling in," Dale said flatly and turned on his heel.

We watched him until he was sitting in the brown and white sheriff's car. Bianca cried. Keith patted her, his face blank and his eyes thoughtful.

The mist had intensified to rain. I began to feel very cold. I gritted my teeth to keep them from chattering.

Marianne rubbed her arms. "Dale said I have to make a statement. What does that mean exactly?"

"He'll ask you what you saw, why you decided to look in the ice house. . . ." My voice trailed.

"I heard the ice machine turn on!"

"Then tell him that." I hugged my jacket to me. The hood covered my hair but rainwater was running down my face. I peered into the middle distance. "What happened to the Search and Rescue volunteers?"

Keith said, "Nelson called them off."

"Where are the interns?"

Bianca gave a large sniff. "They were with Del and Angie, searching the machine sheds. I called Del. He'll take them to the house."

"I think we'd better go to the house, too, Bee." Keith's arm still circled Bianca's shoulders. When she made to pull away from him, his grip on her arm tightened.

"Ow. Let me go, Keith. I want to look in the ice house."

"No," Keith said. "No way. Stop acting like a spoiled brat, Bianca."

She swore at him but she sounded less out of control.

The door of the cop car slammed. Dale strode back to us. "I want you to keep your staff and students from leaving, Ms. Fiedler, and I'd appreciate it if you'd ask them not to talk over what happened among themselves. I need to interview all of them. The sheriff's coming out to talk to you. I told him you'd be at the house."

I was impressed that the sheriff, an amiable political hack, would bestir himself that early on a Sunday morning. Dale had probably asked him to get Bianca out of his hair.

Bianca's jaw stuck out and the intense brown eyes were dark with suspicion. Dale met her gaze. As far as I could tell, neither of them blinked.

Keith said, "Let's go in, Bee. You heard the man."

Abruptly Bianca gave up. She shrugged out of Keith's grasp and stalked down the road in the direction of the house.

Keith jogged after her. "We'll be waiting for you, Nelson."

"I ought to isolate them from each other," Dale muttered. "But hell, I can't be in two places at once." He watched them until they were out of earshot. "If you don't mind, Lark, I'll take Marianne's statement first."

"Okay, but I'm going to walk around. I'm cold."

I thought he might offer to let me sit in the back seat while he interrogated Marianne, but he just nodded in the direction of the retreating figures. "Walk that way."

I started off, flapping my arms. I wanted to run but I didn't want to catch up with Keith and Bianca. So I walked. Twenty paces down the road, twenty paces back. When I tired of that, I did standing stretches, jogged in place, flapped my wings. My shivering eased.

The door of the cop car opened and Dale stuck his head out. "Want a cup of coffee?"

I walked over. "Yes, please."

He ducked back and a moment later handed me a mungy Thermos cup. "It's decaf."

"If it's hot I don't care." It was, blessedly. "Thanks."

" 'S okay." He went back to his interrogation.

I warmed my hands on the cup and sipped. Dale might be a country cop but he had urban taste. The decaf was cappuccino.

I stood for a while looking in the direction of the house. I could see the roof, the kitchen window, the metal roofs of the machine sheds, and a corner of the car barn. There was a lot of activity by the car barn, from the sound of doors closing and engines starting up. I couldn't see anyone but I gathered the Search and Rescue people were leaving. They must have walked back to the staging area along the far perimeter of the farm to avoid using the lane that ran past the ice house.

I had just finished Dale's cappuccino when the door of the cop car slammed shut. I wheeled around.

Marianne said, "I'm through. Your turn." She had been crying again but she looked composed.

"Okay. Will you be all right?"

She nodded. "I'm going to go make a coffee cake."

To each her own. Baking was the last activity I would take up under stress. I watched her head for the house, then went to the passenger side of the car and got in.

Dale grunted a greeting and went on scribbling in his notebook. He also had a tape recorder and a laptop computer.

Probably, like Jay, he made longhand notes while the recorder absorbed what a witness said. Jay entered the crucial bits into the computer afterward, two-fingered.

Dale flipped a page over and set the note pad on the dashboard. "This is one hell of a mess, Lark. How much did you see?"

I swallowed. How much is too much? "I saw his sneaker and enough of the leg to know the body was there."

He digested that. "Then how do you know it's Groth?"

I explained.

He sighed. "Okay. Let's begin at the beginning." He removed one tape cartridge, scrawled *M. W.* on it, and inserted another tape. When it began to whir, he picked up his notebook and asked me to give my name and address.

Dale was still asking me questions when the ambulance and the evidence van pulled up by his car. He got out and conferred. I hunkered down and waited. Dale returned and resumed the interview.

The technicians went into the ice house first. They wouldn't be able to remove the body until the M.E. examined it. They cordoned off a fat ellipse around the building. Daffodil-yellow tape gleamed in the mist. The ambulance crew stayed by their vehicle, chewing the fat. One of them was smoking. Camera lights flashed in the ice house. I heard a roar as one of those little hand vacuums started. Jay had trained them well.

". . . then you knew the victim pretty well?"

I had been explaining my role as Hugo's landlady and book supplier. "Well enough to talk to."

"Can you make the formal identification?"

My stomach knotted.

He twisted sideways and looked at me with earnest blue eyes. "I can ask Ms. Fiedler. . . ." He let his voice trail.

He didn't want to ask Bianca because she was at the top of his suspect list and he didn't need to owe her favors. Ditto for Keith McDonald.

"I'll do it." My voice sounded calm, considering I was repressing a strong urge to scream "no."

"I appreciate it, Lark. It won't be pleasant."

"Was he shot?"

"Stabbed. Hacked, actually. I'm guessing the weapon was a machete, like the ones hanging above the plank table." His mouth crimped. He hesitated, then went on, "I'd rather you didn't say anything about the weapon or the condition of the body to the others. I ought to interrogate the lot of them before we make anything public."

"Even Jay?"

He shook his head. "I want Jay to see the body before we move it, budget or no budget. There's some things don't make sense." He frowned. "I guess Jay could do the identification."

"I don't think he ever met Hugo," I said, with honest regret. Surprising but true. Hugo had paid me his rent at the bookstore.

"Does Jay know McDonald?"

I explained the college connection and Bianca's dinner party. The workshop puzzled Dale.

I babbled for a while about the need to educate journalists. The tape recorder clicked to a stop. Dale flipped the cartridge over. I talked some more. He wanted to know about the Meadowlark staff, the Vietnamese farm workers, and the interns. I saw no reason—certainly not an ephemeral loyalty to Bianca—to conceal anything from him. I told him what little I knew.

The rain eased. The medical examiner drove up. Dale jumped out and had the doctor back his Bronco in behind the cop car. Protecting the crime scene. The M.E. was a local internist with an interest in pathology. According to Jay, he was young and bright, but given to odd enthusiasms.

I stayed where I was. I felt queasy—in retrospect and in anticipation. Hacked to death with a machete. The convenient scapegoats would be the refugees. I disliked that idea a lot, but my mind also shied away from the possibility of anyone I knew murdering Hugo. I thought about Hugo, about the art book he had been reading, about the three wilted daffodils in his apartment.

When Dale stuck his head in the driver's side, I was so absorbed in melancholy thought he made me jump.

"Dr. Riley says the backup car's in place. I told 'em to block the entrance to the farm." He slid in and activated his radio. "I need to warn them to let Jay through." He did that amid much crackling police code, then went back to supervise his evidence crew. They were bringing out plastic garbage bags full of something. It took me a moment to realize they were removing the ice cubes from the bin.

I hoped Jay would hurry. He was going to have to pick up my pieces.

He showed up on foot about ten minutes later. I recognized the set of his shoulders from a considerable distance, jumped out of the car, and ran down to him.

He gave me a hug. "All right?"

"So far. I'm going to identify the body."

He winced. "That won't be good for your health."

"Neither is Hugo's death. I'll be okay, Jay, and Dale needs all the help he can get." I explained Dale's reaction to Bianca.

Jay sighed. "I know the feeling."

"Where's the car?" I asked by way of changing the subject.

"I left it out on the highway shoulder. Hi, Dale."

Dale had materialized at Jay's elbow. He looked harassed. "I didn't see you drive up."

Jay explained, adding, "You don't need another set of tread-marks."

Dale groaned. "They've driven everything through here but a bulldozer."

"Does it matter?"

"You mean, was he killed here? I don't think so. Not enough blood."

My stomach clenched. How much did he need?

"You sure?"

"No. It's weird. I think the weapon's hanging right there in the building, but I won't know for sure until the technicians test for bloodstains. I think he was killed somewhere else and brought here, either in a vehicle—or on foot. He wasn't a heavy man. Then he was stuffed into the ice bin."

"I'd better view the body," Jay said. He didn't sound eager. He looked at me. "Not yet, Lark." Meaning I didn't have to enter the ghastly shed yet.

In the end, I didn't reenter the ice house at all. After a cold forty-five minutes, the paramedics carried a stretcher in. I hunched down and watched through the windshield of the cop car. Eventually they reemerged, and the stretcher bore a lumpy form in a body bag. Dale, Jay, and the medical examiner conferred. The doctor shook hands and left. The stretcher moved slowly toward me. I knew what was coming and shut my eyes like a five year old.

"Are you ready, Lark?" Jay, at the door.

I pried my eyes open and got out, every joint stiff with reluctance.

Dale was standing at one end of the body bag, the open end. He cleared his throat. "His face is pretty much intact."

I nodded.

He jerked the fabric down.

"Yes," I said, "That's Hugo." Then I whipped around and barfed Dale's cappuccino onto the broccoli.

Hugo's face was as pale as a bucket of skimmed milk, and a gash, black with dried blood, sliced down from the left eye to the hinge of the jaw. A flap of skin exposed the jawbone. Cysts showed purple against the pallor. His expression was fixed in a snarl of fear or anger, tongue protruding a little.

When I stopped heaving and turned around, the paramedics had covered the hideous mask. They carried the stretcher to the ambulance in silence. Jay put his arm around my shoulders.

"Sorry," Dale said awkwardly. "We had to be sure."

I nodded. In spite of my revulsion, I hadn't resisted making the identification because I had had to be sure, too.

6 ~

WE MADE OUR getaway by the simple expedient of abandoning my car. Jay's was outside, on the highway. We cut across the backyard of the house and around the conference wing. Jay had a word with the deputy blocking the entrance to the drive. Then we lit out.

When we got home I took a hot, hot shower and Jay fixed sandwiches for lunch. By tacit agreement we didn't talk about the murder, though Jay did say he thought Bianca should cancel the workshop. I was in complete agreement with that.

I drank a glass of wine with lunch and took a nap. Neither the wine nor the nap was typical of me. Naturally, I had a nightmare. I dreamed of Hugo's dead face, and woke with my pulse hammering in my throat and my tongue feeling as if it were too large for my mouth. Like Hugo's.

Sluggish and sick, I got up, showered again, crawled into fresh clothes, and went downstairs to see what was happening. Jay was on the phone in the breakfast nook.

I made a pot of coffee and had drunk half a cup before he finally hung up. "Was that Dale?"

"You're kidding. He won't have time to turn around, let along call bystanders." He tugged his moustache. "It was the Dean."

The Dean was the dean of instruction, Jay's immediate supervisor, since Jay was department head. He had supported Jay through the difficult process of gaining faculty approval of the police science program. He was also, less directly, Keith McDonald's boss. The Dean was a little inclined to suffer from anxiety attacks.

Light dawned. "The interns?"

Jay nodded. "McDonald called him. Dale is interrogating the interns. The Dean was just wondering if maybe I couldn't stop that. I pointed out that we have a murder and the kids are material witnesses."

"Suspects." I explained about Jason and Bill and the ice house.

"Oh, so that's what he was talking about. Interesting."

"It probably doesn't mean anything. All the interns were impatient to go home Saturday. I doubt that Jason and Bill did more than stick their heads in the door of the ice house. They couldn't have seen the body from the doorway."

"No."

"Marianne said they should have reported that the ice machine was switched on."

"That's unusual?"

I explained Marianne's reaction.

"Does Dale know?"

"I expect so. He interrogated her at some length before you got there."

Jay sighed. "So there are suspicious circumstances. Okay, I'd better see if it's all right to go out to the farm again."

"We have to retrieve my car anyway, and I need to talk to Bianca about the workshop."

He picked up the phone. Bianca answered. He told her she could talk to me later and asked if Dale was still at the farm. There was a long pause. Finally I heard a squawk at the other end.

Jay said, "Yeah, I know, buddy. The interns are students at the college, though." More squawks. "I couldn't agree more. All the same, if I come out I can probably get the Dean off your back." A less agitated squawk. "Okay. Lark's coming, too. Her car's still there." Resigned squawk. Jay handed me the phone. "He's putting Bianca back on."

I set my cup on the counter. Bianca was saying something intense about Gestapo tactics.

"Dale has to interrogate the witnesses, Bianca." I cleared my throat. "Listen, about the workshop . . ."

"I won't cancel it. Those Vietnamese women killed Hugo. It's nothing to do with my staff."

A good, liberal viewpoint. *Cherchez l'etranger.* I said, "Well, we can talk it over. There are bound to be changes."

"You're coming out?" She sounded less hostile.

"To get my car."

"Come in the mudroom door when you get here."

"Okay."

"I have to go. Mary Sadat's having hysterics." She hung up.

Jay said, "Dale wants you to bring the shoes you were wearing in the ice house."

That made sense. The evidence crew would need to eliminate my footprints and Marianne's from the general scuffle.

Jay drove slightly over the speed limit. He must have been tense. It had stopped raining, but the overcast sky looked sullen and it was beginning to get dark. Four-thirty. Dale had had a lot of time to interview the people at the farm.

As we came into sight of Coho Island and the narrow southern end of Shoalwater Bay, Jay said, "You're going to have nightmares."

I said I already had.

He glanced at me. "Role reversal?"

Jay's nightmares were a recurrent feature of our marriage. I gave him a constrained smile. "I'll lean on you."

"Do that." He was going at least sixty-five.

The sheriff's car no longer blocked the entrance to Meadowlark Farm. We jounced over the cattle guard and drove around behind the house. The extra cop car was there, parked between Dale's and an upscale civilian sedan. Next to the sedan, my old Toyota looked like a junker, but there were two other rattletraps and the high-wheel pickup I knew belonged to Jason. The interns hadn't gone yet. I left my boots, the ones I had worn for the search, in Jay's car.

I led Jay straight through the mudroom into the kitchen. No way was I going to remove my shoes. Mike Wallace was sitting at the butcher-block table eating something. As we entered, he looked up, eyes wide.

Jay greeted him, and Mike told us the others were in the living room. This was not, strictly speaking, accurate. The interns weren't there. Neither was Dale.

Bianca and Del and Marianne were sitting by the fireplace with a strange man who wore jeans with an expensive pullover. The sheriff had apparently come and gone. Bianca introduced her lawyer, Paul Mayer.

As we were shaking hands, Keith McDonald came in from the direction of the master suite looking frazzled.

He nodded at us and turned to Bianca. "Angie says Mary's asleep. I'm sending Carol and the Carlsens home." I heard slamming car doors and revving engines from the direction of the car barn. Corroboration.

Jay said, "Did Nelson okay that?"

McDonald's mouth set. "Yeah, if it's your business."

"They're students, right?"

McDonald gave a curt nod.

"Then they're my business. According to the Dean." Jay kept his tone cool and conciliating.

McDonald didn't like that. He bit his lip.

"You did call him," Jay said with elaborate patience.

"Yes. I told him they needed a lawyer."

"He called the attorney general. They decided I'm cheaper than a lawyer."

"All right," McDonald said, with bad grace.

Mayer licked his chops. Reflexively, I suspect. There was a definite potential for parental lawsuits, but he would have had a large conflict of interest if he took one on.

The college carried no liability insurance as a matter of state

78

policy. Whenever it got itself into legal muck, it leaned on the attorney general's office. According to Jay, the advice was sometimes good and sometimes not.

Mayer said, "Then you have a watching brief, Mr. Dodge?"

"I don't have a brief at all," Jay replied. "I'm not a lawyer."

"I don't understand. . . ."

Bianca made an impatient noise. "The Dean's covering his ass. Jay will make sure the students aren't railroaded."

I saw Jay's moustache twitch in appreciation.

She added, "It's okay, Paul. You can go home now. I'll call you when I need more advice."

The lawyer took ceremonial leave. Bianca escorted him from the room. We all looked at each other. Del raised his whiskey glass and sipped. Keith offered Jay and me drinks, which we declined. Jay took up a station near the fireplace. I sat.

When Bianca returned, I said brightly, "So, what do we do about this workshop?"

"Cancel it," McDonald said. He didn't hesitate, but he avoided Bianca's eyes.

Del took a belt of his favorite anesthetic. "Aw, Keith, no reason to throw all of Bianca's work out the window. Nelson will pull in that gook woman, whassername?"

"Mei Phuoc," Marianne said.

Del gave a small drunken giggle. "May Fuck. Thas the one. Old Hugo was chopped with a machete. 'S obvious." He hiccuped. "Whodunnit, I mean."

"How do you know Hugo was killed with a machete?" I asked.

Bianca made an impatient gesture. "The sheriff told us." She turned to Del and said through her teeth, "Thank you so much."

"No sweat."

Jay smoothed his moustache. "Mrs. Phuoc is a leader in that community. She's not the type to use casual violence."

Bianca frowned. "How do you know Mei?"

79

"There were rumors of Asian gangs from Portland intimidating local people last winter. The sheriff asked me to sit on a task force."

"Oh. And you interviewed Mei?"

"Mrs. Phuoc was on the committee," Jay said drily. He would see that the Vietnamese women weren't railroaded. I cheered up a little.

Del snorted. "She's a peasant. Illiterate."

Jay ignored him. "She's foreman of your work crew, isn't she, Bianca?"

She nodded. "Hugo and Mei got along. She speaks a little English and he spoke a little Vietnamese. God, how am I going to work with those people? I always let Hugo deal with them." She plunked down on one of the armchairs, muttering something about broccoli.

Del smirked. "I'll handle 'em." Har, har.

Bianca rounded on him. "No, you will not. You will not go near my harvest crew. Do you understand me, or are you too drunk to hear?"

Del blinked.

"Go feel up a sheep," she snarled.

Del flushed. "Now lissen . . ."

"No, you listen. I'm tired of your sexual innuendoes. One more crack and you're out of here. One more—"

"Now, Bee . . ."

She turned on Keith. " 'Now, Bee.' You, too, Humbert Humbert. So you sent little Carol home, did you? I'm surprised you didn't drive her yourself."

A delicate silence ensued. Jay looked at his shoes. I admired the painting over the mantle. It depicted Kayport Harbor in slashing abstraction. Del burped.

Angie Martini stalked into the silence. She was wearing jeans and a sweatshirt, but she managed to look like a leopard defending its cub. I remembered that Mary Sadat was *her* protégé.

"Where is that damned deputy?"

Bianca sniffed. "I put him in the conference room. He and the woman the sheriff brought out are interviewing Bill."

Jay said, "Lisa Colman?"

Bianca nodded.

That made sense. Lisa Colman was a detective lieutenant, Dale's supervisor. She would coordinate the investigation. Since Bianca's prominence made the process ticklish, Lisa would probably keep a closer eye on Dale than in an ordinary case. Still, the department was understaffed. Dale would have a lot of autonomy.

Angie was muttering rude words.

I decided it was time for a distraction. "About the workshop, Bianca . . ."

Bianca glowered. "I'm not going to cancel it."

"Isn't that a little disrespectful? After all, Hugo was an old friend."

"Hugo would want me to go on with it. He Believed in Ecology." She was back to speaking in capitals. She also dabbed at her eyes.

I sighed. "Then consider the practicalities. You'll have half a dozen experienced journalists interviewing Carol Bascombe."

Bianca blinked. Angie snorted. Keith cleared his throat as if he had meant to speak but thought better of it.

"And Del," I added, bringing up the heavy guns.

I could see that I had given Bianca pause.

Del stared into his glass and finished off the contents. It was very quiet. I didn't look at Jay.

Marianne said, "I don't want them poking around in my kitchen."

Bianca glanced from me to Marianne to Del, like a wild creature at bay.

I almost had her. Unfortunately, the detectives had finished with Bill.

The kid was wearing sneakers so we didn't hear him coming. He popped out into the living room from the tiled hallway and stopped short, blushing, when he caught sight of all those adults staring at him.

"You must be Bill Johnson." Jay introduced himself and mentioned the Dean. "Are you okay?"

Bill nodded, blushes fading. "They just asked me a bunch of questions about the ice house. I didn't see Mr. Groth, honest. The lady said I could have a lawyer, but that costs a lot of money, so I said no. They told me I could go home."

"Have they talked to Jason Thirkell?"

"Yeah. The guy, Nelson, talked to him first thing. Now him and the lady are at it again."

"Okay. Well, don't worry, Bill. The killing is probably nothing to do with you."

"I told them that," Bill muttered. "Uh, guess I'll go. Where's Mike?"

"In the kitchen," Marianne said. "If you want a sandwich . . ."

Bill brightened. "Yeah. I'm real hungry."

Marianne went with him. I supposed she was one of those women who look on food as the universal panacea. In Bill's case, she was probably right. Maybe in Mike's, too.

Bill's entrance had given Bianca time to regroup.

"I'll hold a news conference," she announced.

All of us stared at her.

The brown eyes gleamed. "When the workshop participants get here Sunday, I'll hold a formal news conference, give them the facts and maybe some . . . some color. Then I'll lay down guidelines. No interviews with the staff, no photos, no intrusions."

I thought that was almost heroically naive. It was so naive I could think of no way to say so without gross rudeness.

"Besides," she added, "Nelson's bound to solve the case by then. He has a whole week."

Jay cleared his throat.

Keith McDonald said, "You're out of your mind." He sounded weary.

"No, no, really, Keith. They want a story, I'll give them a story. Then we can go on with the workshop. I can't cancel. Not with Eric Spielman and Francis Hrubek coming." She was wheedling.

Keith shook his head.

Marianne reentered on noiseless feet. For a large woman she moved quietly.

Bianca leaned forward, hugging her knees. "It'll work, Keith. You'll see." She exuded conviction.

I said, "What if Dale arrests *you?*"

Bianca stared. Keith tugged at his beard.

Jay was frowning at me, the spousal "pipe down" signal.

"But he won't do that," Bianca said with absolute confidence. "I loved Hugo. I didn't have any reason to kill him. We all loved Hugo."

Dead silence.

Angie said, "Uh, Bianca, listen. Hugo was a great gardener. I'm sure we all respected him. But . . ."

"Where's Bill?"

Jason Thirkell, like his sidekick, was wearing sneakers. He strolled into the room as if he owned it. "Where's Bill? I told him to wait for me." Jason was probably not sneering. His mouth just tilted that way.

"He's in the kitchen," Marianne said.

Jason headed for the kitchen. Jay and I exchanged glances, and Jay followed him.

"I don't like that young man," Bianca muttered.

"Huh? Whozzat? Jason's a good kid!" Del lapsed into stupor. I wondered if he was really drunk or faking it. He was a little too obnoxious. I have a hard time calculating the effects of hard liquor. One glass gives me a buzz.

A clacking on the tiles and low voices resolved into Dale and Lisa Colman, Lisa in high-heeled pumps. She was a short,

square woman, about fifty, who had come into the department via dispatch and stayed on doing scutwork until affirmative action caught up with her. Jay thought she was sharp but a
bit unimaginative. She shook hands briskly all the way around
and took her leave, turning to Dale at the last moment.

"My office. Seven. Get something to eat first."

He nodded.

Marianne led her out through the kitchen. I heard her greet
Jay as the door swung shut.

Dale looked at me. "Got the shoes?"

"In Jay's car."

"Don't forget to give them to me before you leave." He
sounded as if my departure was imminent. That was okay
with me.

Bianca said, "We want to know where we stand, Deputy."

Dale said politely, "I appreciate your cooperation, Ms. Fiedler. When I get the results of the autopsy I'll know a lot
more."

Keith pulled a chair. "Sit down, Nelson. Would you like a
drink?"

"Coffee, if you've got it." Dale didn't sit.

Keith went off to the kitchen. Del was watching the deputy
through half-lidded eyes.

Bianca leaned forward. "When is it scheduled?"

"The autopsy? Tomorrow morning. We're rushing it. The
M.E. had three others slated, but he'll do this one first."

"But what about the Vietnamese?"

"Lt. Colman and I are going to see Mrs. Phuoc tonight. The
lieutenant found a translator."

Bianca leaned back, expelling a long breath. "Good. That's
good. It was probably some . . . some old quarrel we don't
know about."

Dale raised an eyebrow. "And Mrs. Phuoc settled it with an
axe?"

Bianca flushed a little. Her chin lifted. "Mei is a fine
woman. I'm not accusing her. But she has a big crew and all of

those women interacted with Hugo. And they do use the machetes. They like the machetes."

Jay and Marianne reentered, followed closely by Keith with a coffee mug. We heard the distant slamming of a car door and a muted roar as Jason's high-wheeler pulled away.

Jay and Dale exchanged greetings. Dale gulped hot coffee. I made another attempt to persuade Bianca to cancel the conference, but she liked her own plan too well to listen. It was time to go. Past time.

I started making noises of disengagement and Jay, bless him, followed my lead. He asked Angie about Mary Sadat. Rather to my surprise Angie didn't use the opportunity to attack Dale. She just said that Mary had been very upset to discover she was the last of the group to see Hugo alive. Angie had given her a mild tranquilizer. That may have been pharmaceutically incorrect but it was sensible. Dale said nothing.

He did follow us out, however, ostensibly to get my boots. Bianca came as far as the mudroom. As we said goodbye she looked me straight in the eye. "Don't desert me, Lark. I need you."

"I'll be here for the workshop," I heard myself saying, "but I still think you should cancel it."

She nodded, solemn. "I respect your opinion."

Right. I gave myself a swift mental kick.

Jay and Dale had gone on out to the cars and were already deep in police technicalities when I got there. The door to the mudroom closed. I could see Bianca watching us from the porch.

I gave a little wave. She waved back and disappeared.

". . . and there's not enough blood," Dale was saying.

My ears pricked. "How much do you need?"

He gave me a wry smile. "Goddamn, Lark, don't you start pumping me. I've had enough of that from Ms. Fiedler McDonald."

"I'll be good. Want my boots?"

He took them. I watched the two men in my rearview mir-

85

ror as I left. They were still deep in conversation.

As I drove homeward, I tried to think up ways to persuade Bianca to abandon the workshop. I also thought about Hugo. And I thought about Hugo and Bianca. Her reaction to his death was so muddled I didn't know how much of it to trust. "He would have wanted us to go on with it." Anytime somebody performs that kind of ventriloquism for the dead I get very uneasy. If I were murdered I'd want everyone to drop everything.

And why had Bianca insisted that everybody loved Hugo when she knew it wasn't the truth? Hugo had been a hard man to know, and it was clear that Del and Angie, to name two, had found him maddening. To say Bianca was in denial was simply to label a response that in this case was inexplicable. I was beginning to think Bianca was at least as strange as Hugo, that I didn't understand her at all.

The honk of an indignant motorist pulled me back onto my own side of the road and I gave up analyzing Bianca. Psychopathology is not my strong suit.

Jay was a good hour behind me. By the time he got home, I had zapped a packet of frozen soup base in the microwave, taken some bits of leftover seafood out to thaw, and made toast and a salad.

I fed him cioppino. When he looked as if his petals were reviving, I said, "Okay, open up. What did Dale mean by not enough blood?"

He dipped toast in his chowder. "Dale thinks the lacerations may be postmortem."

Inflicted after death. I digested that, not comfortably.

"Of course, the body was on ice for a whole week." Jay chewed, his tone vague as if he was thinking of something else. "That complicates everything."

7 ৵

WE HAD GOOD sex that night of the sort calculated to offend the Pope, e.g. with no thought of generating a baby, at least on my part. Possibly I was just Affirming Life. When I woke from the second nightmare, I thought of that—in capitals.

Jay was sleeping deeply. I gave him a prod with my toe but he didn't respond. I wondered how many times he had wakened with a dry mouth and accelerated pulse to find me snoring away in oblivious insensitivity. As the idea crossed my mind, he rolled over and gave me a pat. He didn't wake up, but he wasn't oblivious.

I leaned back on my pillow, half afraid to fall asleep again, but I did, without incident. When I woke at seven I went for a short run and that improved my mood.

Jay had classes that morning, so I fixed him breakfast and we talked a little. I told him Bianca was determined to go on with the workshop.

He swallowed orange juice. "And you agreed to abet her?"

"Abet!"

He smiled. "You have to say 'no' a lot to that kind of personality. Usually they don't resent it."

"I'm sorry for her. She's in a terrible situation."

He considered that over a last bit of toast. He sipped herb tea. He finished off the orange juice. Then he said, "I'm sure she's grieved and worried. Still, at some level, she's enjoying the drama."

That made sense. Bianca was the daughter of an actress, after all. And of the director of any number of detective flicks. I envisioned the ill-omened press conference. It wouldn't do a damned bit of good, but it was bound to be dramatic. I had once held a press conference.

Jay wiped his moustache on a paper napkin and got up. He leaned across the table and kissed me. "Just say no."

"Gee, Nancy, I didn't think you cared." A stale riposte, not up to my standards. Jay gave me a perfunctory grin and went off to work.

I drank another cup of coffee. I was halfway through it when there was a knock at the back door. Bonnie, who was minding my store, came in, bearing printouts. I waited for her to start cross-examining me about the murder, but she just fed me data, mouth quirking in a dreamy smile.

"What is with you?"

She blinked. "What?"

"I found Hugo Groth's body yesterday at the farm."

Bonnie was suitably horrified and sympathetic. I told her about it, cried a little, and explained the workshop dilemma. Either the story had not yet reached the media or Bonnie hadn't turned on the news. Or something else.

I eyed her. "Why the goofy smile? Did you sell your book?" She had finished the manuscript that week.

"What? Oh, no. Not yet. The thing is, Tom's agent sold the film rights."

Of Tom's new novel, I deduced. "That's wonderful. He deserves it, but . . ."

"He wants to take me to Europe!"

Awk. Aargh. "When?" I croaked.

She laughed. "Hey, not today. Stop worrying. Not until after the store opens."

I quit hyperventilating, but I was worried. Bonnie's mind would be on Europe, not on my bookstore, and my bookstore was not ready for spring vacation. Bianca would have to cancel the damned workshop.

I tried calling her off and on all morning, but the line was busy. I finally got through around two-thirty.

When I had identified myself and before I could launch into a well-reasoned plea, she said, "Have you heard the results of the autopsy?"

"Uh, no. Have you?"

"No, and Nelson promised to contact me as soon as it was over. I can't stand this, Lark. It's awful not knowing what happened. He talked to Mei Phuoc last night. He hasn't told me anything about that, either."

I tried to explain that Dale was not going to confide in her so long as she and every member of her household were suspects. I tried, but I must have exercised a little too much tact, because she went on complaining as if I had said nothing. It occurred to me, not for the first time, that Bianca had difficulty hearing anything she didn't want to hear.

She didn't want to hear about cancelling the workshop. After half an hour of fruitless pleading, I gave up and disengaged.

I was deep in Bonnie's printouts when the doorbell rang, front door this time. It was Dale. He said he had come to consult Jay.

I ushered him into the kitchen, checked the clock—it was almost four—and allowed that Jay would be home soon.

Dale collapsed onto a kitchen chair. He looked exhausted.

"Coffee?"

He nodded without speaking.

Unlike Marianne, I do not bake in an emergency. However, I can thaw stuff. I thawed a coffee cake and fed him two thick slabs. At that point, when he was almost articulate, Jay drove in. I put the kettle on—Jay still doesn't drink coffee—and awaited events.

Properly speaking, I was a suspect in the case. Dale should not have discussed the evidence in my presence. However, since the two men were sitting in the breakfast nook, I cleverly disguised myself as the lady of the house and began to prepare dinner, though it was Jay's turn to cook.

Dale needed a sympathetic listener. Jay listened. So did I, from the kitchen. As the deputy talked, he gave me one or two distracted glances, but I didn't seem to cramp his style.

He began, predictibly, by griping about Bianca. She had called one of our U.S. senators, the governor, and the congressman for our district. No wonder the line had been busy.

Bianca was a heavy contributor to all three campaign funds, so the politicians listened. Then they called. Their calls had blotted up most of Lisa Colman's time, which was one of the reasons Dale felt the need to consult Jay. It was also a solid reason why Dale had not given Bianca the information she thought she was entitled to. I considered telling Dale to explain all that to Bianca, but I didn't want to call attention to myself, so I peeled carrots.

Having got that off his chest, Dale launched into a detailed account of the autopsy results. Egged on by Jay.

As Dale had guessed, Hugo had died, not from the knife wounds, but from a blow to the head. There were signs that he had put up a fight—bruises on his fists and elsewhere. There were also marks that indicated the body had been moved after the killing. The fight went some way toward explaining the uncharacteristic snarl on Hugo's dead face.

Dale was looking for indications that any of his suspects had been in a fight, though a week was time to heal. The lab was working on nail scrapings. The slashes that disfigured the corpse had been administered after death, and not immediately after death, either. Someone was naive. Someone was also vicious. Dale thought the mutilation was an attempt to throw suspicion on users of machetes. I thought so, too.

I rinsed a cup of rice and considered. I could believe Del Wallace was vicious enough and racist enough to incriminate the Vietnamese, but he also raised lambs for slaughter. Angie Martini might see that as further evidence of brutality, but, though he probably didn't butcher the animals himself, I thought Del would have a clear idea of the futility of postmortem wounds. He was stupid when he was drunk, but he wasn't drunk all the time. Of course, he could have panicked.

So who else was ignorant and brutal enough to mutilate Hugo's body? The mutilation was foolish and gruesome, but it was also unnecessarily elaborate. One of the students? Keith? I thought about Keith McDonald. I thought of Carol Bascombe and her unnecessarily elaborate hair.

Dale and Jay were speculating about the time of death. Apparently that was what the M.E. had done also, because the ice made any degree of precision impossible. Mary Sadat had seen Hugo alive at her parents' restaurant Saturday evening. Dale thought it probable Hugo had been killed the next day, although he didn't rule out Monday. It was unlikely that Hugo had ridden his bike out to the farm in the dark, so Saturday and Sunday night were probably out, and by eight or so on Monday there would have been too many witnesses around for the fight, and for movement of the body, to have gone unnoticed. Ergo Sunday. And Sunday meant Hugo had probably had an appointment with his killer. Otherwise he would not have gone out to the farm. It sounded logical but vague. It eliminated no one absolutely, though Marianne had stayed in and around the kitchen during the day, baking goodies for the workshop and freezing them. I had been with Jay.

It was nice to know Dale thought I was in the clear. On the strength of that, I made considerable noise spinning greens for a salad. I also poured Dale another cup of coffee, though he declined the cake. Jay had a piece.

Possibly the sight of the cake jogged Dale's memory. He slewed in the chair and dug an object from his pants pocket. "Want to see something really weird?"

I craned around the end of the cupboards.

"It looks like saltwater taffy," Jay said after a moment. "What about it?"

"Groth was wearing one of those Goretex rain jackets, the kind with big pockets that close with Velcro."

"Yeah?"

"He had six—count 'em, six—small bags of taffy, three in each of the big pockets."

I said, "That's from that little candy shop in Seaside."

Dale sat up. "What shop?"

"I don't remember the name, but they're supposed to make the best taffy on the coast. A house guest brought us a pound of the stuff last spring." My brother-in-law ate most of it.

"How can you tell where it's from?" Dale shoved the piece across the table.

"It's the paper. Most taffy is twisted in plain white paper, very light waxed paper, I think. This stuff has a little flower pattern . . . Flower's! That's the shop. Flower's Candies."

Dale took out his notebook and began scribbling. "Thanks, Lark."

"It still doesn't explain why Hugo had all that candy in his pockets."

"Sure doesn't. Any ideas?"

Dale and Jay starting spinning theories about the taffy and discarding them. Possibly Hugo had been smoking dope and had developed the munchies. I couldn't think of anything useful to contribute to the discussion, so I went back into the kitchen.

Jay gave up, too, after a while. "What about the interns?" he asked. "The Dean will want to know their situation."

Dale shrugged and pocketed the taffy. "Assuming the crime was committed Sunday between eight and four . . ."

"Assuming that."

"You've got the married couple, the Carlsens. They alibi each other, except for half an hour at one P.M. when the guy went to the Quik Stop for potato chips. Of course they would alibi each other. Ms. Bascombe . . ." Dale gave a fey little flip with his hand and pursed his lips. "Carol was with a Friend."

My ears pricked, but I had to laugh at the parody. Dale was revealing hidden talents.

Jay smiled. "Did she identify the guy?"

Dale shook his head. "She was real coy. Married man, I guess. Mary Sadat worked at the restaurant, but she was alone Sunday morning. Jason Thirkell and Bill Johnson drove down to Seaside early and didn't come home until well after dark. Jason's pickup is pretty distinctive. We're looking for corroboration—for all of the kids. I'd like to eliminate them." He rubbed the back of his neck. "I don't see why they'd do it."

My father is a professor. I said, "Come on, Dale. Disgruntled students assault their teachers all the time."

"That's urban high school and junior high kids, mostly. College students are smarter."

I wondered if Dale had ever been a college student in the usual sense of the word. "You didn't mention Mike Wallace. He's an intern, too."

Jay said, "He isn't in the program, Lark. He just lives out there and works for Bianca off and on. He's a student, though, so I'm concerned about him."

Dale sipped coffee. "Mike was in and out all day. No clear alibi."

Jay said, "What about the motives floating around Meadowlark Farm? I mean, the staff's motives?"

Dale set his empty cup down and stood up. "Lark knows those folks better than I do. Ms. Fiedler says they were all devoted to Hugo Groth—her words."

Jay had risen, too. "That wasn't the impression I got," he said mildly. "Bound to be conflicts in a small group like that. I gathered that Groth and Ms. Martini had philosophical differences."

"She's a dyke," Dale muttered.

I said, "She sounds more scrupulous, sexually, than either Keith McDonald or Del Wallace. I don't know what Hugo felt about homosexuals. She said he worked with her well enough."

"She said." Dale sighed. "Those folks are pretty intense about the organic stuff. Maybe there was professional rivalry. Wish I understood more about that kind of farming." He

93

added, wry, "I was raised on a farm, the ordinary kind. Never took to it. When Dad decided to quit, he asked us kids if one of us wanted to take over. We didn't, so he sold the place. My folks like Arizona."

"Doesn't your father miss the farm?"

Dale laughed. "Not so's you'd notice. He's taken up golf."

Jay said, "You talked to Mei Phuoc last night. How did it go?"

Dale shrugged. "Mei was with her family that Sunday. Of course, she'd say that. So will the others. It's a tight community. She was very upset when we told her Groth had been killed."

"They got along?"

"I guess so. She cried some when I said he was dead, but she was defensive about the machetes."

"Natural enough to be defensive."

"Yeah." Dale sounded glum.

He left shortly after that and I took a look at what I'd prepared for dinner. There was a hunk of halibut in the meat drawer. I broiled it.

Bianca called me again that evening. "Lark?"

The human voice is an expressive instrument. Bianca's sounded like an ancient Victrola winding down.

I gritted my teeth and projected perkiness. "Oh, hi, Bianca."

"Trish is here."

I drew a blank. "Trish?"

"Hugo's ex-wife."

I digested that.

"Trish wants to go through his apartment tomorrow. She'll be trying to make funeral arrangements. . . ." The low-energy sound trailed.

I covered the mouthpiece. "Jay, is Dale Nelson finished with Hugo's apartment yet?"

We were sitting in the breakfast nook reading. We sit there a lot.

94

Jay marked his place in his thick textbook with a reluctant finger. "What's that?"

I repeated the question.

"I don't know. You'll have to check with him. Why?"

I explained.

He frowned. "Why would the ex-wife be making the arrangements?"

I was beginning to feel like a relay satellite.

Bianca said, "Trish is Hugo's heir. He left everything to her."

I relayed that to Jay.

"Oh. Well, in that case, she can probably go through his stuff, but not until Dale gives her the go ahead."

I explained the situation. Bianca said wearily, "Okay. I'll check with Nelson in the morning and get back to you. If he's through inspecting the place, will you meet us there and let us in? We don't have Hugo's effects yet. No key."

"All right, Bianca. I was going in to the bookstore in the morning anyway. Call me there."

Before I could segue into an impassioned plea to cancel the workshop she rang off.

I hung up less abruptly and caught Jay watching me.

He smiled. "She's a real fiddler, isn't she? Why are you dancing to her tune?"

"Goddamn, Jay, have a little humanity. The woman needs help."

"She's using you."

We had a quarrel. It was neither wounding nor lengthy but it gave me food for thought.

Later, as I lay in bed drifting off to sleep, it occurred to me to wonder if Bianca's behavior had the same irritant effect on other relationships she intersected with.

I drove in to the bookstore early and Bonnie went with me. She was full of the European trip. That was both threatening and restful—threatening for obvious reasons, restful because it made a change from Bianca's problems. Bonnie and I shelved books. Bianca called around ten and said she was on the way in. Dale had agreed to give Trish free access to the apartment.

I was paranoid enough to call Dale myself, no easy feat. I was just hanging up from my brief conversation with him when Bianca parked her van in front of the store. I watched her get out and go around to the passenger side as I tried to figure out how to deal with Hugo's not-widow.

Bonnie said, "Gee, she's pregnant."

She was. Bianca knocked and I opened the door and Hugo's ex-wife entered. She was a pretty, faded woman, Bianca's age—Hugo's age. She wore no makeup and her eyes were pink-rimmed. She had pulled her shoulder-length hair back on the nape of her neck. Her face looked defenseless. And she was very, very pregnant.

Bianca introduced her as Trish Groth.

She held out her hand. "You're Lark. Hugo liked you a lot."

He did? I mumbled my condolences and introduced Bonnie, who seemed to be taking mental notes for her next novel. I offered Trish a cup of tea, which she declined, and we went upstairs. Bonnie stayed below shelving books.

I unlocked the door and we entered. It was clear that the police had come and gone. Black smudges of fingerprint powder smeared the kitchen cabinets, and the bedding on the futon was bunched and crumpled. Somebody had tossed the wilted daffodils. Bianca made straight for the house plants.

"They need water!" She sounded shocked.

Trish was panting from the climb. She stood in the entry in the classic posture of a pregnant woman, belly thrust forward, one hand on her arched back.

"Shall I get you a chair?" I asked.

She smiled a little. "It's harder to get out of a chair than to stay on my feet. Thanks, though. This is nice." She drifted to the window and looked out. "He said he had a great view of the marina." She stared out at the distant water, face sad.

Bianca bustled back from the kitchen with a small watering can in bright enamel. She revived the failing vegetation and went back to the kitchen, calling over her shoulder, "His papers are in the back, in the bedroom. Did you want to go through them?"

Trish turned. "I suppose I should. I haven't notified his sister. I wonder if the cops did."

"Is she next of kin?"

Trish nodded. "Yes, but she disapproved of Hugo. She's very conventional. Disapproved of me, too." A smile touched her mouth. "If she could only see me now."

Bianca dried her hands. "I'll show you the desk. There's a clothes closet, too. . . ." The two women went off and I decided I might as well wipe the smears off the kitchen cabinets. I found a sponge and a bottle of spray cleanser (Guaranteed Non-Toxic!) and started squirting and wiping. The medicine cabinet in the bathroom was probably a disaster.

I wondered where Hugo had kept his stash of pot. The refrigerator? From the smears on the surface I gathered the police had looked there, too. I wiped the door clean and peered into the freezer compartment. A pint of Ben and Jerry's Tin Roof ice cream and two trays of ice cubes. No Baggie. I saw nothing suspicious in the hydrator, either.

I rinsed the sponge and cleaned the cupboard doors. There was no sign of illicit substances on the shelves. A covered glass dish caught my eye and I lifted it down to the counter. It was a handsome piece of crystal—Venice green, and expensively plain. I lifted the lid. Three pieces of Flower's taffy lay on the bottom of the dish. I wondered if Dale had noticed the candy—probably not, if he had searched the apartment before going through Hugo's personal effects. I set the dish on the small table and made a mental note to call it to Dale's attention.

It didn't take me long to clean the rest of the smears. I found a feather duster, gave the living room surfaces a once over, and straightened Hugo's bedding. The place had been tidy when I saw it last.

I was plumping the pillows when Bianca and Trish came back down the hall, Trish stuffing papers into her purse. They came within sight of the dining table. Trish stopped.

"What is it?" Bianca asked.

Trish burst into tears.

Between us, Bianca and I managed to seat her at the table. I had left my handbag in the store, but Bianca came up with a wad of clean tissues. Bianca patted and I murmured and we stared at each other. It couldn't be good for anyone to cry that hard.

Finally Trish seemed to pull herself together, though she continued to shiver as if she were cold.

I found a tea kettle and put it on. Hugo had left a box of herb teabags in the cupboard. I brewed three cups. I scarcely knew Bianca and didn't know Trish, so I was feeling distinctly out of place. Perhaps Trish sensed my discomfort.

When I brought her her cup she thanked me. "I'm sorry to let you in for that. It was the candy dish."

I stared at her blotched face and then at the green glass of the dish.

"Organic c-candy." She cried a little more and wiped her eyes. "Hugo had an awful sweet tooth. We used to joke about it. He was crazy about Flower's taffy."

I lifted the lid. "Only three left."

She took them out. "Then let's eat them. For Hugo."

I hate taffy. I chewed mine—it was some kind of mint—as long as I could stand it and then gulped it.

Trish gave a watery giggle. "I can't stand the stuff. It feels as if it's pulling my fillings out."

Bianca swallowed. "Mine was peanut butter. Kind of nice."

Trish sighed—a long uneven sound. "I gave him the dish when I got the job with the county library. He never kept anything in it but Flower's taffy. Oh God, I wish he wasn't d-dead." She cried some more, but she was no longer helpless with grief. She blew her nose and shoved the damp tissue in her bag. "I'm going to take the dish home with me."

I said, "I have a box it would fit in. Shall I wrap it for you?"

"That would be awfully nice."

I hesitated. "And there's the Zen book. You ought to take that with you, too. He was reading it when . . . it was the last book he read, I think." I went to the armchair and closed the Zen master. "It's wonderful if you like gardens."

Trish slewed around, sniffing. "I like to look at them, but Bianca will tell you I have a brown thumb. They never let me work in the garden at the commune."

I brought her the huge book. "You loved Hugo, didn't you?"

She nodded, swallowing. "You're wondering why we divorced, right? I wanted a healthy baby. Hugo's babies . . . died." She closed her eyes, then opened them and gave me a very direct look. "He had major exposure to Agent Orange. I lost three deformed fetuses. When they told me the fourth was deformed, I had an abortion. Hugo was raised Catholic." She shook her head. "So was I, for that matter, but he just couldn't deal with the idea. So I divorced him."

Bianca said, "Trish . . ."

She was getting upset again. "I wanted a baby, a nice ordinary kid, so I divorced Hugo. He told me he'd always think of me as his wife—not in a threatening way, you know—it was just the truth. I thought I might remarry, but I never found anyone I liked half as much as I liked Hugo." She bit her lip, which was trembling.

"But the baby . . ."

"Artificial insemination." She gave a short laugh. "Hugo hated that. He said it was like cattle, but it's giving me a nice healthy little girl. I don't know the father and don't want to. I think of her as Hugo's daughter."

I was starting to cry.

Trish said, "Can we go? I want to get out of here. I want to go home."

8 ❧

I JERKED UPRIGHT in my office chair. "My God, we ate the evidence!"

Bonnie handed me a tissue and I blew my nose. We were in the back room. Trish and Bianca were long gone. I had been telling Bonnie Trish's story, a three-hanky tale if there ever was one.

"Evidence?" Bonnie said cautiously.

I stood, jiggling the computer desk. "Dale found saltwater taffy in Hugo's pockets. I just discovered more of it upstairs in the green candy dish."

"The one you wrapped up like a birthday present?"

I had shrouded the candy dish in foam wrap, set it in a small box, and protected it with styrofoam pellets. Trish could have dropped it from an airplane.

I fumbled in the desk drawer and found the key to the apartment. "I'm going upstairs. Back in a minute."

Bonnie gave a resigned nod. She knew she'd get the whole story eventually.

I had tossed the candy wrappers into the wastebasket by Hugo's reading chair. I retrieved them and sat in the chair. Time to stop emoting. I supposed I ought to call Dale, though the candy was probably not crucial in and of itself. It just confirmed Hugo's little secret.

The dish had been nearly empty, though. If Hugo thought he was going to need a taffy fix he would have headed for the supplier. Did the shop sell its stuff in Kayport?

I wanted a phone. Hugo had kept his in the bedroom/office. I stood up to go back there, then changed my mind. I stuffed the bits of paper into my jeans pocket and clattered downstairs instead.

I entered the bookshop from the back entrance. Bonnie was out in the store dusting shelves. I could hear her humming "April in Paris." I grabbed my jacket and purse, and her jacket and purse, and went in pursuit. I found her dusting off World War I.

"Come on, Bonnie. We're going to Seaside."

"Seaside? Whatever for?" She gave a biography of Marshal Petain an extra fillip with the feather duster.

She came with me under protest. Before we left, she made me call the cops. I tried calling Lisa, Dale, and Jay, without result. I left messages all over the place. What more could I do?

Seaside is a honky-tonk beach town of the kind people from the city used to take their kids to in the 1920s when an excursion train ran from Portland to the coast. The drive from Kayport took about an hour. I used the time to fill Bonnie in, not just about the taffy but about everything, including Bianca's refusal to cancel the workshop.

Bonnie thought I should just quit. I explained about Bianca's ability to radiate guilt.

"What can she do to you?"

"Sue?" I was joking. Then I remembered the high-priced lawyer. Bianca and I had an oral contract. I wished I knew more about Washington law.

Fact. The main drag of Seaside is called Broadway. It is one lane wide and runs due west from Highway 101 to the ocean with unmetered parking on both sides of the street. On that blustery day most of the parking spots were empty. I drove down the street very slowly trying to find the Flower's Candies sign.

Broadway ended in a tiny turnaround rimmed with concrete sidewalks. A bronze statue of Lewis and Clark, shrunk to three-quarter size, stood in the center. The explorers gazed at the Pacific beyond a sign that informed us we had reached the end of the Lewis and Clark trail. Daffodils encircled the statue. The sandy beach lay a good ten feet below the level of an old-style esplanade. The beach curved south toward a forested headland like something out of Robinson Jeffers. For once it was not raining, but the ocean was dreadnought gray flecked with whitecaps.

I negotiated the tight curve of the turnaround and looped back for another pass at the street. Bonnie suggested we park and walk. The likeliest territory for taffy shops was only seven blocks long. I parked by an empty arcade that was blasting out rap music and we got out.

We found Flower's Famous Saltwater Taffy tucked into an alleyway between a kite shop and a charming little bookstore. Bonnie pulled me away from the bookstore, which, in any case, was closed, and we entered the shop.

There was an immediate reek of warm chocolate and refined sugar. I blinked and looked around. All the wood surfaces were enameled white and yellow, and the famous taffy in its neat paper twists overflowed faux-country barrels. Miniature silver scoops dangled from plastic cords.

I couldn't see anybody, but reassuring noises emanated from a back room. I approached the glass display counter and saw a bell. A sign said "Ring for Assistance," so I did.

"Pralines," Bonnie purred.

In addition to every conceivable flavor of taffy, the glass cases held an opulent variety of fudges, nougats, and, indeed, pralines. The smell was making me queasy.

"Can I help you?" A big woman, who wore a white baker's apron over jeans and a striped T-shirt, gave us a wide professional smile. I could see she found customers an annoying interruption. I knew the feeling. It wasn't exactly the high season and she probably hadn't yet geared up to meet the public.

I said, "Do you sell your taffy through other candy stores?"

She tucked a wisp of hair behind one ear. "Nope. Just here. We're thinking of starting a mail order line next fall, if you're interested."

I explained hastily that I wasn't a wholesale candy buyer. Then I launched into a muddled account of Hugo's death.

Rather to my surprise the woman didn't toss us out on our ears. She seemed intrigued that her confection had been taken in evidence at a murder site.

"What did you say his name was?"

"Hugo Groth."

"I guess it wasn't on the news last night."

"Probably not." I did my best to describe Hugo. When I mentioned the ponytail and the boils that marred his complexion, her face brightened.

"Gosh, yes. A week ago Sunday, like you said. When he came in I remember thinking he was going to buy fudge. People with skin problems usually do. I was wondering if I ought to steer him to the healthy stuff." She flushed a little. "I know all this candy isn't real good for you. Did you see the sugar-free taffy?"

"Yuck!"

She grinned and relaxed. Candy shop proprietors probably suffer from health nuts the way bookstore owners suffer from self-appointed censors.

"I think it's awful, too, but you'd be surprised at the parents who drag kids in here and then won't let them buy candy with real sugar in it. I mean, why not take the poor little devils to a granola store?" She laughed heartily. Bonnie and I smiled.

"Hugo?" I prompted.

"You say he was killed?"

"Not long after he left here. The sacks of your taffy were still in his pockets."

She made a sad clucking noise. "It's a crazy world."

"Do you remember what time he came in?"

"You don't ask for much." Her mouth compressed in the

effort to remember. She shook her head. "Early, I think, but I can't say exactly. We open at ten, so it was after that. Business was slow. I was in and out, making a big batch of fudge."

"Well, thanks anyway. I'll tell the deputy in charge to call you." I got out a notepad and started to write Dale's phone number down for her.

"You could ask his friends what time they was in town."

"What did you say?"

She blinked at my tone. "His friends. They was waiting outside for him—by the kite shop."

I felt a moment of pure exhilaration followed by panic. "Friends. What did they look like?"

She shook her head. "It was raining, see, and the window was a little steamy. I just saw these blurs hanging out by the kite shop and when he left they left, too. I figured he was going to share all that taffy with his friends."

I drew a breath. "How many of them were there?"

"Two," she said without hesitation. "One tall, one shorter."

"How much shorter?"

The candy maker's mouth tightened. "Look, I got a bunch of taffy pulling back there. I'm sorry your friend got killed, but that's all I can tell you."

I thanked her profusely, took her card, and gave her Dale's number.

Bonnie said in a small voice, "May I buy some pralines?"

The woman made the transaction in silence, handing Bonnie a small white paper bag and her change. "Thank you and come again."

Bonnie promised she would.

The woman turned to me. "I wouldn't swear it in court, mind you, but I think it was a man and a woman."

"The people waiting for Hugo?"

She nodded.

I thanked her and we left.

She had thrown me for a loop—two loops. I had been assuming Hugo was alone. When I took in the fact that he wasn't, I had leapt to the conclusion that the waiting pair were Jason Thirkell and Bill Johnson. Jason and Bill had admitted they spent the day in Seaside. What man and what woman?

The question kept me quiet all the way to Astoria.

As I drove onto the long drawbridge across the slough on the west side of Astoria, I noticed that the mud flats were exposed. Low tide. Way above us in the distance, the bridge over the Columbia showed pale green against darkening clouds. The wind had picked up.

Bonnie was nibbling a praline.

"Is it good?"

"Yum. Want one?"

"Not without coffee."

The Toyota chugged onto the main drag and I turned left for the bridge. The ramp coiled up and up, high over the ship channel, then swooped down to a long straight stretch. On either side at mid-river, the wind pushed small combers at the exposed mud flats. The bridge is nearly five miles long.

The speed limit on the straight was fifty-five, as for any two-lane highway, but the wind was ripping across the water, throwing spray onto the windshield, so I went slower. I turned on the wipers and gripped the wheel. The car shuddered with every gust, and half a dozen sassy seagulls, beaks into the northwest wind, were pacing us at eye-level. In gales, the state police close the bridge because waves wash over the roadbed.

The Sunday Hugo was killed the wind had blown a steady twenty-five knots from the south with gusts of fifty. Surely even Hugo would not have ridden a bicycle across the bridge in that kind of weather. How had he got to Seaside? Who had given him a ride?

I posed the question for Bonnie as we finally negotiated the raised section of the bridge over the Washington channel.

"I suppose it was too far for him to ride his bike."

"The distance wouldn't have bothered Hugo, but I think the wind would have."

"Maybe he took a bus."

That was the logical answer. "Or maybe his murderer drove him."

"Or murderers."

I settled in behind a slow-moving camper. "The woman did say there were two people waiting for him."

"Who?"

I shook my head. "Nobody but the two boys said anything about going to Seaside that day, and they denied seeing Hugo."

"A man and a woman," Bonnie reminded me.

"Possibly a man and a woman—or a man and a slight boy. She wasn't sure. Probably Jason and Bill. Bill isn't very big."

That was idle speculation, of course. I indulged in it because I had a bad conscience. The candy woman was Dale's witness. I had found her for him, but I should have left the questioning to him. I tried to remember whether I had said anything likely to distort her recollections. Bonnie didn't think so. That was some comfort.

So were the pralines. When we got back to the bookstore, Bonnie made a pot of coffee and I ate one. It was excellent.

Jay and Tom were in the kitchen when we got home, Tom full of his ghastly European plans. He whisked Bonnie off before I could blurt out that I didn't want them to go.

"What's for dinner?"

"It's either beef stew or beef soup. We'll find out." Jay gave me a long, considering look. "Why don't you sit down and tell me the day's misadventures?"

"That's not fair!" Misadventures indeed.

I came more or less clean. Jay bawled me out. He also called Dale—and got through. When Jay hung up he said Dale was coming to the house.

The beef soup was nice—lots of veggies from Tom's garden. I was finishing the dishes when Dale appeared at the back door. I gathered he was taking my information seriously. I gave him the candy wrappers and the woman's business card. He drank a cup of coffee but he didn't say much, except that everybody at the farm, including the interns, was lying to him. I thought that was probably true.

When Dale left he told us he was going to interview the candy maker the next day. Maybe she'd remember something about Hugo's "friends."

I had barely showered after my run the next morning when Bianca called. She was still adamant that the workshop would go on, so I didn't bother to tell her about Seaside. She said Trish wanted to hold a memorial service and invite Hugo's friends and fellow workers.

"When?"

"Friday. At the farm."

I sighed. "I suppose the police won't release the body."

"No. And Trish needs closure. She's due in ten days."

That made sense, unfortunately. "Can I help?"

She gave me a list of people to contact, mostly gardeners. I had been so much in the habit of thinking of Hugo as a loner, it hadn't occurred to me that other people in the community would also have known him. I told her I'd do the calling, took down the time of the service, and hung up on a subdued note.

That was the day Mary Sadat disappeared.

Bonnie and I drove in to the bookstore to work on a window display. Bonnie was full of her plans for Paris and insisted on telling me all about them. So far I had kept my chagrin to myself. I bit the insides of my cheeks and exercised self-control.

The display, featuring kites of all kinds, including a handsome Chinese number, was going up fast, so I decided to take a break and call the people whose names Bianca had given me. I was halfway through the list when Jay rang up.

"What's with the busy signal?"

I explained.

"Well, okay," he grumbled. "Listen, Dale just called me. They think that dark-haired intern, Mary Sadat, is missing. She didn't show up for a work session this morning. You know what this means?"

"Among other things, that the Dean will be camped in your office all afternoon."

He groaned. "You got it."

"Shall I drive to the farm and see if I can find out what's happening?"

"If you have time. I tried calling Bianca a couple of times without getting through."

"Okay," I said. "After lunch."

I finished the funeral calls and Bonnie finished the display window. We went out for deli sandwiches. When she heard of my mission at the farm, Bonnie said she'd call Tom to take her home. That was kind. They were, she said, planning a side trip to northern Italy. That was less kind.

There were no cop cars in the parking area by the Meadowlark car barn, so I gathered that Dale hadn't sent for the Search and Rescue people. I knocked on the mudroom door and went in. When I entered the kitchen, Marianne dropped a ladle.

"I didn't mean to startle you," I said. "I did knock."

"It's okay. I'm just jumpy." She rinsed the ladle off at the sink. "You heard about Mary?"

"I heard she didn't show up this morning."

"No." Marianne went back to her kettle. Something smelled of garlic and onions.

"What does Bianca think happened?"

Marianne sighed. "God knows, but she's frantic. They're out at the greenhouses."

"Tell me how to find them and I'll get out of your hair."

She started to give me directions, but Mike came in from their wing of the house, so she sent him with me.

Mike was a shy young man and I'd never really talked to

him. We trudged past the car barn in silence. As we came to the machine sheds, he burst out, "D'you think somebody hurt Mary?"

"Hurt" was a euphemism for "killed." I said gently, "I don't know, Mike. I hope not."

"She's so little." His voice was anguished.

I stole a glance at him. His face was suffused with emotion. "Tell me about Mary. She was quiet the day I met the interns. I felt I didn't get to know her at all."

He mumbled something. Another glance showed he was near tears, so I didn't press him. I thought about shy people. They do a lot of the world's work.

"Dad doesn't like her," he burst out.

That was my impression, too. I could think of nothing comforting to say.

We walked along a path springy with bark dust. I supposed it kept out the mud. I could see the greenhouses, ultra-modern metal and vinyl constructions, in the near distance.

"I wanted to go out with her." Mike sounded half-ashamed. "But her folks are strict with her. And anyway she said she liked older guys." He glanced at me. "She's not a lesbian, you know."

I was startled. "I didn't think she was."

"Dad says Angie's hot for her."

I kept my mouth shut. I was not about to criticize Del Wallace to his son, but I did wonder about the depth of Del's malice toward Mary. What had he called her? Sadsack Sadat? Mary was from the Middle East. Her parents ran a place called the Phoenician, and I suspected they were fairly recent immigrants. That might be a clue to Del's attitude. He was a born Know-Nothing.

Partly to lighten the mood, I said, "I'm surprised you like Mary. I thought all the guys would go for Carol Bascombe."

Mike cleared his throat. "Carol's kind of cute but she's a real airhead."

Either that or she gave a good airhead imitation.

Up close the greenhouses seemed built on a larger scale than the distant prospect had led me to believe. In spite of myself I was impressed. Oriented east/west for maximum light, they loomed well over my head, with odd vents and extrusions marring their smooth lines. The greenhouses were big enough to get lost in—or hide in. A tall stack of wooden flats leaned against the nearer of them.

"Was this where Hugo's bike was hidden?"

Mike hunched his shoulders against a wind gust. "Yeah. I guess so. I mean, there aren't any other stacks of crates."

I could see why the bicycle wasn't found immediately. The stack was as high as my head and quite close to the north wall of the greenhouse. If the bike had been shoved back into the crevice, it would have been hard to see. I walked to the door and started to open it.

"They're in the other house, Mrs. Dodge."

I followed him around the corner of the first greenhouse to the entrance to the second. The two greenhouses were offset so one did not shade the other. As we approached I could hear voices—a male rumble and sharp female response.

Mike stopped on the step. "They're arguing."

I said, "Well, thanks for showing me the way out, Mike. I'll see you later."

"Okay. Bye." He loped off toward the house, looking relieved not to have to go into the greenhouse.

I took a deep breath and pushed the door open without knocking. A strong herbal odor, not unpleasant, weighted the warm air. I shut the door with care.

"... and you were the last one to see her, Del," Bianca was saying.

"What's that supposed to mean?" Del's voice rose.

They were standing with Angie about halfway down the long walkway between two rows of seedlings in long flats.

"She was working for you yesterday afternoon."

"What if she was?"

"Damnit, Del, I just want to know when she left and

whether you said anything to her to drive her away."

At that point, Angie's head came up and she spotted me. She waved and the others turned.

"Oh, Lark," Bianca said. "Have you heard . . ."

The floor was concrete covered with some kind of outdoor matting, dark brown. I unzipped my jacket and walked toward them. "Jay called me."

"And you knew I'd need you." Bianca gave me a melancholy smile. "How thoughtful of you."

The other two stared at me as if I was an intruder—an unwelcome one. I didn't blame them. However, Bianca's assumption meant I didn't have to explain my presence.

I said, "Tell me what happened."

"Nothing's happened," Del snorted. "Not a damned thing."

"You wish." Angie's lip curled. "Mary was supposed to help me thin the spinach." She made a wide gesture that encompassed the trays of greenery. "When she didn't show up at eight, I waited for her ten minutes or so, then I started in working. I thought she'd show up. Sometimes she oversleeps."

"Lazy cunt," Del muttered.

Angie took a step toward him. "If I were you, Del, which thank God I'm not, I would speak softly and watch my words."

"I'll say what I damned well please." Del's response seemed automatic. I thought he looked worried.

"Because . . ." Angie cleared her throat. "Because you are the only one on this farm who disliked Mary, and when the police find her body . . ." Her voice broke. She stared at Del, blinking back tears. "You shit. I hope you hang. We hang murderers in this state."

Bianca said, "Now, Angie, we're not sure Mary's been harmed."

"Her parents don't know where she is." Anger steadied Angie's voice. "I called them at ten, Lark, when she still hadn't come. Her mother said her bed hadn't been slept in, and she didn't work at the restaurant last night. It's closed Mondays. Mary is missing, goddamnit."

Bianca removed her tweed hat and stuffed it in her pocket. Her bangs stuck to her forehead. "I spoke with Mrs. Sadat, too. She said Mary's book bag is gone, and the car. I got the license number from her."

Del snorted. "Kid drives an old Volkswagen Beetle, bright red. The cops should be able to spot it."

"Dale Nelson told me they won't do an official missing person's report until Mary's been gone twenty-four hours." Bianca ran a hand over her face. "He took the license number, though. She is a witness." She drew a long breath. "I'm asking you again, Del, and I'm not accusing you of murder. Did you say anything to upset Mary yesterday?" She touched Del's arm.

Del shook her hand off.

"If you scared her," Bianca said, "or made her mad, she may just have gone off to brood about it. Kids do that."

Del opened his mouth to reply, but Angie rounded on her employer. "You people make me sick. Here's Hugo hacked to death and you're trying to deny the obvious. There's a killer on the loose. How many victims do you need?"

Bianca spread her hands. "One is enough."

Del Wallace was as red as a turkey cock.

Angie stared at him. "This man gets a kick out of castrating sheep. Mary's a mere female. Why should he hesitate to kill her if she knew something incriminating?"

Del roared and went for her, hands clawing. Bianca shouted a warning and I took a step forward.

Angie kneed him. He dropped to the floor, moaning.

She looked at me. "The first week I worked here, Del called me a ball breaker. Gee, I guess he was right." She turned to Bianca. "Get him the hell out of my greenhouse."

"What's going on?" Keith McDonald's voice, behind me.

I turned. Bianca stared at him, too.

113

"Ask Del." Angie was brushing potting soil from her sleeve. Del's charge had shoved her against the flats of seedlings. She began to straighten them.

"Somebody at school said Mary Sadat was missing." Keith paid no attention to Del or Angie. He was asking his wife. "Is that true?"

Bianca nodded.

"How long?"

"We don't know. Probably overnight."

"This is awful. A student. Mary wouldn't harm anyone. We have to do something, Bee."

Her eyes narrowed. "I notified Nelson. He said he'd send out a bulletin on her car."

"Her car! What if . . . We've had one killing. We have to search the farm."

I was trying to understand Keith's reaction. He seemed genuinely upset. His hands shook and his eyes were scared. I said, "Was she a student of yours, too, Keith?"

He gave me a distracted glance. "What? Oh, yes. She took my ballad class last term. The Dean will have fits," he added in a more normal voice.

I mentioned Jay's call to me.

"He's checking on campus?"

"Yes."

"Good, good." He shook his head as if to clear it. "I have a bad feeling about this."

"Thank God somebody has sense," Angie snapped.

Del levered himself to his feet, wheezing. He shambled down the corridor without looking at anybody. The door slammed behind him.

9 ⬧

"I THOUGHT YOU had a one o'clock class." Bianca tossed Keith a glance over her shoulder. She was helping Angie tidy the work area.

He touched his beard with a shaky hand. "I dismissed them early. What are you going to do about Mary?"

"We could search," Bianca said without enthusiasm.

Angie slammed a tray of seedlings back in place. "*I'm* going to search, whether the rest of you do or not."

"Are the other interns here?" I asked.

It appeared that Jason and Bill were moving sheep, the Carlsens were plowing lime and compost into fields that would be planted with spinach, and Carol Bascombe was home with the flu. Or so she had said when Angie called to see if *she* was missing.

Bianca pulled her tweed cap out of her jacket pocket and settled it on her head. "We can't search the whole farm, Angie. The best we can do is the outbuildings. I presume you've already looked through the greenhouses."

Angie nodded.

"Then we should pair up. Keith, you and Lark can look through the machine sheds and the car barn. . . ."

"Let Angie go with Keith," I said with elaborate nonchalance. I had reason to think she could handle him should he fondle her thigh. "You and I need to talk, Bianca."

Keith's blue eyes narrowed.

Bianca shrugged. "Okay. I have to stop by the house for a flashlight. Then I'm going to drive straight to the old barn." She buttoned her jacket and turned to the other two. "Lark and I will do the ice house and the sheep sheds on our way back."

Angie glanced at her businesslike watch. "Rendezvous at the house at four?"

That seemed agreeable to everybody. I thought Keith was pouting a little. Del probably was, too. Or maybe he was castrating a sheep.

Angie and Keith decided to double-check the greenhouses, so Bianca and I set out for the house without them. When we were out of earshot, I raised the subject of the workshop. I waited until then because I thought an audience just made Bianca more stubborn.

She stopped walking and turned to me. "I can't think about the workshop now." Her eyes darkened under the cap. "I'm too worried about Mary."

The implication was that I wasn't.

Bianca shook her head, mournful. "Mary, of all people. How could Mary threaten anyone? She's so quiet."

"I would have said that of Hugo."

Bianca lapsed into grim silence. I felt fairly grim myself. We trudged along.

I was thinking that her detour to the house was a pretext, that she'd dally to telephone the congressman and assorted government agencies, but she just stuck her head in the kitchen and asked Marianne for messages.

Half a dozen reporters had left their numbers on the answering tape, Marianne said, and Dale Nelson would be at the farm at five. Bianca grabbed one of the small electric lanterns from the mudroom and we went to the car barn. She indicated that I should get into a pickup so ancient it had lap-restraint seat belts. There were five other vehicles in the barn.

To my surprise she didn't follow the lane past the ice house. She drove down to the highway, turned east, and rattled along the road to the top of the crest. There an old-fashioned three-barred gate led into scrub forest. I got to open the gate. And close it.

The barn sat in a natural meadow filled with incurious sheep. I gathered that Jason and Bill had come and gone. Like many old barns in the area, this one was built of unpainted vertical boards under a peaked cedar roof. Weather had turned the wood silver. Inside, it was darker than a deconstructionist short story.

"Watch your step." Bianca turned her electric lantern on and swept the beam over decaying stalls and cribs. "Floor's rotting."

I followed her in, placing my feet with care. The interior smelled of mold, musty hay, and ancient manure. We searched the main floor methodically. It was a silent place but the silence seemed to breathe. Darkness watched us from every corner, from behind us and above us. I saw nothing but a few old implements and an abandoned saddle that had fallen from the wall in a heap. Somebody had cleaned the place out long ago.

I sneezed once but the sound was swallowed up in the watching stillness.

When we had circled back through the labyrinth to our starting place, Bianca pointed to a rickety ladder nailed to the wall of the barn. "If she's here she's in the loft."

"Will that thing hold me?"

She shrugged. "I think so, but not both of us at once. You go first. I'll light the ladder for you."

I inched my way up into a huge space that was half-lit by the unglazed window through which hay had been winched. A timber protruded over the yard from the peak of the gable, but the pulley used to raise bales was long gone. Inside, heavy beams crossed the width of the building about twenty feet up, one on each wall and one across the center. A thick post supported the central beam. Patches of gray sky showed through the roof. Mold-blackened hay bales stacked as high as my head in some places rimmed the walls. Some had tumbled to the plank flooring atop ankle-deep drifts of loose timothy. Plenty of room to hide a body. I didn't see how we could hope to find it, if it was there.

Bianca was more inventive than I, or better acquainted with barns. She stuck the lantern in her jacket pocket and hauled an old pitchfork up the ladder. The handle of the fork had broken off halfway down and the tines were brown with rust. "Stay away from the window." She lifted the pitchfork in both gloved hands. "The floor's rotten over there where the rain blows in." She strode to the far wall and began probing between the bales.

I waded through the loose hay at a more cautious pace. When I reached the tallest heap of bales I began to climb. Unseen creatures skittered away from my tread. Mice, probably. I thought about spiders.

The bales formed a surprisingly steady stairs, rather like the steps of a Maya pyramid, though the loose hay at their base was slick. As I scaled the top, I jarred one of the bales with my left hand.

Something brushed my face and a low cry rang in my ears. My heart stopped.

"Barn owl," Bianca called from the far side. "She's probably nesting."

She was. I watched her flutter out the opening, still emitting mournful hoots. I had just escaped dislodging her nest with my hand. It was a good thing I had stopped to pull on gloves. I sank back on my bale-mountain and breathed through my nose, in, out, in, out.

My peering and poking discovered nothing more startling on that wall than the owl. Relieved, I scrambled across to a tumble of loose bales.

I was almost enjoying myself, and I remembered my father's stories of the family farm in New York. The Daileys were prosperous Quaker farmers. By my father's time, the farm itself had shrunk to a handful of symbolic acres, and the great cobblestone barn with its iron weathercock was used for family gatherings. Dad swore a century of hay had polished the hardwood planks of the second story floor like the surface of a huge ballroom. The local square dance club used to hold its dances there.

I was envisaging a happy hoedown when something alien caught my eye. I stopped dead and peered. I couldn't recall the color of Mary's anorak. A fold of dull fabric protruded from the loose hay. It looked purplish in the dim light.

"Bianca!" I croaked. I cleared my throat. "Bring the lantern over here. I'm afraid . . ."

I heard her slither toward me. "What is it? Jesus!" The beam of Bianca's light whirled and steadied.

"Your turn." I had had enough of finding bodies.

She swallowed and nodded. I held my breath as she waded toward the telltale scrap. I even looked away, so I was startled when she gave a short yip of laughter.

"Shit. Some other birds have been nesting."

I walked over and peered down. A plaid stadium rug lay rumpled in the hay. Further probing revealed a couple of empty beer cans and three used condoms.

"Yuck."

"Have you no romance?" Bianca swept her light around the immediate area. "Jason holding court, no doubt. The kid's a stud, or thinks he is."

Reaction made me cranky. I bit back a comment about the other candidates for stud-dom at Meadowlark Farm. The blanket was thick and looked expensive. The beer, on the other hand, was a cheap brand sold at every twenty-four-hour market.

Bianca snorted again and went back to her methodical probing.

I worked slower, and I uncovered nothing more harrowing than an ancient gunnysack. It was empty. "I'm finished."

Bianca didn't reply. I turned around. She was sitting on a bale near the ladder, face in her hands, shoulders heaving.

I will confess my first feeling was exasperation. I stood

119

there flat-footed, telling myself that she had a right to be upset, that she was not manipulating me. Then I went over and gave her a pat on the shoulder. "Need a Kleenex?"

She drew a tissue from her pocket and blew her nose. "I'm sorry. I was thinking about Hugo."

"You said he liked the old barn."

"Yes." She gulped and blotted her eyes. "It was September when we bought the place, after the harvest was over. The autumn weather was wonderful that year. The first thing we decided to do was clean out the barn. We looked for pesticides and chemical fertilizers, and we found some, not a lot. The previous owners had kept horses, so there was old tack down below. When we finished clearing that out, we climbed up here—Keith and Hugo and I, and the three kids. It was great, full of fresh loose hay. Hugo . . ." She blew her nose again. "He climbed up on that beam and did a perfect double flip off it. We were all laughing."

I looked at the beam, impossibly high overhead, and tried to imagine Hugo doing acrobatics.

"I can't cancel the workshop," Bianca said with real desperation. "Don't you see? I have to salvage something."

Lost innocence, perhaps. I did see, unfortunately, and never mind that Hugo had refused to attend the opening night celebrations. Bianca was trying to save an ideal.

I sat down on the bale beside her. "Okay. It'll be a media circus, though. What do you want me to do? Extra, I mean."

"Oh, God, just back me up."

"That I can do."

We drove down the rutted lane in a fair state of understanding. When we reached the broccoli fields, she said she was going to have to harvest the first crop while the workshop was in session. Otherwise, it would start turning yellow. The Vietnamese crew had agreed to come Monday.

The ice house was still officially off-limits behind a yellow tape barrier, but we got out together and looked in the door. The ice had melted from the bin. The place stank of mold and something less tolerable, but it was empty. So were the two sheep sheds I had watched Jason and Bill enter the day before I found Hugo.

Keith and Angie reported that they hadn't seen any sign of Mary either. Angie was calmer. I suspected Bianca had done the search to calm Angie down. Marianne fed us coffee and cookies in the kitchen. She said Del and Mike had driven in to town. It was only four thirty, so I decided not to wait for Dale.

As I drove home I began to think about backup strategies, in case the worst happened and Dale arrested Bianca as the workshoppers arrived. But I didn't really believe Bianca had killed Hugo. Her grief, however theatrical its outward signs, seemed honest. Besides, I couldn't think of a motive. Hugo's death was a disaster for her. So who had killed him? And how was Mary Sadat tied to the killing?

If the Vietnamese crew were eliminated, the suspect list was short. Dale had excluded transients for obvious reasons. Hiding the bicycle and burying the body under a load of ice required knowledge of the farm. That meant Hugo had been killed by one of the interns, by Mike Wallace, or by one of the staff.

Del, Keith, and Bianca were my favorite candidates, but Marianne had been there that Sunday, and she had demonstrated a thorough knowledge of the farm. And there was Angie. Angie was ambitious and opinionated. It was clear she coveted at least some of Hugo's territory. And, if I had doubted her ability in a knock-down drag-out fight, that afternoon had dispelled my illusions. She was hot-tempered and lethally able, but would she harm Mary?

Del, Keith, Bianca, Angie, and, of the interns, Jason and Carol Bascombe. Jason because Hugo might have threatened his academic future, and Carol because she was the only one who had expressed hostility to Hugo directly. The others were dark horses. I had no clear picture of the Carlsens. Bill seemed too much the follower to initiate action, but he might have collaborated with Jason. And Mary was missing.

A log truck passed me going the other way. The Toyota shuddered in its wake and I gripped the wheel. A pair of killers. Bill and Jason, Jason and Bill. The two had gone to Seaside. Had they offered Hugo a ride home, and quarreled with him on the way back? If so, how had the bicycle got to the farm?

And what of Mike Wallace? I didn't want to think negative thoughts about Mike. He was not an intern, not part of the team, but he was more disturbed by Mary's disappearance than casual acquaintance warranted. I doubted that Mike would have collaborated with Jason, but he might have abetted his father. Mike seemed to take Del's opinions seriously. And Del was a dominant baboon. He could have fought with Hugo, killed him, then gone to the house and demanded his son's help.

I reached the turnoff for Shoalwater and drove through the tiny town at a sedate twenty-five. What was true of Mike was even more probable of Marianne. Del could have intimidated her into helping him dispose of the body.

I wound out of town on the beach road, drew up at our garage, and set the brake. My head ached, and it was my turn to cook dinner.

It was a comfort to discover that my marriage wasn't going to rise or fall on my cookery. I fixed scrambled eggs and pancakes and Jay didn't seem to notice. He was preoccupied by a tall stack of reports he had to mark by eight A.M. the next day.

When Jay first set up the program at Shoalwater C.C., he startled his wannabe cops and the English department by requiring formal reports in all of the police science classes. They were technical papers, for the most part, and not exercises in creative imagination, but he demanded literacy, attribution, and organization. A surprising number of the first-year students changed their major to P.E. and Recreation by the end of the second term. It was the end of the second term.

Between papers Jay told me of Dale's efforts to find Mary. Mary's three large brothers had showed up at the Dean's office. Jay had rescued him, an experience Jay said made him nostalgic for his old hostage negotiation days in Los Angeles.

Then Dale had called all the interns to Jay's office and grilled them about Mary there. Nobody had a hard and fast alibi for the period in which she had gone missing. It interested me that Carol Bascombe had showed up on campus. She was supposed to be suffering from the flu. Dale had also taken Jason and Bill through their statements about Seaside. They stuck to their story. They had not seen Hugo the day he was killed. Dale thought they were hiding something but couldn't figure out what.

The interrogation and the Dean's hand-wringing had occupied most of the afternoon, as predicted. Jay thought he'd put in an all-nighter with the reports. I made him a large pot of herb tea and went to bed.

The next day, which was Thursday, both press coverage of Hugo's death and the search for Mary Sadat heated up. I noticed the press first, because a reporter from the *Oregonian* was camped outside the bookstore. Kayport is off the beaten track, and the first police report of Hugo's murder—sans mutilation, a detail Lisa Colman withheld—had been insufficiently sensational to attract metropolitan coverage. Now that Mary was missing, our grace period was over. I wondered whether television crews had reached Meadowlark Farm yet.

I gave the reporter a couple of platitudes and a lot of blank incomprehension. He finally left. Since Bonnie had gone off with Tom in search of a travel agent, I was alone. I hid in the back room and played the telephone answering tape. The little red light was blinking like a lizard in a sand storm.

The first three calls were from reporters, one of whom was enrolled in the workshop. Her I called. She wanted to know whether the workshop would go on as scheduled and, when I admitted it would, asked about Hugo's death. I told her

Bianca would make a statement. The reporter didn't let it go at that, of course, but I managed to disengage without outright rudeness.

Two customers had called to order books—Danielle Steel's latest and a tome devoted to poultry-rearing. The second sounded more interesting. I noted the phone numbers and the books' titles and looked the poultry book up on my database. It was out of print. I had Steel in stock. I called the customers.

The next-to-last message was a breathy female voice, rather garbled. I had to play it twice. It was Carol Bascombe. She said she had to talk to me and asked me to call her back as soon as I could. I would have, but she forgot to leave her number.

I stared at the telephone in exasperation. I had not the faintest idea why Carol was picking on me, but I knew I wouldn't be able to concentrate on my inventory until I had at least tried to reach her. Perhaps she had called back with the phone number.

I stabbed the play button and picked up a pen, but the last message was from Bianca. She asked me to call her when it was convenient. Her voice was in plaintive mode. It wasn't convenient, so I didn't call her. I called Jay, got the building secretary instead, and explained about Carol. Nancy, bless her heart, said she'd try the registrar's office.

I sat at the desk entering ISBN numbers into my inventory program until the phone rang. Nancy with Carol's home number. I thanked her and hung up. When I tried the number, though, I got another answering machine. The message was brief and to the point, but the male voice sounded familiar. I left a short, and possibly short-tempered, response and hung up.

It's not uncommon for women living alone to ask a male friend to tape the message for their answering machines. The sound of a male voice eliminates some of the heavy breathers. As I turned back to the monitor screen my mind made the connection. The voice was Jason's.

I sat in my padded office chair, staring at the monitor until the screen-saver pattern came on. Jason and Carol. Mike thought Carol was an airhead. Jason might be more susceptible. He probably preferred airheads. Carol had disliked Hugo, Jason had had a grudge. Had they conspired to kill Hugo? Had Carol called me to confess? Why me?

I tried to reach her again and hung up when Jason's voice came on the line. It was half past eleven. Jay was still in class. Disgusted and worried, I went out for a sandwich.

Between shelving books and fiddling with my inventory, I kept trying to reach Carol all afternoon. At three I called Bianca and got *her* answering machine. I was about to give up and leave for the day—after all, I was still on vacation—when the phone rang. It was Jay. He said that the police had found Mary's car.

My stomach knotted. "Where?"

"Astoria. It was parked behind a Dumpster in the Baylor lot."

The Baylor was a historic hotel that was being renovated. I swallowed. "Do they think . . ."

"They're sifting through the debris right now."

I thought of Mary, shy and pretty. I thought of Carol, too. "I hate this."

"So does the Dean," Jay said.

10 ❧

THE MEMORIAL SERVICE for Hugo was scheduled for Friday evening. I woke on that thought after a restless sleep troubled by nightmares.

Dale had come over after dinner Thursday night looking exhausted. Mary's body was not in the Dumpster, nor did the Astoria police find other signs of her there, and there was no evidence of a struggle in the car, which was locked. Dale had spent the day interviewing her family, the interns, and the farm staff, without result.

"They're lying!" he burst out when he finished his second cup of coffee.

Jay yawned. He'd had only two hours of sleep the night before, but he had finished marking the reports. "Of course they're lying. Crime suspects always have irrelevant secrets to protect, and that farm is bound to be full of secrets. It's an unnatural setup."

"Unnatural!" I scowled at him.

Jay said patiently, "People who work together don't usually have to live together, too. If I had to live in the same place as the Dean I'd wind up strangling him."

I contemplated living in the same household as Bianca.

Dale sighed. "*Somebody's* guilty as sin."

Carol. I had not yet reached Carol. I opened my mouth to mention her call, then thought better of the idea. Carol had called me, not Dale and not Jay. Maybe she wasn't going to confess to murder. Maybe she just wanted to know whether I had the latest Danielle Steel in stock.

Jay was rubbing his eyes with the heels of his hands. "I don't like this business of Mary Sadat. She must have seen something." He dropped his hands. "And probably not at the farm. She was supposed to be in Kayport working at the restaurant when Groth was killed. Did you verify that?"

Dale's mouth tightened. "I asked her folks. She waited tables."

"What time does the place open?"

"It's popular for lunch as well as dinner. I assumed . . ." Dale yanked out his notebook, reached for the phone, and dialed. A voice responded and he asked what the restaurant's Sunday hours were. "Thanks." He hung up slowly. "It doesn't open until four-thirty on Sundays."

Jay whistled.

"Yeah. Lots of time." Dale slammed his hands on the table. The mugs jiggled. "She was lying to me. I just asked her parents if she worked that Sunday and they said yes, but I damn well did ask Mary Sadat what time she went to work. She lied." He rose, energized. "I'm off. Thanks for the coffee, Lark."

"Don't mention it."

Jay said, "Look at all the times, Dale. She wasn't necessarily out with another student."

Dale nodded. "I'll look, but I want a crack at those interns tomorrow. Did I tell you they were lying?" He left with a bang of the back door.

I got up and gathered the mugs. "Maybe Mary lied to her parents, too."

I caught Jay in mid-yawn. He blinked at me.

I was chasing a small idea. "Her brothers came to confront the Dean?"

"Yes. Three of them."

"Sounds like a traditional family."

"So?"

127

"Women in traditional Middle Eastern families are traditionally deceptive. They have to be if they want any kind of independence. She was probably seeing somebody her parents wouldn't approve of."

He got up, eyes on me. "That's a shrewd observation. I doubt that they'd allow her to go out with a man at all. Her brothers kept harping on her virtue. At the time, I thought the concern was irrelevant, that they ought to be worrying about her life."

"Poor kid."

"Yeah. Hell, I can't think." He rubbed his eyes again. "I'm beat, Lark. I'll talk to Dale tomorrow."

When he had gone up to bed, I picked up the telephone and tried to reach Carol. My mind was on Mary, so I was startled when Carol answered my ring.

I identified myself.

"Where are you?"

"At home, of course." Where else at nine-thirty on a weeknight?

"Is your husband there?"

"Yes, but he went to bed."

Long, breathy pause. I could hear an unfamiliar rock group thumping in the background. At last she said, "Uh, I need some advice. I need to, like, talk to you alone."

Girl talk. How sweet. I was losing patience. "If the phone won't do, I'll be at the bookstore all morning."

"Can I come by around noon? I work at the farm Friday mornings."

"Okay. We can go get a hamburger or something."

"I don't eat that junk. It's unhealthy," she said with conscious virtue. "See ya."

Oh, Carol. I sat in the nook for a while speculating about Carol's problem, but I didn't have a clue. My mind drifted back to Mary Sadat. Now there was a woman with problems.

So I went to bed early and had a double dose of nightmares, this time featuring women in peril, not my favorite fantasy pattern. I wouldn't even watch *The Silence of the Lambs,* and here was my head creating horrors. After the second nightmare, I got up and drank a cup of warm milk. It tasted awful, but I did fall asleep again.

Jay's first class was at ten, so he hung around making phone calls Friday morning. Bonnie came over and showed me a bunch of brochures and a "French for Travelers" tape. I fled to the bookstore in self-defense, though I had little left to do before my reopening. At eleven, Bianca called to ask if I could pick Trish up at the bus depot at four. I could, though it was going to be inconvenient to shuttle Trish to the farm, dash home for Jay, feed us, change, and dash back out. Bianca wanted me at the farm at half past six.

It was idle to suppose Carol would show up at noon. I didn't expect her to be on time and she wasn't. I took out the feather duster and settled in to a good, thorough dusting. Then I began rearranging the fiction. Alphabetically by categories is the best way, but placing a book in the wrong category is embarrassing, and unfair to the writer. I removed Danielle Steel from Romance and placed her in Best-Sellers. And Toni Morrison from Best-Sellers to Literature. And so on. I probably created chaos. Finally, a scratching at the front door announced Carol's arrival. It was one o'clock, and my stomach snarled at her.

When I let her in, she looked around. "Gosh, have you read all these books?"

She was in airhead mode. I thought of saying, "I don't read 'em. I just sell 'em," but that was too unkind. I said, "Some. What did you want, Carol?"

"Well, like I said, to talk." She wriggled.

"I'm hungry." I led her to the back room and began closing the place down.

"That a Mac?" She indicated my computer.

"A PC." I blanked the screen and grabbed my purse and jacket.

"Cool." She wriggled again. "Do you keep your inventory on disk?"

I stared at her. Her hair was artfully tangled and her outfit, including a bright rain jacket, was color-coded. Teal blue, this time. She had gone home from the farm and changed clothes.

"Where are we going?" She whipped out her lip gloss.

"Aho's. I want a decent sandwich."

"Is that private?"

I glanced at my watch. "It will be by the time we get there."

Aho's is the best bakery on the Peninsula. It ought to be downtown, but the owners opted for a boring mall on the edge of Kayport. I drove to the mall and we went in. Carol wanted a cup of cappuccino. I ordered turkey on wholemeal dill and a hazelnut latte. There were only three booths. As we sat, the four businessmen occupying the booth nearest the display case rose and crowded around the cash register. We watched them leave. Apart from Carol and me, they were the last customers.

Larry Aho, the baker, retreated to make my sandwich and left us alone with our coffee.

"Okay," I said. "Out with it."

Carol took a sip of cappuccino. "You're married to a cop, right? I mean, Professor Dodge, he's working with the police."

I explained that Lisa Colman was the detective in charge of the murder investigation and that Dale Nelson was doing most of the field work.

"Yeah, but your husband . . ."

"Jay is a reserve deputy, and the sheriff's department sometimes hires him as a consultant." She looked blank, so I went on, searching for short words, "He's not doing anything official on this case, because the Dean wants him to keep an eye on you and the other students, in case you need help."

"Cool." She looked relieved.

"Do you?" I prompted. "Need help, I mean."

"Uh, yeah . . ."

"Turkey on dill."

I got up and retrieved my sandwich. "Thanks, Larry."

Carol had stuck her perfect nose in her cup.

I sat. When Larry disappeared into the back room once more, I said, "I ought to warn you, I guess. Jay won't withhold information from the police, and neither will I. If you tell me something incriminating . . ."

"Well, it's not. That is, not exactly." She twiddled a strand of hair.

I took a bite of sandwich.

"It's about the day Hugo was killed. I mean, well, you know . . ."

I chewed. "A week ago Sunday."

She nodded.

I was a little slow to catch on, but I began to understand that Carol felt embarrassed. "You were out with somebody. A married man?"

"I was with Angie."

I narrowly avoided choking.

Carol said dreamily, "She's so cool."

I felt a large twinge of disappointment in Angie Martini. She had been so self-righteous with Del about coming on to students, so scrupulous. "You had a date?"

Carol blushed. "Gosh, Lark, I'm not gay."

I drew a long breath. "Then why all the secrecy?"

"Well, we figured, I mean, she figured the cops would react the way you did, so she said she'd just tell them she was out looking at nurseries, and she was, only I was with her."

"All afternoon?" What with his trip to Seaside by whatever means, Hugo could hardly have reached the farm before one or two. Dale now thought the murder had occurred between one and four.

Carol said, "I want to open a nursery—you know, the kind with a flower shop—and my Dad's going to finance it, but he said I should learn the business first."

"And Angie is your mentor?"

131

"I guess." She eyed me doubtfully.

"She's showing you the ropes."

"Ropes?"

"How to run a greenhouse."

She beamed. "Yeah. She says I don't have to be organic if I'm careful with pesticides, but I'm not supposed to say that to Bianca. Or Hugo, only Hugo's dead now."

"And Angie asked you to lie for her?"

"Well, it wasn't a lie, exactly. I just said I was out with somebody." She wriggled. "I can't help it if the cops thought I meant with a guy, can I?"

I went back to my sandwich, partly to give myself time to think.

Angie was paranoid—or was she? Dale had called her a dyke. Her impulse to conceal an innocent meeting with a female student was understandable, if not very wise. Surely being suspected of sexual shenanigans was preferable to being suspected of murder.

I patted the mayo from my lips. "You should ask to speak to Dale Nelson. Tell him the truth. If you want to warn Angie, go ahead. Or I'll tell Jay, if you like."

She looked hugely relieved and thanked me several times, though I had just pointed out the obvious course. When we got back to the bookstore, I let her use the phone. She called Angie first, then Dale. Dale came to the store and took her amended statement. He wasn't happy, but he wasn't hard on Carol, probably because he was glad to be able to eliminate two suspects from his list.

That blotted up the afternoon. At three forty-five I closed up and drove to the depot to wait for Trish. I didn't have to wait long. She waddled down from the bus and I got out of the car. She seemed surprised to see me instead of Bianca but not upset. I found her overnight case and tucked it into the trunk.

She squeezed into the passenger side and wrestled with the seat belt while I got in. Seat belts are mandatory in Washington. When she finally fastened hers, she gave her huge belly a

132

pat. "One more week, then thank godalmighty I am free at last."

I laughed.

"If my bladder holds up that long."

I said, "Do you need to use the restroom?"

"Always." She cast a dubious glance at the bus depot.

"Let's make a pit stop at the bookstore. We have time."

She smiled. "Thanks."

She used the loo and declined a cup of tea, and we got back into the car.

She leaned back against the headrest. "I'll be glad when the service is over."

I pulled out onto Main Street. It was raining a little.

"But it was nice of Bianca to organize it." She shifted in the seat. She sounded doubtful.

I stopped at the solitary red light. Bianca had said Trish needed closure. Maybe Bianca needed closure. The dynamics of the relationship baffled me.

"Tell me about the commune," I blurted.

"What?"

"The commune. Isn't that where you met Hugo?"

"Oh, no. Hugo and I went to high school together. We met Bianca and Keith at the commune."

"What was it like?"

She gave as much of a shrug as the seat belt allowed. "A big old farm. The house was falling down. So was the barn. There were about a dozen of us. We lolled around and smoked dope and listened to Keith's guitar. We were just a bunch of kids trying to put off growing up."

I reached the highway, stopped, and looked both ways. A log truck rattled past with the trailer up on the truck bed. Going home. I said, "Except Hugo."

She nodded. "Except Hugo. He was the only grown-up around and he was barely twenty-one."

"So how did you live?"

"As in the clichés. We mooched off Bianca, who had a generous allowance from her mother. Hugo grew vegetables. As long as we had brown rice and Hugo we weren't going to starve."

"It sounds kind of boring."

Trish chortled. "It was. I'm a book person. Every time Keith drove his rattletrap pickup to town I'd hitch a ride with him. I'd pad into the public library in my earth shoes and granny dress and check out as many books as the law allowed. Hugo used to tell me I was rotting my brain."

Silence. The windshield wipers swished.

"Hugo wasn't bored," she added, sad. "Neither was Bianca. He taught her everything he knew about gardening, which was a lot, and she worked at it. Really worked. Even when she was pregnant with Fiona."

"That's impressive, considering her background."

"The hotel?" Trish nodded. "She may be a hothouse plant, but she's tough. She's a leader, too. Bianca organized the commune. Otherwise, it would have folded after six weeks. Hugo could have organized things, but he wasn't about to give anybody orders—or take them."

"He did what he wanted to do?"

"It was the only way he could function." She cleared her throat. "One of the best things Bianca did for Hugo, when he came to work for her at Meadowlark Farm, was to give him a free hand. On the commune, Bianca was the leader. She could do that for two reasons. She had the people skills to get us to work—she bullied and cajoled and flattered and threatened. Of course she had money, but it wasn't just that. She was also a believer."

I glanced at her.

She was frowning. "What do you know about utopias?"

"Uh, Sir Thomas More and Amana."

"Right, and Salt Lake City and the Amish and the Hutterites. After we left the commune, I read up on American utopias. They succeed when there's a strong central ideal. It's usually religious. In our case, it was organic farming and environmental purity."

"Kind of vague . . ."

"No. There's a solid body of literature and a surprising amount of research. Bianca and Hugo read everything, and they were believers, Hugo for obvious reasons. I never quite understood why Bianca was so passionate, but she was. Bianca's a leader," she repeated, as if she couldn't summarize her perception any other way.

A gust of rain hit the windshield and the wipers whined. "How did Hugo learn about plants?"

"He grew up on a dairy farm. He was the youngest of six. His mother taught him to garden. His dad was an old-fashioned German Gauleiter, a real tyrant. He bullied those kids something awful, worked them before and after school. Hugo hates . . . hated cows. Bianca bought one when she found out she was pregnant. Hugo taught her how to milk it and told her she was on her own."

I smiled.

"He wouldn't even drink the milk. We made really awful natural yogurt." She shifted in the seat again and loosened the seat belt. "He wouldn't eat that, either."

I glanced at her. She had teared up. "What about Keith McDonald?" I asked by way of distraction.

Trish gave a shaky laugh. "Good old Keith. He never changes."

"I suppose you mean he's just a kid at heart."

"I suppose so. Keith was our troubadour. He looked like Donovan."

"Who?"

"Such is fame." She sounded amused. "Donovan was a sixties singer—fake folk. He was good-looking in a baby-faced way, with big soulful eyes. Keith looked like Donovan, sounded like him, dressed like him. All the women buzzed around Keith like flies going for flypaper."

"I know from flypaper."

She chuckled. "We were all very careful of Keith's hands. He got out of a lot of work because he didn't want to ruin his hands. I think he slept with every woman on the place." She added, rueful, "Including me."

"Good heavens."

"It was a different era."

"Must have been. Wasn't, er, anybody jealous?" I was thinking of Bianca.

Trish said, "Hugo? You bet. That's why I decided Hugo and I had better get married, even though it was against my principles."

"And Bianca married Keith?"

"Yes. I always thought I got the better deal."

An early tourist passed me going eighty. Muddy spray blanked the windshield. I squirted detergent and increased the speed of the wipers. "I understand that Keith still, uh, plays the field. Why does Bianca put up with it?"

Trish didn't answer.

I added, "He came on to me. That's why I ask."

"You didn't like it."

"He's not my type," I said, a bit defensive. "And I didn't like the circumstances."

Trish gave a sigh. "I told you Keith has never changed. Time passed him by. Hugo kept growing and changing. So did Bianca. So did I. I guess Keith didn't see any reason to change." As I pulled off and we passed below the MEADOW-LARK FARM sign, she added, "He can be very charming. There are the kids to consider, too. And of course, Bianca has a thing about divorce because of her father."

That made sense. I drove around behind the house and parked by the stairs to the mudroom.

Bianca and Marianne came out to greet Trish, and Marianne took her in for a cup of tea. Bianca invited me to join them.

I stayed firmly behind the wheel. "I need to get home. I'll see you later."

She said she had called the workshop speakers and explained about the murder investigation. Both had agreed to come anyway. I wondered what she had really told them.

When I got home, Jay was marinating a flank steak. Potatoes were baking in the oven. He had rinsed greens for a salad.

I gave him a large kiss. "Wow, a major production."

He returned the kiss with interest. "If I'm going to have to listen to Keith McDonald sing, I want to be fortified."

"Will he do that?"

"Do you doubt it? They're holding the service at the farm and Bianca is in charge. She's sentimental about the commune. McDonald was the official minstrel."

"Horrors," I said, but I was curious. I hadn't heard Keith sing. Jay's favorite singer is Leadbelly.

I told Jay about my conversation with Carol, but he wasn't surprised. Dale had phoned him.

At half past six we turned off onto the drive to Bianca's huge house. It was lit like the QE2, lights twinkling through what had turned into a steady rain. We were not the first arrivals.

"Looks like a stock car rally," Jay muttered. Half a dozen extra vehicles already jammed the asphalt lot beside the car barn. Jay let me out. "I'm going to turn the car and park it so we can get away from here. Tell Bianca she ought to send somebody to direct traffic."

"Okay." I held my purse over my head and dashed for the side entrance. I could feel my hair frizzing.

Marianne and Trish were sitting in the kitchen. I think I startled them, but Marianne nodded and Trish gave me a constrained smile. I explained about the jumbled cars. Marianne went off to find Mike.

"Where's Bianca?"

Trish toyed with her cup. "With the priest."

I sat in one of the kitchen chairs. "Priest? Will there be a religious ceremony?"

Trish said, "Not if I have anything to say about it. Hugo was very bitter about Cardinal McIntyre."

I stared.

"The good cardinal saw Vietnam as a holy war. Hugo didn't desert the Church, the Church deserted him."

"Oh."

"I'm afraid I disgraced myself." She didn't look repentant. "The priest said something gooey about Hugo's child, so I told him Hugo and I weren't living together."

I controlled the urge to smile.

Trish said through her teeth, "I told him to say whatever he says about lapsed Catholics, that he must have some words for them because there are so many of them."

"Wow."

"Bianca is mending fences."

"Is she Catholic?"

"Lapsed."

I didn't envy the priest. In the distance a door chime sounded.

Trish cocked her head. "More people?"

"Gardeners," I said. "I called a bunch of them myself."

She relaxed a little. "Well, that's all right."

At that point Jay entered and I introduced him to Trish. Then I excused myself and went in search of Bianca. It sounded as if she needed propping up. The first person I ran into was Del Wallace.

11 ᷂

I WENT IN through the dining room where we had eaten with the staff on our first visit to Meadowlark Farm. Del was standing by the sideboard, wearing a gray suit and looking lost.

He blinked at me. "Where's my wife?"

"Marianne went to get Mike." I explained about the cars.

"Oh, yeah, okay." He drifted past me to the kitchen. I smelled whiskey, but Del didn't sound drunk, just confused.

I could hear conversation from the living room and Keith's voice in the front hall. I headed for the living room.

Bianca and crew had transformed it. They had removed all the furniture from the center of the room, and replaced it with padded folding chairs of the sort that can be rented for wedding receptions. Thirty chairs, five deep, were arranged to focus on the fireplace with its raised hearth. A fire crackled. Soft music played on the sound system. Perhaps a dozen people, scattered in twos and threes, were talking in subdued voices. When I stepped down into the room, they looked at me. I nodded and smiled.

I didn't see Bianca at first. Then I spotted her with a fifty-ish man I took to be the priest, though he wasn't wearing a dog collar. He sat in an alcove near the French doors, and Bianca, in solemn brown, stood facing him. They were talking. She glanced around, caught my eye, and gave a half-hearted wave. I decided not to intrude.

Keith ushered an elderly couple in and seated them near the

front. The woman was wearing the stereotype of all garden club president costumes—a pink lace dress of a kind I didn't think was sold outside the Midwest. She looked to be in her seventies. The man, bent over a cane, was older.

When he got the couple settled, Keith beckoned to me. I followed him out into the hall.

"Will you take over the front door? Angie's supposed to, but she hasn't showed up yet. I need to tune my guitar." Keith was wearing dress slacks and a sweater over an actual necktie. The tie picked up the blue of his eyes. He looked somber.

I said, "Of course. What do I do?"

"Welcome people, take their coats, show them where to sit."

"Does it matter where?"

"No, though the Dean should sit in the front row. He's going to speak."

I must have winced because he flashed me a grin. "Briefly."

"Thank God."

He nodded and went off in the direction of the family apartment.

Over the next quarter hour, I ushered in half a dozen elderly gardeners and the Dean. He had come without his wife, which meant the service was second level priority. When the governor spoke at Shoalwater C.C., the Dean's wife tore herself away from her tax-consulting firm and made an appearance. Hugo didn't rate that, at least not at the end of March.

I smiled at the Dean, and he smiled at me. I thought he might balk at sitting in the first row, but he came meekly enough. The door chimed. As I went back into the hall, I saw Bianca, the priest trailing her, surge across the Berber carpet to greet the Dean.

More elderly gardeners. The Peninsula is rapidly turning into a retirement community, and retired people have time for gardens. I tried to visualize Hugo lecturing to them in a group. I failed. He had to have met them individually.

I seated them, and noticed that the Carlsens and Carol had

slipped in the back. Jason and Bill were missing. And Mary, of course. It was interesting that there were no farmers—"real" farmers, Del would have said—and no politicians. Bianca was not trying to use the occasion to make points. These were people Hugo had met face to face.

The chairs were almost all taken. The room buzzed with low-voiced conversation. I spotted the new editor of the local paper, which featured a gardening column, and wondered if any other media people had sneaked in. I doubted even Bianca would invite reporters.

I was back at my post by the door, waiting, when Angie came up behind me.

"I'll take over now."

I turned.

She was wearing a silver-gray jumpsuit in washed silk. She greeted me without warmth. "I hear Carol talked to you."

"You were a fool not to tell the police you were with her."

She shrugged. "I knew I could if I had to. I was hoping I wouldn't have to."

"Any word on Mary?"

Her mouth tightened. "No. And I wish this farce was over."

"You and Trish."

Her eyes widened but she didn't say anything. The doorbell chimed again. I left her to answer it and went in search of Jay.

The service was scheduled to start at seven. At seven-fifteen, Bianca walked across the room and stood on the raised hearth. When the buzz of conversation had ceased, she made a nice little speech about Hugo, omitting any reference to murder or missing students, and asked the priest to say a few words. His name was Kramer and he obliged. Considering the encounter with Trish, I thought he comported himself with dignity.

He offered half a dozen platitudes in a pleasant baritone, concluding, "In the midst of life we are in death. Of course, the reverse is also plausible. In the midst of death, we are in life, and a gardener must know the truth of that paradox. By all accounts, Hugo Groth was a good gardener and a good man. God rest his soul."

Several people murmured "amen." I noticed that the sound system was still playing. Fortunately, the music was classical and unemphatic.

The Dean is a sociologist by training and speaks like one. At Bianca's request, he offered some sad generalizations about the prevalence of violence in America, and some positive ones about the utility of hands-on education. He affirmed the college's support of the sustainable agriculture program.

Jay shifted in his seat, and I suppressed a grin. When one of the college authorities announces support for a program in public, the program is in deep trouble. Bianca's internships could continue without the college's backing, but there was no doubt that academic credit and the tie-in with an accredited degree were an inducement to students. I wondered if Bianca understood the Dean's subtext. Her calm face betrayed nothing.

When the Dean finished his benediction, Bianca returned to center stage. She reminisced a little about the commune, though she didn't call it that, introduced Trish, who thanked everyone for coming in a nearly inaudible voice, and made a smooth transition to Keith. The sound system fell silent, and Keith brought his guitar up to the hearth. Jay shifted again. I imagined I could hear his teeth grinding.

Keith was rather good. It's true his guitar-playing was rudimentary and his Scots accent, when he used it, was awful. But his voice, a light tenor, was flexible and pleasant, and most of his selections made sense.

He did "Amazing Grace" and "All Things Bright and Beautiful," which even pagans tend to know. The audience warmed to him and joined on the refrains. Next, he sang an English ballad about ravens and a dead knight. That was fine, if a little odd. It probably went over a treat in his ballad seminar.

Then he sang a Scottish lament for the departure of Bonnie

142

Prince Charlie. The verses seemed irrelevant to Hugo's life and death, but it was clear from the intensity with which Keith sang that the song had private meaning for him.

Better loved ye canna be.
Will ye no' come back again?

A simple enough refrain, with a good high passage for a tenor. Keith's voice broke on the chorus after the third verse. I stared at his handsome, bearded face and wondered what was going through his head.

He collected himself and finished with "Study War No More." That was a suitable conclusion for Hugo, who had exchanged his sword and shield for a ploughshare down by the side of a particularly beautiful river. It's a rollicking song, despite the seriousness of the subject matter, and the elderly gardeners really swung into the last chorus. Trish cried, but everyone else seemed to find the song cheering.

And that was that. Because of her condition, Trish retired at once to Hugo's old room. Bianca thanked everybody for coming and said there were refreshments. Marianne stood in the arch to the dining room. She served coffee, punch, and cookies to anyone who wanted to stay and chat. Half the people left immediately, among them the Dean. The other half included the interns, the president of the garden club, and Lt. Colman, who had been one of the last of the mourners Angie had shown in.

Bianca and Keith stood by the fireplace in an informal receiving line, in case anyone should be so old-fashioned as to expect one. A number of the gardeners did. They left gradually. Angie was minding the door. Del and Marianne stayed in the dining room with the interns and a handful of gardeners. Del was on his best behavior, but he kept blinking like an owl. He said Mike was out controlling traffic.

Jay and I drank punch, sampled Marianne's cookies, and drifted back to the living room. As the last of the gardeners departed, we began folding and stacking chairs. After a few minutes, Del joined us. I wondered why he was being so helpful. Keith and Bianca were deep in conversation with Lisa Colman.

"Where were Jason and Bill?" Jay asked.

Del said, "Bill don't like funerals. Jason didn't like Groth." He gave a halfhearted bark of laughter.

Jay carried a stack of chairs to the inside wall. Del folded the remaining row and followed suit. As they returned together, Angie stalked in from the hallway, hands in the pockets of her jumpsuit.

"Is that the last of them?" she asked.

I peered into the dining room. "I think so."

"Thank God."

"Thank God," Del said at the same moment.

Angie scowled at him. Del blinked.

Lisa Colman was shaking hands with Bianca. When she saw Jay, the detective gave him a wave, a mere flip of the hand. Jay nodded, and Keith and Bianca escorted Colman out.

We stood in the middle of the empty room in a silent clump, waiting. I could hear Carol's voice in the dining room and the flat burr of Adam Carlsen's. Marianne came out, looking tired but not displeased, like a woman who has done her duty.

Angie said, "Any coffee left?"

Marianne nodded.

Bianca and Keith returned. Bianca said, "I'm glad you're all still here. I want to talk to you. You, too, Angie."

Angie had taken a step in the direction of the dining room. She shrugged and came back.

Bianca glanced around. "Let's shove the easy chairs back near the fireplace."

The men leapt to comply.

When they had re-created a conversation area, Bianca sank onto her favorite hassock. I sat in the chair beside it, Keith took up his station on the hearth, and Jay remained standing.

Del wandered to the drinks cabinet and poured himself a neat whiskey. Nobody followed suit.

Bianca said, "Keith and I talked with Lt. Colman."

Angie shifted in her chair. "We saw that."

"Why the hell didn't you say you had an alibi? Why did you lie?"

Angie said sullenly, "I didn't lie. I just didn't mention that I was with Carol."

"Carol!" Del exploded, his drink slopping. "Carol Bascombe?"

Keith smirked. "Miss Congeniality."

Del shook his head like a bull shaking off a fly. "Not Carol. She's can't be . . . ."

"She's not," Angie snapped. "Carol and I were looking at nurseries. It was strictly business."

"Business?" Del seemed to be suffering from echolalia. He wiped whiskey off his hand with his handkerchief. "Funny business, you mean, you two-faced bitch. By God, kick a man in the balls for a little plain language, and then go off and . . . and corrupt that innocent kid." Del's historical sequence was muddled. "You ought to be shot."

Angie rolled her eyes.

"What price sexual harassment?" Keith said to the ambient air.

"Yeah." Del leaned forward, hands clenched on his knees. The drink wobbled on the arm of his chair. "Yeah, bitch."

Bianca's intense eyes flickered from one face to another.

Jay said, "You're overlooking something, Wallace."

Del gaped.

"Whatever Ms. Martini and Carol were doing together that Sunday afternoon—and Carol is well over the age of consent—we know they weren't killing Hugo Groth."

"Look, fella, whose side are you on?"

"The students'," Jay said crisply. "If Carol has a complaint, I'll listen to it."

"What complaint?"

Our heads swivelled.

Carol, hands on her hips, stood in the archway. She wore a dead-black wool dress that ended halfway up her perfect waxed thighs, and her hair had been teased to the status of Importance. She wore three gold chains.

Bianca said, "How long have you been listening, Carol?"

Carol ignored her, eyes on Del. "I know what you're saying, Mr. Wallace, and you're full of shit." She stepped down into the room and took two long strides toward us. "Excuse me, but you're really pissing me off. Angie showed me this cool place in Raymond and we talked to the lady that her and her husband own it. She says I can come back whenever I like."

Del snorted.

"Unlike some I could name," Carol went on, "she didn't make me feel stupid every time I asked a question. She was a real nice lady. Angie and me looked at two other nurseries and then I went home. That's what happened."

Del said, "D'you expect us to believe—"

"I don't give a shit what you believe." Carol's chains swung as she turned to Jay. "Angie never came on to me, and she never came on to Mary or Letha either, but I know who did."

Angie said, "Don't overdo it, Carol."

Carol ignored her, too. "Letha and me know how to deal with old guys, so it wasn't a problem for us, or not much. But Mary's a real baby. She doesn't know diddly about men. She used to cry and ask us what she was doing wrong. It helped some when Mr. Groth talked to her. . . ."

"When?" Jay cleared his throat. "Excuse me for interrupting you, Carol. When did Groth have this talk with Mary?"

She shrugged. "A couple of times. Once in the fall and once in February, during the lambing."

Jay said, "I see. Go on."

Del was spluttering.

Carol turned back to him. "Me and the Carlsens have been

talking, Mr. Wallace. There's two things bothering us. Where's Jason and Bill? They said they'd be here tonight and they weren't. And where's Mary?"

"How the hell would I know?" Del roared.

"I don't know." Carol tossed her important locks. "I'm asking."

"We're all very distressed about Mary, and I'm sure the police are doing their best to find her." Bianca's voice was as smooth as silk.

Keith said, "Did somebody call Jason?"

Carol nodded. "Adam's in there now, trying again. I called and got Jason's answering machine. I recorded his message, you know? On the tape? So it was, like, creepy to call up and get my own voice. Bill's mom said he was out with Jason."

Jay headed for the hall. "I'm going to phone Dale Nelson, if Adam hasn't reached him."

Bianca got up from the hassock. "Thank you for sharing your thoughts with us, Carol."

Carol twisted a strand of hair. "That's okay, Mrs. McDonald, but there's one other thing."

Bianca shut her eyes and opened them. "What is it?"

"I spoke my mind. I don't want Mr. Wallace evaluating me."

Bianca said, "We'll arrange something, Carol. Don't worry."

Carol expelled a breath that fluffed the strand of hair over her left eyebrow. "Okay. That's all, I guess."

Angie said, "Thanks, Carol."

Carol blushed. "It's all right. Bye." She turned and went back toward the dining room.

We stared at each other. Del got up and left the room. He didn't say anything. He just picked up his drink and walked out. Marianne watched him go, her face impassive.

When Jay came back a few minutes later he looked worried. "I got through to Dale and told him to check out the student haunts. I called the Johnsons. The boys took Jason's pickup, as usual. They were planning to attend the memorial service."

Bianca rubbed her arms as if she were cold. "God, I hope nothing's happened."

"The kid drives like a maniac," Keith said.

Jay nodded. "He's had two DWIs, big fine the last time. They should lift his license."

There was a commotion in the hallway. Mike came in, dripping. "Hey, where's Dad? There's a TV crew down at the gate." He took off his glasses and wiped them on his shirt front. "Channel Five!"

Keith and Bianca exchanged glances. Keith said, "I'll go get rid of them."

"Don't say anything." Anxiety sharpened Bianca's voice.

He nodded. "I know better."

Jay ruffled his moustache with one finger. "Lark and I ought to leave, Bianca. Dale will phone you when he finds Jason."

"Okay." Her mouth quivered. "Lark . . ."

"I know." I was resigned. "You'll need me tomorrow. Call me in the morning."

She gave me a tremulous smile. "Thanks. And thanks for coming."

"It was a good memorial service," I said by way of consolation.

Once he had threaded his way past the television lights, Jay drove home like a bat out of hell, and he didn't turn the windshield wipers off even once. He didn't say much, either.

As we slowed for the Shoalwater turnoff, he muttered, "You saw Carol this afternoon, so I suppose she didn't surprise you."

The wipers whirred. "What she had to say didn't surprise me, but, yes, Carol surprised me."

He grunted.

He was halfway into the house by the time I had disentangled myself from the seat belt.

It was only nine. Bonnie's lights shone across the street—

148

she and Tom laying plans, no doubt. I thought about running across to tell her the latest, then thought again. Bonnie could wait.

Jay was on the phone when I came into the kitchen area, so I went upstairs and changed into sweats. I stood awhile looking out across our little balcony at the ocean. It was dark, but I could make out the white crests of combers rolling in. A light rain spattered the windows. Bonnie's lights flicked off.

Down in the kitchen, Jay was still on the phone. I made myself coffee and put the kettle on for tea. Since his side of the conversation consisted of unintelligible noises of encouragement, I couldn't make out the subject. Jason and Bill was not a bad guess, however.

The kettle shrieked and I poured hot water over a tea bag. Jay could have drunk decaffeinated coffee, but he said it tasted like warm spit. I thought the herb gunk he favored tasted like stewed hay.

He finally hung up. I brought him his tea. "Heavy conversation?"

"Thanks. I wanted to find out whether Bill and Jason had classes this afternoon. I had to roust somebody to access the registration files. They're enrolled in a biology lab from two to five."

"On a Friday?"

"We're hurting for lab space. There are labs on Saturday morning, too."

"Ugh."

"Lots of absentees. I called the lab tech. He said Bill and Jason were there, horsing around, in his words. They left at four-thirty." He toyed with the cup.

I had poured myself a mug of coffee. I sat beside him and sipped. Too hot. "Is the lab important? The memorial service wasn't until seven."

"Bill lives in Shoalwater."

"And Jason rents an apartment near the college?"

"Right. Bill's parents said he hadn't been home, so the two

of them probably went to Jason's place and had something to eat. To drink, too, if I understand Jason."

The college lies on the east side of Shoalwater Bay. As the crow flies, the distance between our house, just outside Shoalwater, and the campus isn't far, but the bay is large. The drive around the south end takes Jay forty minutes on a good day. It was still raining out, and it had rained hard earlier.

I sipped my cooling coffee. "How long does it take to drive to the farm from Jason's apartment?"

"Almost an hour on the highway."

"There's another way?"

Jay rubbed the back of his neck. "I think so. Something McDonald said once about a shortcut. If there is one, and if those guys went on horsing around, there's a good chance Jason used the shorter route. Do we have a county map handy? There's one in my car."

"Drink your tea."

He ruffled his moustache. "I hope I'm wrong, but I'm feeling a lot of urgency about this. I took it for granted Bill and Jason had just skipped out on the service, but Carol expected them to show up. If I find out they drove over to Raymond and spent the evening boozing and playing video games, I'll skin them alive."

"Drink your tea," I repeated. "I'll find the map."

Easier said than done. We had lived in the house for a year, but, what with assorted renovation projects, our belongings were not well-organized. The map finally surfaced in a drawer in the hall closet where we dumped car junk.

Jay got out his reading glasses and stuck his nose into the east county. "Jeez, I don't know. Looks like a logging road." He picked up the phone again. This time he called Dale. Without result.

"You could call Carol."

He stared at me, then gave a sharp nod. "I'm a dolt. She lives in the same apartment complex."

I found the number for him and he dialed. Carol must have picked the phone up on the second ring.

"This is Jay Dodge, Carol. I have a couple of questions for you. Yeah . . . okay." He covered the mouthpiece. "Turning the stereo down."

When Carol came back on the line, he said, "Have you checked to see if Jason and Bill are at Jason's apartment? They're not? Okay. Listen, Keith McDonald said something once about a shortcut from campus to the farm. Do you know about it?"

Carol spoke at length. Finally, Jay thanked her and hung up. He looked worried.

"There's another road?"

"Yes. She says it's pretty primitive. There used to be a fishing resort up there—steelhead—before the clear-cut. The road's paved and the county patches it, but it's in poor shape, unlit, and winding. It's icy in winter and the drop-offs are steep. Carol doesn't use it, but the others do when they're late for a work session."

"That doesn't sound good."

"It sure doesn't. Damn." He picked the phone up again and dialed Dale's number. It took conversations with three dispatchers, but Jay got through at last. He explained about the shortcut, listened to Dale beef, and hung up.

"Well?"

"They can't search it tonight. Two injury wrecks outside Kayport. First thing tomorrow." He got up and took his cup to the sink. "I hate waiting."

12 ~

IT MAY BE possible to collaborate on nightmares. Jay and I spent the night tossing and turning, more or less in unison. I gave up at six and went for a run, though it was still semi-dark. When I got back, Jay was in the shower. He had made coffee for me, so I drank some and mixed muffins before running up for my own shower.

I came back down in jeans and a sweatshirt. "I suppose you're going to drive to that awful road and take a look."

He blinked at me over his tea mug. "How do you figure that?"

"I know the way you think." I popped the muffins in the oven.

"It'll be a couple of hours before Dale sends a crew out there...."

"And every second counts."

He sighed. "That's right."

"I'm coming."

"I thought you had to go out to the farm."

"I hate it when men whine."

He grinned. "Okay. I know I'm outflanked."

"Leave my flanks out of this. You can drop me at the farm afterward."

We ate breakfast in companionable silence, uninterrupted by the telephone. The sun shone between squall lines, turning my kitchen into a riot of daffodil yellow. I was going to have to do something about the color.

We were halfway out to the car when I stopped. "The map?"

"Got it."

"The cellular phone?"

"What?"

Jay's brother, Freddy, had given him a car phone for Christmas. Since Jay had spent more than half his working life tied to a beeper, it was one of those gifts that evoke the "just what I've always wanted" response. Jay had never used the phone.

"I'll get it. If we find the pickup, we'll need it."

"Maybe the battery's dead," he said hopefully.

I unlocked the back door and went in. It took me fifteen minutes of hard searching, but I finally found where he had hidden the device. For good measure, I brought one of those aluminum emergency blankets, too, a thermos of leftover breakfast coffee, and half a dozen highway flares, though Jay kept a good supply of emergency equipment in his Honda. It was almost eight by the time we got started.

When we reached the Ridge Road and turned south, I tried out the phone. I called Meadowlark Farm.

Marianne answered from the kitchen. I could hear the coffee maker burping away. I gave her my number but didn't say where I was going. When I told her Jay would bring me out to the farm later on, she didn't sound thrilled.

Jay drove all the way to Shoalwater College, past the huddle of cheap apartments that housed most of the students who didn't live at home. The apartments were privately owned and managed, not dormitories.

The college has a beautiful setting. Jay's office overlooks the bay, and the grounds crew does good things with native plants. Still, the architecture is basically early biscuit factory. The student population exceeded capacity two years ago, but there are no new classrooms in sight.

Jay drove past his own building to the parking lot behind the science labs. A dozen or so parked cars indicated that some unlucky students were attending a lab. Jay got out and walked around for a while, hands in the pockets of his jacket. A light wind ruffled his hair. I was about to jump out and join him, when he came back.

"What were you looking for?"

He started the engine and put the car in gear. "Just visualizing. I want to try to retrace their route."

He eased onto the highway, drove half a block, and made a right turn at a 7-Eleven. Again he got out. He was gone quite a while. I read the booklet that came with the phone, even though it sounded as if it had been translated from Japanese by a computer. I even considered telephoning my parents in New York to see if the phone worked for long-distance calls.

"That was a good guess," Jay said as he got back in the car. "They stopped for a six-pack of Bud and a frozen pizza."

"The clerk remembered?"

"It's a family place. The owners are on the premises night and day, apparently. The man says he remembers them because he carded Jason, thought he looked too young to buy beer. Jason turned twenty-one in December."

"You know a lot about these kids."

"The Dean did ask me to look after them." He wheeled into the parking lot of the apartment complex. "Bill's nineteen."

"I thought he looked young." I began to have a clearer understanding of Jay's urgency. He tends to take responsibility seriously. If the Dean had trusted him to look after the students, he would do his damnedest.

Jay got out. So did I. He looked at me over the top of the car. "Jason's apartment is 722B. It's over there. Second floor." He gestured. "Will you knock on the door? Just in case. I want to look around the parking area."

The apartments were strictly motel modern. I climbed an openwork stairway and walked along the passage until I came to the bright red door of 722B. The paint was beginning to peel. I knocked and listened. No answer. I knocked again. Silence.

"What a dump," I said as we pulled out of the lot. "Carol lives there?"

"It's the social place to be."

"Hey, are you saying Carol's a sosh? That young woman is not stupid."

"No. She aced organic chemistry."

"But not English?"

"A C in composition."

"From Keith McDonald?"

"No. She's never had a class from McDonald. Mary Sadat took his ballad seminar. So did Letha Carlsen. Not Carol."

"He mentioned that Mary took it." It was just possible that Keith's feeling of concern for his students was as protective as Jay's. Keith had seemed far more shaken by Mary's disappearance than by Hugo's death.

Half a mile south of the campus, Jay slowed the car. We crept along to an illegible signpost and turned left.

"Are you sure this is the road?"

"Pretty sure. Carol said it wasn't well marked."

For the first few miles the road was not bad. We passed farmhouses, a collapsing machine shed, a fishing cabin. Then the road began to climb and the surface got bumpier. Nobody had painted the white line along the shoulder or the yellow line down the center for a long time. Winters on the Peninsula are not severe by eastern standards, so the frost damage was subtle. The county's road crew had tossed a mixture of gravel and asphalt into the worst cracks. Even so, the roadbed was rough.

We wound through second-growth forest, almost ready for harvest, for a few miles. Then we hit the first clear-cut. It was recent and it looked like hell.

I know the timber company propaganda in favor of clear-cutting trees, but the fact remains that it's an insult to nature and an insult to the eye. This area hadn't been cleaned up and replanted. It would look better in a few years. In a few years it would look like a Christmas tree farm, which is what timber companies want. Now, early in the season, before the bushes had leafed out, the clear-cut looked like photographs of Belleau Wood circa 1917.

We climbed past the blitz into another stretch of second-growth. As we rounded a curve, a log truck loaded with one mammoth cedar barreled toward us, horn blaring. Jay bumped the Honda onto the shoulder as the noise Dopplered. Gravel sprayed, but we didn't spin out.

Jay's knuckles showed white on the steering wheel. "Good thing we met him here. No drop-off."

I drew a breath. "That was an old-growth cedar log."

"Are you looking, Lark?"

"For signs of the pickup? Yes. Pity it's silver and black. If it was fire-engine red, it'd be easier to spot. Do you really think we'll find it?"

"I hope it's not out here."

We continued to climb. The road surface was dry. The previous evening, it would have been wet and treacherous. We passed the derelict fishing lodge. Stumps surrounded it.

We pulled around another curve and I made a noise that may be represented as "Ulp." A sheer drop-off skirted my side of the road. The cliff ran several miles, with the misty foothills and a bend of the Coho visible below in the blue distance. I made myself look straight down.

"Stop!"

Jay slowed the Honda but didn't stop. "What is it?"

"Never mind. Sun on water." A creek must run at the base of the canyon.

Jay grunted and drove on.

About a hundred yards farther along, I glimpsed something else. I squinched my eyes. "Better stop. I can't tell. Could be water . . . damn." A tree that must have grown straight up the side of the ravine blocked my sight. "Slow down, damnit. There. You have to stop, Jay."

"I can't stop yet. I need a straight stretch or a wide place." He kept going.

I had lost sight of my glittering patch. I blinked hard.

It was a good quarter mile before the road straightened, the shoulder widened, and Jay could pull over without endangering us or the car.

He set the brake. "We'll have to walk back."

"I know. Do we need a flare?"

"Not yet."

We got out. I zipped my all-weather jacket and tugged my gloves on. Jay reached into the glove compartment on my side and took out his binoculars. "Show me."

Every ten yards or so Jay lifted the binoculars and scanned the canyon below us. It was brushy and had been logged, but noble firs had begun to rise above the deciduous undergrowth. We trudged to the tree that had blocked my view.

We had already passed the tree when I glimpsed the metallic reflection. I jogged back toward the Honda about ten yards and looked down. At first I didn't see anything but the brown of the undergrowth and the somber greens of the dominant conifers. Then I stepped sideways and there it was. "Come here."

Jay walked over to me.

I pointed.

He steadied the binoculars and focused. "Yeah. That's it, about halfway down. They must've been flying. I don't see . . ."

My pulse accelerated. "It's the pickup?"

He lowered the glasses and looked at me, his eyes grave. "I can see the sleeve of a jacket in the underbrush. One of them was thrown. I don't see the other. The truck smacked into a blackberry patch, so it's half-hidden."

I gulped. "What now?"

"We get help fast. Then I'm going down with a medical kit. Let's hope I need it."

It took us about four minutes to jog back to the car. Jay

called the sheriff's dispatcher while I set flares in front of the Honda and at the curve behind it. We would have to trust the next log truck to avoid it.

I retrieved Jay's first aid kit from the trunk, his emergency blanket, and a canteen of water. I got my aluminum blanket and more flares from my side of the car. When Jay finished talking, I reached for the telephone.

He grabbed my wrist. "Who were you going to call?"

"Bianca."

"No."

"But I'm obviously going to be late. . . . Oh."

"I don't want those people to know what's happening. We'll take the phone, though, in case I need to relay information on the injuries. I gave the number to the dispatcher. Did you bring the rope?"

"Rope?"

He popped the trunk again and got out, leaving me to retrieve the phone. I was laden like a camel. I lumbered around as he pulled a coil of climbing rope from behind the black plastic box of snow chains we had never used. He also took out his point-and-click camera with the built-in flash, which he stuffed into one of my pockets.

I regarded the rope with interest. "You're taking up mountain climbing, and I'm your faithful sherpa."

"Very funny. I want a lifeline. I'll use that tree by the road. The first ten or fifteen feet are steepest."

We redistributed the load and slogged back to the marker tree. Jay would have to lower himself through the brush, then make his way along the milder slope to the wreck. I was ready to go down, too, but he made me promise to wait for the rescue car. We wrapped a bight of rope around the trunk of the tree. It was some kind of native evergreen and probably shallow-rooted. I hoped it would hold.

"Phone?" Jay said, reaching for it.

"Why . . . oh, in case you need to describe the injuries."

"Come on, Lark. Get it into gear."

He stuffed the phone in one pocket and the emergency medical kit in the other, and draped the canteen across his chest. He also managed to squish both blankets into his jacket. They folded up small.

I held the rope against his weight as he picked his way down the slope. Once he lurched off-balance and the rope jerked at my hand, but I dug my heels in and held on. When I felt the rope go slack I peered down at him.

"I'm okay. Set the flares out," he called.

"Okay," I yelled back.

I set four flares both ways from the tree, with attention to the curves in the road and the probable speed of the rescue vehicles. I also had instructions to photograph the skid marks and the point at which the truck had left the road. Neither of us thought the photos would substitute for professional work, but the rescue vehicle might arrive before the patrol car. Rescue crews tended to take first things first, and as far as they were concerned preserving evidence came a long way behind saving lives. That was a viewpoint I could sympathize with. Nevertheless, I did my best with the camera. Just in case.

The marks were fairly obvious, now I knew they were there. I wondered how many other, less lethal times Jason had burned rubber. His tires had ground treadmarks into the weedy shoulder before the pickup became airborne. I shot the treadmarks from a couple of angles. The natural light must have been adequate because the flash didn't discharge.

Then I stuffed the small camera back in my pocket, walked to the tree, and watched Jay's uncommunicative head bobbing in the brush. I hoped the paramedics and the cops would hurry.

Since I knew where the pickup was, the path it had cut was visible. It had sailed over the edge, hit the ground beside a noble fir, and rolled down through the blackberries until it came to rest on its side against an alder. The blackberry vines had whipped back, partially obscuring the truck so I couldn't see which side was down. Blackberries are the kudzu of the Pacific Northwest.

Jay stopped by the patch of color that was one of the boys. He squatted there a long time. Then he inched his way through the vines to the pickup. Once, I thought I could hear him talking on the phone, but the wind had picked up and a stream gurgled nearby, so I couldn't be sure.

I didn't see how anyone could have survived a crash like that. I thought of Bill's ingenuous face and Jason's twisty little mouth, and I began a kind of preliminary mourning. It was such a stupid waste. Jason was a rotten driver, however youthful his reaction time, capable of running the truck off the road on his own. He was the personification of adolescent male insurance rates. I was no expert but, from the look of the tread-marks, he had been speeding. Was the wreck an accident, a nasty coincidence, or had it been engineered? I shivered in the rising breeze.

I also thought of Mary Sadat. Mary's car had been found in Astoria. If someone had murdered her, the killer could have dumped her body along this road with perfect confidence. Hunters were always getting lost in the hills. Sometimes the ground searches found them, sometimes not. Sometimes their gnawed bones showed up years later, a nice academic puzzle for forensic anthropologists.

"Hey!"

I jerked back to the scene before me.

Jay indicated that he wanted to come up. I took up the rope and braced myself. He needed it more coming up than going down. He grabbed the tree when he reached the top and scrambled onto the road. His face and hands were scratched and bleeding.

"Blackberry vines?"

"What? Yeah, it's a jungle."

"Are they dead?"

He shook his head. "Both unconscious, though. I don't like

the look of Bill Johnson. He was thrown. Head injuries, possible spinal damage. The damn fool wasn't wearing a seat belt."

"What about Jason?"

Jay divested himself of most of his gear. The canteen clanked on the gravel. "Jason's trapped in the truck, but he was moaning a little. They're both dangerously cold. I wrapped Bill in one of the blankets. Couldn't get to Jason." He sat on the edge of the road and took out the phone again. "Reception's lousy down there. The rescue team will need the Jaws."

The Jaws of Life. I wondered if the chrome roll bar had done Jason any good.

Jay was talking to the dispatcher. She crackled back. After a while he signed off. "That line's not clear, but I think she said they're on the way."

It was a good half hour before the fire department rescue truck and the first of the sheriff's cars arrived, time for us to carry our gear back to the Honda. I was expecting Dale Nelson, but I didn't recognize the deputy who came.

The rescue crew was smooth and professional. The paramedic in charge questioned Jay, as the others, who included a young woman, readied stretchers for the descent. Then they went down. They were at it a long time.

Jay talked to the deputy about the skid marks. He also made it plain they should check the pickup for evidence of tampering. There was a lot of radio chatter back and forth. Eventually, the paramedic called for the Life Flight helicopter from Kayport.

I felt like a fifth wheel. Still, the process was interesting in a horrible way. After a long while, Jay came over to me. His scratches had scabbed.

I gave him a hug. "I'm cold."

"Me, too. Won't be long. They'll fly Bill out in the chopper. Jason's in somewhat better shape, though he's still unconscious. They'll transport him in the ambulance."

There was no ambulance. Even as I formed the idea, one

roared up from the south, from Kayport. The driver slewed the vehicle around importantly and parked behind the rescue van. Then Dale showed up, light flashing. He liked the revolving light. It wasn't necessary.

Jay said, "I can ride back with Dale. Why don't you take the car on down?"

"I'll wait until the helicopter comes."

He smiled at me.

"Well, I've never seen a helicopter rescue." I felt defensive as well as redundant. Jay didn't argue. He gave me another hug and walked off to talk to Dale. I remembered the thermos of coffee and went for it. Sitting out of the fitful wind felt good, so I drank a lukewarm cup of the stuff in the car. As I walked back to the rescue scene, the ambulance screamed past me, heading for Kayport. I caught a glimpse of Jason, bundled in blankets, with an IV hanging over him and a tense paramedic at his side.

The rescue squad was bringing Bill up to the road in a basket-like stretcher. They had been arguing whether to move him up or have the helicopter hover over the canyon. They were being very careful. Apparently they decided the risk of gusts was too great. The helicopter was going to land on the road.

Once that decision was made, the first deputy who had arrived began, rather officiously, to clear an area on the road. I was standing on the shoulder and he waved me off. He probably expected me to go on down to the Honda, but I walked back to Jay and stood beside him as the rescue crew inched Bill's "basket" up the hillside. As the carrier reached the shoulder, one of the rescuers slipped and fell halfway down the side of the ravine. He wasn't seriously hurt but his sudden movement jolted the stretcher.

Jay reached down to steady it and I caught a glimpse of Bill's face. I looked away. Bruises had swollen and turned black, reducing both eyes to slits, and one of the many lacerations had torn his nose, exposing the cartilage. When the para-

162

medics had slipped the stretcher onto a gurney they wheeled it over to the rescue van. They changed IVs and the woman began monitoring his vital signs.

Beside me, Jay stirred and cocked his head. "It's coming," he said quietly. I could hear nothing, but Jay was a medic in the army and he tends to recognize the sound of helicopters.

He was right. The Life Flight copter landed on the road about five minutes later, churning an amazing amount of dust and debris into the air, considering it had rained the night before. The helicopter medic and the rescue crew had Bill aboard and secured within two minutes, and the aircraft took off. I watched until it was a speck in the sky above the Coho River.

Jay and I walked back to the Honda. He had changed his mind. He was going to drive the Honda to the hospital and stay there as long as he was needed.

He drove slowly, carefully. At the base of the shortcut the road came to a T. One arm led east toward the farm, the other to Kayport.

"Do you want me to drop you off now?"

I started. I had been brooding over the meaning of the accident. "No. I want the car."

"Okay." He turned right in the wake of another log truck. "Don't say anything, not a damned thing, about this business. Pretend it didn't happen."

"All right. The workshop starts tomorrow. There should be enough adrenaline flowing about that to keep their minds off Bill and Jason."

He sighed. "I can't believe that woman didn't cancel the conference."

Neither could I. And I was beginning to get stage fright.

13 ~

"I JUST TALKED to Frank Hrubek," Bianca said. "Can you drive to Portland tomorrow to pick him up?"

Hrubek was the first of the two science writers who were going to address the workshop. I admired his writing. Even so, I was not tempted.

"No," I said with great firmness. "Rent the man a car."

"He doesn't drive."

We were standing in the seminar room of the conference wing of the house. In spite of catastrophe, chaos, and the memorial service, the room had been freshly dusted and vacuumed, and Marianne, arms folded, stood silent witness to the conversation.

I drew a long, careful breath. "You did not hire me as a chauffeur. I'm supposed to help you run the workshop."

Bianca thrust a hand through her hair. "I know. I apologize. I was going to get him myself, Lark, but you must see that I can't be away from the farm for six hours, not now."

The drive from Kayport to Portland International Airport took two and a half hours in good weather. It was raining again. "More like seven hours altogether," I said coldly, "what with waiting around and claiming luggage. Let Keith do it."

She shook her head. "He's distraught over the students— Mary missing and now Jason. Keith's on medication. He shouldn't drive." She didn't mention Bill. Maybe Bill was too much Jason's shadow for her to think of him. He was lying in the hospital, probably with a broken neck. Bianca didn't know that yet. I gritted my teeth.

"Come on, Lark," she wheedled.

"Why not Angie?"

"Angie and Del will be putting in a half day of work. Farming," she added with maddening complacence, "operates on its own time line. They have to plant the spinach."

"Send one of the interns." I was flailing around and knew it. "Send the Carlsens."

"What if they had a wreck on the way? With the others missing . . ." Her voice trailed and the intense eyes pleaded.

I got the point. Parental lawsuits. "What if *I* have a wreck?"

"You won't," she said with superb confidence.

"Send Mike."

"No." Marianne didn't even bother to raise her voice. She knew how to deal with Bianca.

"If I agree to drive to Portland tomorrow to fetch Francis Hrubek, my husband will divorce me on the grounds of mental incompetence."

Bianca smiled a sad smile. "You have a great sense of humor."

"When does Hrubek's plane arrive?" The moment I asked the question I knew I was defeated.

Bianca did, too. Her face lit. "Ten. Nine forty-five, actually."

"In the morning?"

"Of course in the morning. He wants to be here for the reception."

I groaned. "I'd have to be on the road by half past six." I tend to wake at six spontaneously, so six thirty wasn't all that horrible, but Bianca didn't need to know about my internal clock. I wanted her to owe me big-time. I gave another artistic groan. If she could manipulate, so could I.

"Come and have some lunch," Marianne interposed.

I glanced at her. She looked grave and sympathetic. I hadn't had lunch, as a matter of fact, and it was past one o'clock. The muffins were ancient history.

Bianca turned the big brown eyes on me. "You'll go, won't you? That's wonderful. I'll get the flight number for you."

In my own defense, I will say that I didn't stick around to be manipulated further. I left the farm. After lunch.

I drove straight to the hospital in Kayport. The receptionist told me Bill was in surgery and Jason in intensive care.

"Second floor?"

She frowned. "You can't see either of those patients."

"I know. My husband is here . . . probably in the nearest waiting room."

"He's a relative?"

I stared at her, unwilling to explain that Jay stood *in loco parentis*, as far as the college was concerned.

"Second floor. West elevator," she conceded. "The waiting room's across from the nurses' station."

"Thanks."

Shoalwater Hospital is one reason the Peninsula is becoming a retirement center. It has excellent diagnostic and immediate treatment facilities, good stroke therapy, an attached nursing home for long-term care, and the Life Flight service, which can airlift patients to Portland as well as rescuing them from obscure country roads. The average age of patients was around fifty. Bill and Jason were bound to be oddities.

I don't like hospitals. Most people don't. A woman I knew had died of a stroke in this one a few months earlier and memory was making me edgy.

The elevator decanted me opposite an empty alcove with a philodendron and a built-in sofa upholstered in soothing shades of blue and purple. A tasteful watercolor of the Kayport marina hung over the bench. I stood for a moment looking at it and thinking of the view from Hugo's apartment. Then I made myself peer around the corner.

At the far end of the long corridor, a small knot of people stood talking in hushed voices. I could see Jay, head cocked, hands in his jacket pockets, listening to someone. As I watched, a figure emerged from the clump and strode toward me. Dale Nelson. I retreated to the alcove and sat waiting.

He spotted me as he was reaching for the elevator button. "Hey, I thought you were at the farm."

I stood up. "I was. What's happening?"

He made a face. "The usual waiting game. Jason Thirkell hasn't regained consciousness yet. Jay's dealing with Bill's parents, thank God. Kid got out of the operating room half an hour ago. He's in post-op. Thirkell's there in intensive care."

I cleared my throat. "Bill's pretty bad, then."

"They think he'll live, but . . ." The elevator arrived. "Hey, I gotta go. See you." Dale hopped in and the doors slid shut.

I watched the illuminated buttons until Dale reached the ground floor. Then I sat again. In a surprisingly short time, a middle-aged couple, the woman crying, the man with his arm around her trying not to, came around the corner and pressed the elevator button. Bill's parents, I suspected. I got up and started to say something, offer my sympathy, but they were speaking in low, intent voices and it was apparent they didn't notice me. I decided not to intrude. What could I say?

When the elevator doors had closed on their anguished faces, I stuck my head into the corridor again. Jay was still standing by the nurses' station, but there was only one other person with him. As I passed the first of the two-bed wards, the man shook hands with Jay and went off in the other direction. Jay took a seat on the dispirited sofa in the hallway and picked up a magazine.

He looked up as I approached and gave me a smile that was half grimace.

I sat beside him. "I saw Dale."

Jay sighed. "Then you know about Bill."

"I know they operated on him."

"He's a healthy kid. He'll live." His face was bleak.

"Is he . . . will he be paralyzed?"

Jay shrugged. "It's too soon to tell. At the moment, the doctors seem more worried about brain damage. His skull was fractured. They operated to relieve the pressure."

I tried to digest that. "What about Jason?"

"He's still in a coma and there's a strong possibility he'll develop pneumonia. He was damn cold."

"What about injuries?"

"Bruises, some lacerations. Nothing like Bill."

"I think I saw Bill's parents."

Jay's hand clenched on the *National Geographic,* but he didn't say anything.

"Have you talked to the Dean?"

"Left a message for him."

"Did you eat lunch?" I asked because Jay is a little apt to forget the practicalities in stressful situations.

He blinked at me. "No."

"You must be Jay Dodge."

Both of us started and stood up. A young woman in a flowered dress, pumps, and a blue raincoat looked up at us. She was about five-foot-two, heels and all.

She held out identification so Jay could inspect it. "I'm Louise Callender. Dale said you'd fill me in." She had round pink cheeks and blond hair and might have been Dale Nelson's sister.

Jay shook hands and introduced me.

Dale had called Deputy Callender away from a shopping spree at the mall. She was detailed to sit outside Jason's room until he regained consciousness. Dale wanted to question Jason, of course, but I gathered that Callender was also supposed to guard the boys. That was interesting, but not entirely surprising. I tried to envisage her wrestling with a large man, Del Wallace, perhaps.

When Callender had conferred with Jay and was sitting on the couch with the *National Geographic,* we headed down the hall, bound for the cafeteria in the basement.

Jay leaned on the elevator button. "How are things at the funny farm?"

"Uh . . ."

"That bad, huh?" The doors opened and we got in beside a couple of nurses in polyester uniforms—pastel pants outfits, one with stylized daisies all over it. The nurses smiled and went back to a conversation about the Portland Trailblazers. They rode with us to the basement and also made for the cafeteria. Bill's parents huddled in a far corner over coffee. It wasn't until Jay and I were sitting at one of the tiny ice-cream parlor tables that we could say anything of significance.

In other words, I had some time to think up a rationalization for my wimpishness in the matter of Francis Hrubek. As I had expected, Jay was outraged. Between savage bites of turkey sandwich, he forbade me to go, told me I was a dolt and a patsy, and offered me the use of the Honda. My ancient Toyota is not suitable for long drives.

I dallied with my cup of bad coffee. "I'll be back by one-thirty."

"Ha."

I said, "I'll have two and a half hours to persuade him to sign all his books."

"Wonderful."

I eyed him over my mug. "Let's go home."

He finished chewing the last of his sandwich, patted his moustache with the paper napkin, and laid the crumpled napkin on the table. "I can't leave the hospital until Jason regains consciousness."

"That could take days!"

He explained that he was convinced the accident had been rigged and that Jason had seen something incriminating.

I leaned back. "Was he blackmailing the murderer?"

"Maybe, maybe not. The timing is suggestive."

"Hmm. Hugo is killed. Ten days pass. Mary disappears . . ."

"And things start to happen. I think Jason and Bill saw her in Seaside with the murderer."

"Does Dale agree?"

"He's willing to think about it."

"Hence Louise Callender."

"Yeah." He took a last swallow of tea.

I got up. "I thought your opposition to my little Portland jaunt was uncharacteristically feeble. If you're going to camp out at the hospital, I'll bring you a razor and a toothbrush."

"Thanks." He actually looked guilty.

"Do you want me to wait with you?"

"No. It could . . ."

"Take days," I finished. "All right, Jay, but I don't think Jason is your responsibility."

He shrugged back into his all-weather jacket. "I don't have a legal obligation to him, but he is a student. His father's driving down from Seattle, and his mother and stepfather should be here any minute. I'll have to talk to them."

I shivered. "Good luck."

He walked me out to the Honda. As I unlocked the car, he said, "Don't let that conniving female bully you into anything else."

I gave him a peck on the cheek. "I won't. See you later."

I didn't stop at the bookstore. From then until the end of the workshop, it would have to wait. When I got home, I discovered Bianca had left a message on the recorder. She sounded urgent. I called Bonnie.

That absorbed a good hour. I took a nice hot shower and changed into sweats. I read the paper. I packed a duffel with supplies for Jay. He might as well be comfortable. Then I called Bianca.

Angie answered, sounding tired. When I had identified myself, she said, "Del just drove Trish home to Raymond. She was having false labor pains. At least, she thinks they're false."

"Wow. Bianca called me. Do you know why?"

"It's probably about Bill and Jason. You knew about the wreck, didn't you?" She sounded mildly accusatory.

"Uh, yes."

170

"Oh, here she is. She wants to talk to you."

Bianca wanted to rank me down for not telling her about the wreck. When she paused for breath, I said, "Bianca?"

"What?"

"Shut up. If you want me to drive to Portland tomorrow you will speak to me very, very softly."

She made a sound of protest.

"Jay and I found the boys this morning. I didn't tell you because Dale Nelson told me not to."

"But I was so worried about them . . ." She broke off. When she spoke again, her voice sounded scared. "Was it . . . did somebody cause the wreck?"

"I don't know, Bianca, and I'm not going to talk about it." I had just talked about it to Bonnie in considerable detail, including speculation, but Bonnie was a friend and Bonnie was discreet.

After that Bianca made a disheartened attempt to get me to hang around the airport for another hour waiting for two of the workshop participants. She wasn't up to her usual form, however, and I managed to resist.

I drove back to the hospital at six. Jason was still unconscious. It would be days, of course, if not weeks, before Bill could be interviewed. The doctors now thought he was paralyzed from the waist down, though there was some possibility of partial recovery of movement. They still had no firm opinion about permanent brain damage. Jay had been dealing with the Johnsons and Debbie Davis, Jason's mother, all afternoon.

I dragged Jay down to the cafeteria again and we had a macaroni and cheese casserole for dinner. A noisy family group dominated the restaurant area, so it wasn't until we got to the Jell-O pudding that we had an opportunity for real conversation. The family dissolved, leaving us alone except for the servers, who were doing a desultory cleanup.

I don't know what it is with cafeterias and the Jell-O company. You can go for years without seeing a Jell-O pudding—

except in cafeterias. I toyed with mine. It tasted of cocoa and cardboard, except for the blob of white stuff on top. That tasted of plastic.

Jay dug into his without hesitation. He scraped the last of the chocolate from the glass cup and shoved the cup back, swabbing his moustache with a paper napkin. "Dale got preliminary results from the crime lab this afternoon." He crumpled the napkin.

He meant the state crime lab's analysis of the scene of Hugo's murder. I wondered what the lab would make of my pudding. "And?"

"This is confidential . . ."

"For God's sake, Jay."

He scowled. "You don't seem to be able to resist Bianca Fiedler's blandishments. We want Bianca and her staff kept in the dark."

This was unsurprising, but I was interested to observe that Jay was using the pronoun "we" without consciousness. That meant he thought of himself as inside the investigation. He wouldn't think that unless Dale did, too.

"My lips are sealed." I shoved my unfinished dessert away. "Probably permanently, by that fake mousse."

"Aw, it wasn't that bad. Comfort food."

"Jay," I said gently, "tell me about the lab report."

"They found traces in the wheelbarrow."

The wheelbarrow he was referring to was one of those large, low-slung carts used to haul plant clippings. "Hugo was carried to the ice house in the wheelbarrow?"

Jay nodded. "Postmortem."

"So he was killed near the greenhouses." I brooded. The wheelbarrow was stored near the greenhouses—Angie's territory. Not Del's. "But Angie . . ."

"Has an alibi." He smoothed his moustache. "At least, she does if we can definitely establish that Hugo was alive until one in the afternoon. I think we will."

"When Jason wakes up?"

"Maybe."

"Then the mutilations and the ice house business were a sort of post-meditation—whatever the opposite of premeditation is."

"Maybe." He drew a breath. "I think Groth had an appointment with his killer at the greenhouses, probably around one or one-thirty. They quarreled for whatever reason, and Groth was killed in the fight. The M.E. thinks he took a while to die from the head wound, as long as an hour, though he would have been deeply unconscious. The body was moved maybe as much as two hours after he died."

Envisaging the scene was making me sick. Or it may have been the Jell-O pudding. "So he was transported to the ice house in the wheelbarrow and there was a time gap. I don't see that that gets you further along. You still have two suspects."

He raised his eyebrows.

"Del and Keith."

"Five," he said. "Wallace, McDonald, Marianne Wallace, Bianca Fiedler, and Angie Martini. But we're pretty sure now that we're looking for an impulsive personality."

"An improviser." I nodded. "But Angie's alibi . . ."

"Could be after the fact, or even before it."

"So the timing is crucial. I don't see Marianne."

"She's not very likely—no apparent motive—but she would have had the opportunity." He stood up. "Dale is going to do another round of interviews."

"Tomorrow?" I thought of Bianca's probable reaction and groaned. "That should enliven the morning."

"What's it to you, my sweet? You'll be in Portland."

I groaned again. I also wondered whether I might not return to discover the show was over—that Dale had made an arrest. It was not that I wanted to be in at the kill, but I didn't want to miss anything crucial either.

We went back upstairs and I met Jason's mother. She was a cocktail waitress and seemed more worried about missing work than about Jason, but that may have been my imagination.

14 ❧

I DROVE TO Portland International Airport via Interstates 5 and 205, bypassing Vancouver and catching a picture-perfect view of Mt. Hood from the Glen Jackson Bridge. Sunday traffic was light on the bridge, and had been on Highway 30, all the way from Astoria to Longview, where I crossed back over the Columbia. The weather was brilliant, our first real spring day.

I took the cellular phone with me. The evening before, I had left Jay prepared to spend the night at the hospital. He wasn't beside me when my alarm woke me at five-thirty, so I gathered that Jason must still be unconscious. I didn't call the hospital before I left. It was too early. Once I reached the highway on the Oregon side and saw how beautiful the weather was, I forgot to call.

When residents of the area say "the mountain is out," they mean that the native fog, smog, and low-hanging clouds have finally cleared away, and the mountain, whichever mountain it may be, is visible. Or it may have gone away and come back, who knows?

That morning *all* the mountains were out. Just before I crossed the Lewis and Clark Bridge at Longview, I saw the truncated cone of Loowit, Mt. St. Helens. Approaching Vancouver, I saw Mt. St. Helens again, its shy twin, Mt. Adams, and, a bit farther on, Mt. Hood. I thought I also caught a glimpse of Mt. Rainier in my rearview mirror, but that may have been an illusion.

I did not forget murder and mayhem, but my mind was tired of running in futile circles. Getting out of the Shoalwater area filled me with something like exuberance. Nothing is so beautiful as spring.

I swept along in my spring daze, ten miles an hour above the limit on U.S. 30 and five on the Interstate when I reached it. At the airport, I left the car in the short-term parking facility and headed across the zebra-striped crosswalk to the terminal. As I approached the wide revolving door, a mellifluous male voice welcomed me to Portland International Airport. It went on to assure me that parking was limited to the curb lane for a maximum of three minutes, and that the middle lane was for active loading and unloading. "Violators," the voice said sadly, "may be cited and towed."

Undaunted, I whisked past the clump of smokers standing near a vast concrete ashtray and whirled through the door. I took the north entrance because Hrubek was coming in on a Delta flight. I rode the escalator up behind an impenetrable barrier of passengers with large suitcases, checked the monitor above one of the Delta desks for the gate number, and trotted on in.

PDX is an airport like any other with one small exception. It has a superb bookstore. Powell's City of Books had opened a branch at the airport after the last remodeling session. Most airport book displays are marginally less interesting than the ones at supermarkets. Sometimes an airport has a Dalton's or a Smith's. The Powell's airport branch at Portland is a store for people who actively love books. It does very well. It also opens at nine A.M. It was ten of nine.

I drank a cup of espresso in one of the many coffee boutiques, then strolled across the teal-and-purple carpet to the bookstore. Thanks to my light heart and lead foot, I had forty-five minutes to squander. I admired the displays, chatted with the clerk, bought Jay a pioneer diary in facsimile and Bonnie a guide that laid out walking tours of Paris. I also found a slim collection of Francis Hrubek's early essays I didn't have in stock. As I paid for my loot, I mentioned that I'd come to the airport to meet Hrubek.

The clerk's face lit up. "One of the gods," she breathed. "Do you think he'd autograph our books?"

I had no idea, but I agreed to raise the issue with Hrubek. Then I headed for the D concourse. The remodeled north wing featured skylights that would brighten even a gray day, and that morning the effect was dazzling. I laid my handbag on the conveyor belt of the nearest metal detector and walked through the little gate without setting off the alarm. The man behind me was less lucky. I glanced back and saw him unbuckle his big studded belt.

I retrieved my bag and strolled along, shunning the people mover and admiring a row of live trees that marched down the center of the wide corridor beyond the conveyor. Hoardings with cutesy murals of workmen and bemused passengers covered a series of gaping holes. The murals announced in large letters that the holes would transmogrify into pubs and fast-food emporia when construction was done. I believed them.

When I reached the assigned gate, I still had fifteen minutes to kill. As I stood waiting, I flipped the essay collection over. A benignant middle-aged face twinkled at me. The nose was long, the mouth curved in a wry smile, the moustache drooped heroically. I thought I'd recognize my quarry. I opened the book to the first chapter and began to read.

A 757 taxied up. The flight was announced. I stuffed the book back in its sack and watched the passengers stumble up the carpeted ramp into the waiting area. A few grandmothers, one younger man with skis, baggy-eyed salesmen. The bulk of the passengers were business-suited executive types, male and female. No Hrubek. I waited. More businessmen, several carrying laptop computers. The flight had originated in Cincinnati, but Hrubek lived in Pennsylvania. He had had to make a connecting flight, probably very early, even allowing for the three-hour time difference. Maybe he'd missed the plane. I waited.

Passengers dispersed. Behind the check-in station, airline personnel shuffled papers and made computer entries. I was about to walk over and ask whether Hrubek was on the flight list when I spotted the gnome.

A short, elderly man with a cane, back curved, stood at the head of the ramp, blinking through thick spectacles. I went over to him. "Are you Francis Hrubek?"

He squinted up at me. "Who wants to know?" The voice was gravelly and humorous. I recognized the eyes even through the distorting lenses.

I had been assuming that Francis Hrubek didn't drive, like Hugo, as a matter of principle. Probably Hrubek didn't drive because he couldn't see well enough to pass the driver's exam.

I thrust out my hand, thinking publishers ought to be forced to update jacket photos. He had shaved off his moustache. "I'm Lark Dodge. Bianca Fiedler sent me to get you. Welcome to the Pacific Northwest."

He gave me his claw. "Thanks. Lark?"

"Like the bird. Did you check your luggage?"

We began to move, very slowly, down the corridor. I wondered if I ought to ask the airline people for a wheelchair.

"Long flight," Hrubek observed. "Feels good to stretch my legs." We inched along. "I have one suitcase, assuming it didn't get lost in transit. I checked it through. Didn't want to wrestle it into the overhead rack."

"No problem."

We used the people mover. As we passed the security guards stationed by the metal detectors, Hrubek said, "What's this about an accident at the farm?"

The nearest guard turned and stared.

"I'll tell you all about it," I said with resignation, "but let's find your bag first."

He seemed amenable to that. We crept through a swirl of

177

incoming skiers. Off to Aspen, probably, or Alta—Salt Lake City was a frequent Delta stop. Finally we reached the escalator I had ridden up. There were two escalators down. The logic of that escaped me. We had a little hesitation and shuffling but managed to get onto the center track without falling. Hrubek shifted his cane to his left hand and grasped the rail. I stood behind him, silent and, alas, impatient.

A few feet down the escalator I remembered Powell's Books. I was considering whether to mention the clerk's request for autographs, when I glanced at the people riding the up escalator. Two women stood side by side, chatting and blocking the way for a tall businessman with a briefcase. I noticed him first because he was grimacing. Then I saw the women's faces. The man said something and the heavier of the two women turned to him. The slimmer woman took a step upward, her companion moved in behind her, and the businessman passed them, briefcase swinging.

"Mr. Hrubek," I croaked. "Please wait for me at the baggage claim area. It's to your right. I just saw someone I have to speak to."

He turned round, frowning, and stumbled as we came to the bottom of the escalator. I caught his elbow and steadied him. "Really," I said, "I am so sorry. I'll be back within fifteen minutes."

I pointed him the right way and he went off grumbling. Then I wheeled round and began to run up the escalator in hot pursuit of the women. One of them was Mary Sadat.

Naturally, in the interim, both women had disappeared and a gaggle of baggage-laden passengers had debouched onto the escalator ahead of me.

"Pardon me. Sorry. Excuse me. I beg your pardon." I don't know why people don't stand to the right on an escalator. Near the top a woman with frosted hair was spending a week in Reno with three matched suitcases. The largest, which could have held a wedding dress, a fur coat, and the *World Book Encyclopedia,* squatted on the left. When we reached the top and she began wrestling with it, I leaned my left hand on the stainless-steel barrier between the escalators and vaulted over the suitcase.

I came close to smashing the woman's face with my elbow. I also stumbled when I jumped, but I scrambled to my feet and ran. I could hear her squawking as I sped off.

A waiting area under the skylight led to D and E concourses. I stopped in front of a chair upholstered in striped fabric and I dithered. Where had they gone? If they had stopped at the Delta ticketing area, they might still be there, standing in line behind a dozen skiers. Perhaps I should wait. They hadn't had suitcases, though. I was about to sit when I glimpsed them. They had got ahead of me after all. They were strolling away from the security check toward the D corridor. The older woman was laughing. Mary slung her handbag over her shoulder by its long strap. I dashed to the same gate, flopped my purse on the conveyor belt, and zipped through the gate ahead of two startled businessmen. Then I grabbed the purse and ran.

The two women had almost reached the people mover when I caught up with them.

"Mary!" I was puffing a little, more from excitement than the exertion. "Please, Mary. I need to talk to you."

Mary Sadat whirled, hands at her mouth. The other woman had stepped onto the conveyor.

I took a step toward Mary.

"Oh, no! I can't . . . Sarah!"

"Please," I said. Mary was going to bolt.

The other woman, Sarah, turned around.

"Excuse us."

I stepped aside and so did Mary as three impatient passengers strode onto the people mover. Such is conditioning. Sarah tried to start back. They trapped her. I could see her mouth working as the conveyor bore her away from us.

I took Mary's arm and drew her over to the adjacent passenger area, which was blessedly empty. "We have to talk."

Mary said nothing. She looked like a rabbit frozen in a hunter's sights. The nearest seats faced away from the corridor, so I walked her around and sat her down with her back to the people mover.

I stood over her. "Do your parents know where you are?" By all accounts, they had been frantic.

She shook her head.

I stared down at her pallid face. I could not conceive of doing anything that cruel to my family. "Why?"

"She'll kill me, too," Mary whispered.

"Who?"

Her mouth compressed in a line. She shook her head. Her eyes glittered with tears.

The other woman, Sarah, bustled up panting. She had run back the length of the people mover. "Who are you? What are you doing to my sister? Let her go or I'll call the guard."

I turned. "Do that. Mary has been the object of a two-state search by at least three police departments. Maybe *I* should call the guard."

We stared at each other and Sarah's face sagged. "She's in trouble, isn't she?"

"Not so far, but a lot of people are worried about her, including your parents." Including my husband.

The older woman's eyes fell. "She begged me not to tell."

"They'll make me go back." Mary began to sob. "She'll kill me, too."

I was getting a little tired of Mary's indefinite pronouns. "Who will make you go back and who will kill you?"

Mary sobbed.

Sarah moved to her shoulder and patted it. "Now, Mary . . ."

The PA system announced the arrival of a Delta flight.

"Oh, God," Sarah said. "I'm supposed to meet my husband."

"Where?"

"Gate twelve."

"Well, stand so you can see the arriving passengers. When you don't show up, he'll page you or come on down the corridor looking for you."

She sighed.

I said, "You have to explain, Mrs. . . . ?"

"Pierce," she said. "I'm Sarah Pierce."

"I'm Lark Dodge. I met Mary at the farm when we were searching for Hugo Groth." I clarified my connection with Bianca and described my trip to the airport. I was conscious of time ticking away, and of an elderly man with poor vision waiting for me near a strange baggage carrel.

"Then you weren't looking for Mary." Unlike her sister, Sarah Pierce had a faint accent.

"No. Spotting her was pure luck." I didn't specify good or bad.

Sarah heaved another sigh and gave the sobbing Mary another absentminded pat. "Mary's been hiding. She's afraid. . . ."

"So I gathered," I interrupted, "though I don't understand why, exactly."

Mary said frantically, "No, don't tell her. She works for them. They'll find me and kill me like they did Mr. Groth."

"Who," I said with as much patience as I could muster, "is or are going to kill you? I don't understand."

Mary sobbed.

I looked at Sarah.

She shrugged. "I won't force her to go back."

I said, "Mary is a material witness in a murder investigation. Believe me, the police can force her to go back."

"Sarah?"

Both of us turned. Mary sobbed.

A blond man with a hunter-green carry-on came over to us. He wore Nikes, jeans, and an anorak over a Ragg sweater. He looked puzzled. "What's the matter?"

Sarah said, "This is my husband, Jerry." She turned to him. "I'm sorry we weren't there to meet the plane. Mrs. Dodge

181

spotted Mary. She knows her." They were a great family for foggy pronouns.

"Uh-oh." Jerry Pierce set his bag on the carpet.

"She wants Mary to go back to Kayport."

Mary sobbed harder.

I said, "I do not personally care what Mary does. I don't have the authority to force her to do anything, either. But I saw her, I know she's alive, and I'm going to let the police know where she is. I not only want to do that, I have to do that."

Pierce said, "Yes, I can see that."

"What do you do for a living?"

He blinked. "I'm a social worker."

"A public employee? Then you'd better call the police, too, if you value your job."

That was the wrong approach. His jaw set.

I backtracked. "I'm just trying to explain to you that this could be a serious matter. If Mary comes forward now, voluntarily, I don't think there will be any penalties, but she's going to have to tell the police everything she knows about the killing."

Mary choked out a muddled statement to the effect that she hadn't seen anything.

"Then why the panic? You didn't witness the murder?"

"No!" she wailed.

I slung my shoulder bag to my other shoulder. "I don't understand." I looked at Pierce and his wife. "And I don't understand how you two could let Mary's parents imagine she was dead. That's what they think. That's what everybody thinks."

Sarah said nothing but her eyes filled with tears.

Great, I thought. It runs in the family.

Pierce said, "Look, Mrs. . . . ."

"Dodge," I said. "Lark Dodge."

"Well, Mrs. Dodge, Mary is with us because she's afraid of her family."

My eyebrows shot up.

"Not of her parents, exactly," he added. "Of her brothers. They bully her. Hell, that's a euphemism. They treat her like a caged animal. And Sarah and I don't owe the Sadats anything. They opposed our marriage, and when we went on seeing each other, Sarah's brothers took me out behind the restaurant and beat me to a pulp. I spent three days in the hospital."

"Oh." I remembered the Dean's reaction to the Sadat brothers.

"I got myself transferred to Portland as soon as I could, and when I'd found a place to live I sent for Sarah. We got married two years ago in Reno and her parents haven't communicated with her since. As far as they're concerned, Sarah is dead."

"Not my mother," Sarah said. "I let her know I was all right."

Pierce scowled. "Yeah. Well, when the boys beat me up, they beat Sarah, too. If Mary says she's afraid of them, I believe her, and I'm not sending her back. She's Sarah's sister and she can stay with us as long as she wants to."

I said, "Then what do you think we should do? She can hide from her family, but she can't hide from the police. Not indefinitely. And I still have to report that I saw her."

Pierce rubbed his forehead. "Gawd, what a mess."

"All right." I was conscious of Francis Hrubek waiting alone in the baggage area. "Look. I'll leave you to work it out. At the very least, Mary should call Dale Nelson or Lisa Colman in the Shoalwater County sheriff's office. What I want is your address and telephone number, Mr. Pierce. Maybe, when Mary explains the situation, the police will take her statement here. She'll have to go back eventually to testify. If she doesn't know anything much . . ."

Pierce said unhappily, "She knows something. I couldn't get it out of her."

"She'll kill me, too," Mary wailed.

I drew a breath. "If by 'she,' you mean Bianca Fiedler, I think you're wrong, but if she is a murderer, then I want her

183

brought to justice. If you don't give evidence, Mary, Hugo's killer may never be caught. Please stop blubbering and think a little."

Mary just cried harder.

Sarah said, "She won't calm down now. And she won't tell you anything, either. Leave her alone."

I looked at Pierce.

He shrugged and dug out his wallet. He handed me a business card.

"This isn't your home phone."

"You're a hard-nose," he said without rancor and got out a pen. He took the card from me and scribbled on the back of it. "There you go. Address and phone number. We won't go away."

"Word of honor?"

He nodded.

I stuffed the card into my handbag. "Okay. I'm a fool to trust you, Jerry, but I do. Call the sheriff."

He nodded.

"I'm going to," I said. "Immediately."

"Give us time to get her calmed down."

I stared at Mary's heaving shoulders. I admit it. I don't understand weepers. Mary was getting her way, though. If it works . . .

Pierce picked up his bag. "Haul her up, Sarah. I'm taking the two of you home."

Sarah levered Mary to her feet and the three of them started off toward the terminal, Sarah supporting her still-weeping sister. I paced them as far as the first bank of telephones. Then I dug out Pierce's card, opened the phone book, and verified that there was indeed a Gerald Pierce at the number he had indicated. I tried to call Jay without success. I also called the sheriff's office and left a message that included Pierce's name and phone number.

The whole melodramatic episode had taken twenty minutes. It was past time for me to rescue Francis Hrubek.

15 ⨾

I FOUND HRUBEK with some difficulty in the scrimmage of passengers near the Delta baggage carrel. He did not look happy. When I spoke his name, however, he composed his features into a kind smile and asked if I had found my friend.

I drew a long breath. "Yes. I do beg your pardon. I'll explain everything. . . ."

He was handing me his plane ticket. "Look for the black bag with a green plaid ribbon on the handle, and point me to the nearest men's room."

I walked him to it and went back to the carrel. Luggage was still tumbling down onto the conveyor belt. The passengers scrabbled and bumped each other. I stood back and watched. Eventually I spotted the bag. When I heaved it from the conveyor, I realized that Hrubek had exercised a mild revenge. I came close to rupturing a disc. Books, no doubt. The bag had wheels and a telescoping handle, though, so I pulled it after me to the carpeted hallway and waited until he emerged from the restroom. When he didn't see me, I said his name again.

"Ah, you found it." He beamed at me through the thick lenses.

"Yes. Do you want me to drive the car around or shall we walk to it?"

"Walk," he murmured. "My legs need stretching."

So we crept across the zebra-striped walkway to the parking structure, me trailing the black bag with the green ribbon.

I even remembered where I had left the Honda.

When we finally reached I-5 North and the traffic thinned, I said, "I owe you an explanation."

"Eh?"

"For abandoning you in the baggage claim area."

"My dear young lady," he said with the elaborate courtesy of his generation, "it is I who am in your debt for meeting the plane."

I shot him a sideways glance and decided he was as mad as a hornet. Hrubek was a major writer, after all, and I was supposed to cosset him. I had even forgotten to mention the clerk at Powell's books.

Too late for autographs. I swallowed. "It's this murder, you see."

"Murder?"

"Didn't Bianca tell you that a member of her staff had been murdered?"

"Oh, the young man who was killed. Murdered, you say."

I felt the flame of pure rage. Damn Bianca. "Murdered," I said firmly. "The woman I chased after is not a friend. She's a material witness and she's been missing for more than a week."

He twisted to face me. "Missing?"

"And presumed dead." I explained. In fact, fueled by my anger, I talked from Vancouver to Clatskanie.

Though I was furious that Bianca had not made the situation plain to him, Hrubek seemed more interested than appalled. He listened with the murmurs and cues that signal encouragement, but when we drew up at the town's sole light, he said, rather plaintively, "I don't suppose you'd be willing to stop for a burger?"

I looked at the dashboard clock. It was eleven-thirty. "Lord, your stomach's on Eastern time, isn't it?" I negotiated an abrupt right-hand turn and pulled into the parking lot of a restaurant I knew. "We can do better than a hamburger."

The least I could do was to buy him lunch.

He did want a burger—a double cheese with a mountain of fries—though the restaurant specialized in seafood. I had the shrimp salad. We ate in friendly silence. I finished first.

He bit into a large greasy french fry with the relish of a man who has fallen off a low-cholesterol diet. "That's more like it. Hadn't you better telephone your husband again?" I had explained my futile attempts to communicate with Jay and Dale.

"Will there be anything else?"

Distracted, I looked up at the waitress. "No, I . . ."

"Another cup of your splendid coffee, my dear." Hrubek contemplated the final french fry.

The waitress gave him a professional smile. "Right away, sir."

"Uh, I'll take the check," I muttered. She handed it to me and went off for the coffee pot. I stood up. "I'll call Jay and then settle this." It was the kind of restaurant where you pay the cashier.

"Take your time, Lark. Thanks for the snack."

Snack? It occurred to me as I paid the tab that Marianne was going to enjoy Francis Hrubek. Irks care the crop-full bird?

The hospital switchboard paged Jay again and this time he picked up the phone.

My relief was disproportionate.

He had gone home for a couple of hours for a shower, he said. Dale had driven him, and he'd returned in the Toyota, so I wouldn't have to pick him up. Jason had still not regained consciousness. Worse, he had developed pneumonia, but the doctors thought it would respond to medication. Jay sounded very tired.

When I told him I had found Mary, though, he perked up.

"Holy shit! You mean she's alive? Is she with you? Christ, this puts a spin on everything. . . ."

"Jay!"

He gave a laugh that was pure exuberance. "I love you, babe."

"Well, I, er, love you, too." The phone was quite near the

187

cashier's counter and the people lined up to be seated were listening to me with every sign of interest. "Mary isn't with me."

"What!"

"Jay, pipe down. I didn't have any kind of authority over her and, believe me, she doesn't want to come back to Kayport." I moved closer to the phone and gave him a recap of my encounter with Mary in a low voice. He kept making small sounds of astonished disbelief, but I knew he was drinking it all in, even the irrelevancies. I finally wound down. "And get through to Dale, will you? I tried."

"Right away."

"Will he accuse me of tampering with his witness?" I was feeling a little anxious, because I had already tampered with the candy maker in Seaside.

Jay gave a snort. "He's more likely to kiss your feet—if Mary doesn't take off again. What was the address?"

I read it to him and the phone number as well. He said Dale would probably ask the Portland police to interview her. I wondered if they would take her into custody. I didn't like that thought but I didn't express it. I did emphasize Mary's emotional fragility and I think Jay listened. He told me again that he loved me, a sign of extreme ebullience and some kind of record. I said I'd see him in a couple of hours.

I went back to my captive writer with a huge sense of relief tempered by uneasiness. Hrubek rose when I started to sit down again and said he wanted to use the rest room. I followed him as far as the lobby and stood there looking at the old photos of logging camps that decorated the walls between shelves full of kitsch and costume jewelry. The place was a tourist mecca in summer, but the crowd that Sunday were locals. My thoughts drifted to my bookstore. Two more weeks and I'd be dealing with tourists myself. I could hardly wait.

U.S. 30 follows the cliffs along the Columbia, except for a few recent straight cuts through the forest above it. The driving can be tricky in bad weather, but that day the road was dry and almost free of traffic. Hrubek's long flight—and the cheeseburger—put him rapidly to sleep, so I had time to think about things.

Mostly Bianca. I was by then convinced she had killed Hugo, though I still had no idea of her motive. In this judgment I was influenced by pure fury. It was bad enough that she had manipulated me. That she should practice gross deception on a man of Hrubek's stature seemed to me both immoral and foolish. Clearly she was capable of anything.

I glanced at the snoozing writer. He had reacted to my revelations with some shock, but he hadn't seemed angry. I supposed Bianca had conned him, as she had conned me.

Mary had said repeatedly that "she" would kill her, too. The "she" couldn't be Angie. Angie had an alibi. Of the two other women, the obvious choice for the role of murderer was Bianca. It had taken me that long to admit the obvious because I was in denial. I hadn't wanted Bianca to be the killer because I hadn't wanted to admit what a patsy I'd been. It was that simple.

I screeched around a curve marked 35 MPH and the rear end of the Honda slewed. I slowed down. No point crashing the car because I was mad at myself.

Crashing. Could Bianca have engineered Jason's wreck? Would she have known he was likely to take the shortcut? Not impossible, I told myself firmly. Besides, the crash might not have been rigged. Jason was more than capable of running the pickup off the road without assistance.

As we approached Astoria, the highway reverted to its 1930s origins and began twisting. I geared up and down repeatedly and Hrubek began to stir. At Tongue Point a camper pulled out in front of me going twenty and I had to brake hard.

Hrubek sat up with a snort. "Where are we?"

"Astoria. We cross the river again here. It takes about forty-five minutes from the bridge to the farm."

"I had quite a nap, then."

We crawled into Astoria. "Feel better?"

"Less mush-brained." He burped. "Sorry. Tasty burger."

The sluggish camper turned off at a supermarket and I speeded up to thirty-five.

Hrubek was peering out the window. "Nice town?"

"I like it. Lots of nineteenth-century carpenter gothic architecture, big Scandinavian population."

"Fishermen."

"Yes, though the salmon runs are vanishing."

"According to William Clark, salmon jumped out of the river into the Indians' nets in 1801."

I eased through a yellow light. "The salmon die-off is a rotten shame."

"What's causing it? The dams?"

"Partly. Partly clear-cutting. That raises the temperature of the streams the salmon spawn in. The loggers deny it. They blame the Russian and Japanese fishing boats offshore."

Hrubek clucked his tongue. "Plenty of blame to go around. I wish I could see better. I have the feeling I missed some spectacular scenery."

"And some spectacular clear-cuts." We were approaching the bridge. From the east, the sheer height of the span over the ship channel is stunning. I knew when Hrubek caught sight of it because he drew a sharp breath.

"We're going up on that? Looks like a roller coaster."

The traffic lights were with me. I eased onto the winding ramp that leads up to the bridge. As we reached the apex of the the span Hrubek said, "Freighters?"

Three cargo ships lay at anchor below in the river. "Astoria is the first port of call for a lot of trans-Pacific shipping. Most of the vessels go upriver to Portland, but they take on their pilots here and let the crews loose for a little R and R."

"Must make for lively Saturday nights."

We swooped down onto the lower segment of the bridge. The incoming tide had covered the mud flats at mid-river, though meandering lines of foam betrayed their presence. Across the water the hills on the Washington shore stood out

190

in sharp focus, for once. Sometimes they disappear in a gray mist. The water was a deep blue-gray.

Hrubek wriggled his shoulders in the seat harness and gave a small sigh. "You'd better tell me what I need to know about Spider Woman."

There were no flies on Francis Hrubek.

I gave him a restrained evaluation of Bianca's life and accomplishments. I did my best to sound neutral.

He said, "You're a loyal employee."

That was too much. "I'm not an employee at all," I said grimly. "I'm an independent book-dealer she conned into helping her with the workshop. I was also the murdered man's landlord and I liked him. In my opinion, Bianca should have cancelled the workshop when Hugo's body was found. At the very least, she should have warned you that you're being thrust into the middle of a murder investigation. She is . . ." I hesitated. "She's a suspect," I finished lamely.

"I see. What shall we do about it?"

I eased to a stop at the end of the bridge. "I don't know, Mr. Hrubek."

"Frank."

"Thank you, Frank. I threatened not to show up, and Bianca got around that. It's too late to cancel the workshop."

"Oh, the workshop will happen. You misunderstood me. I meant, what shall we do when the sponsor is hauled off to the pokey?"

"Contingency planning?"

He smiled.

So we talked it over. By the time I turned off the highway at Meadowlark Farm, I felt much less panic-ridden. I also learned some interesting things about Hrubek.

He was not a naturalist by training, as I had assumed. He had a degree in journalism from Columbia and had worked on several urban dailies before deciding that modern journalism offered no room for thoughtful discussion of long-term issues. Growing up on a Depression-era farm, he understood gardening, as Hugo had understood it, from his mother. Sometime in the 1950s Hrubek had begun serious reading about the environment, and his work had grown from those roots. He was, in short, the ideal writer to guide young journalists through the ecological wilderness. Bianca had found him, had persuaded him to lead off her workshop. She deserved some credit for that. Doubt nibbled at me. Maybe she wasn't a killer. Maybe she was just annoying.

The farm looked idyllic in the soft spring sunlight. I slowed for the cattle guard and inched my way up the empty drive. As we neared the house, I felt my anger and apprehension sharpen. How was I supposed to deal with Bianca, believing what I did? I had encountered murderers in the past, but I had rarely had to deal with them once I knew they were killers. By that time they were in custody. Bianca would probably read my suspicion the moment she clapped eyes on me.

I parked the car in the lot near the car barn, beside the red Cherokee Keith usually drove. It looked as if it had just been washed. When I had set the brake and killed the engine, I turned to Hrubek.

"If you don't mind, Frank, I'd like to make another brief call to the hospital. Then I'll take you in and get you settled."

He made no objection and I picked up the phone. The switchboard operator paged Jay several times with no result. Something must have happened. My stomach knotted. "Will you page Louise Callender?"

Fortunately Louise was the deputy on duty. She picked up the phone almost at once.

I identified myself.

"Oh, Mrs. Dodge, you just missed him. Jason regained consciousness about an hour ago. Dale and Jay took a statement and then they left."

Apparently Dale had not come out to the farm yet as planned. He was probably on his way. Bianca was going to appreciate that. "Did they say where they were going?"

"Dale meant to phone the lab, and he wants Judge Kononen

192

to swear out a warrant. . . ." She broke off as if she'd said too much.

I felt a prickle of excitement. "A search warrant or an arrest warrant?"

I wasn't surprised when her voice cooled. "I'm afraid I can't say, Mrs. Dodge."

I thanked her and replaced the receiver.

"Good news?" Hrubek asked.

"I don't know," I said slowly. "Something's happening." I released my seat belt and turned to him. "Thanks for your patience. I suppose we ought to go in."

He smiled. A nice man. I popped the trunk lid and got out of the car.

I lugged Hrubek's bag as far as the mudroom and left it there. Then I led him through the kitchen. I heard voices and was not surprised to find everyone still seated around the dining table. Marianne had told me she was going to serve the main meal at one so she could take her time arranging goodies for the reception.

As we entered the dining room, Bianca jumped up and turned around to greet us. She homed in on Hrubek as if I weren't there, charm at full wattage. I gritted my teeth.

Keith rose from the far end of the table and Del and Mike stared. Angie gave a tentative smile. Marianne got up and sidled past us to the kitchen.

When Bianca had finished her effusions and introductions, she turned to me. "We thought you might make it back in time for lunch." Her tone conveyed mild reproach.

I found myself immune to the tiny manipulation. In fact, what I felt, looking into her intense brown eyes, was embarrassment. She had done something shameful and I was embarrassed for her, for the human race, possibly.

"Frank's bag is in the mudroom." I was sure my face was red. I blush when I'm embarrassed. I looked away and met Keith McDonald's blue gaze. He smiled. Trust Keith to spot my discomfiture.

Marianne poked her head through the swinging doors. "Dessert?"

"In the living room." Bianca made a wide gesture. "I'll show Mr. Hrubek the conference facilities and Mike can take his bag to Hugo's room, er, the guest room. Then coffee and chocolate mousse in the living room."

At "chocolate mousse" Hrubek's face lit up. He followed Bianca off like a puppy trailing a brass band. Bianca probably expected me to join the grand tour but I stayed behind.

Mike stood up.

"I left the bag in the mudroom," I muttered. "It's heavy."

He nodded and slid from the room, silent like his mother.

"Good trip?" Angie swallowed from a tall water glass.

"Okay. Good view of the mountains." I hesitated, irresolute.

Without rising, Del pulled Marianne's chair back. "Take a load off, Lark."

I sat, rubbing my right leg. I hadn't driven that far in some months.

"Glass of wine?" Del was downright cozy.

Keith seemed bemused. Tranquilized, perhaps. I considered relieving him of part of his anxiety. Keith cared about Mary Sadat. But Jay had said to keep my mouth shut.

A warrant. I took the glass of red wine Del poured me and sipped. It had to be an arrest warrant, and Dale and Jay had to be coming out to the farm. I could—should—have gone home, but I had no intention of missing the climax of the action. Besides, there was Marianne's chocolate mousse to consider. I wriggled my shoulders and felt the wine warm my stomach.

Angie stood up and began to clear away the dishes. After a few more sips of wine, I joined her. The men made no attempt to help us. In fact, Keith got up and went out into the hall. I could hear him on the telephone. Del sat like a lump. If he had put in half a day's work already, so had Angie. I expected her to make some comment but she just glanced at him and went on stacking plates. I gathered glasses and napkins.

In the kitchen, Marianne was pouring water into the coffee maker. "Trays," she said, without looking at us.

Angie handed me a gleaming teak tray and took one herself. "Keith's feeling a bit rocky today."

"What's Del's excuse?"

She grinned. "Terminal clumsiness. He drops things."

I felt my mouth twitch in response. "Convenient."

"Passive aggressive."

I had to laugh. Del was just plain aggressive.

Angie and I had the table cleared in no time. When we had stuffed the dishwasher to capacity and started the wash cycle, Marianne began spooning mousse into sherbet glasses. She slapped the brown gunk into the goblets and somehow it wound up looking like rose petals. It was an education to watch her.

Mike reappeared and his mother directed him to set up the small tables in the living room. He nodded and vanished. Marianne was piping a white substance from a squishy tube onto the pudding. I had the feeling the substance wasn't Cool Whip. Angie and I watched. Marianne gestured for a tray and began setting the sherbet glasses on plates that held two thin ginger wafers apiece. She set the loaded plates on one of the trays and picked it up. "Coffee'll be ready in a couple of minutes. Get the cups, will you, Angie?"

Angie put eight stoneware mugs and a stack of paper napkins on the other tray. "I suppose Hrubek uses sugar and cream."

I thought back to Clatskanie. "Cream. So do I."

She got a cream pitcher from the refrigerator and a fistful of spoons. "Coming?"

"I'll bring the coffee."

She hefted the tray. "Bring the whole shebang and plug it in in the dining room."

"Okay." The machine was into its final phase. I waited for it to finish burping, unplugged it, and carried it out the swinging doors, through the tidied dining room, and into the big sunken living room.

Under all this soothing domesticity I felt, like heartburn, the heat of my anger at Bianca. I was not going to be able to conceal it for long. Well, with luck I wouldn't have to. I kept my ears pricked for the sound of car engines. Where were Dale and Jay? Had they had to drive to Raymond? I tried to remember where Judge Kononen lived. Maybe he was in church. No, it was nearly two o'clock. He'd be home.

Keith, Del, and Angie lined up for coffee. Mike loped in from the residential wing and poured himself a mugful. I laced mine with cream. We made small talk, and I kept reminding myself to say nothing about Jason regaining consciousness and nothing about finding Mary Sadat. Something stirred at the edge of my mind.

Angie was asking Keith if he was going to play the guitar at the reception. He said no. He sounded depressed.

I sipped and poked at my memory. Then it came to me. I had been careful to say nothing about finding Mary myself but I had forgotten to warn Frank Hrubek not to.

16 ~

SURELY HE'D REALIZE . . .

I was sitting on the ledge of the hearth, clenching the handle of my coffee mug. I set the cup down, rose, and, elaborately casual, began to move toward the conference wing. I could hear Hrubek's voice quite near. Bianca laughed.

I glanced back to see if anyone was watching my furtive end run, but Angie, Mike, and Marianne were still chatting over their coffee, Keith stood at the French doors, sipping from his mug and gazing out at the spring scene, and Del had gone over to the whiskey decanter. I slid around the corner and started down the tiled hall.

". . . so I ducked back inside the lobby just as Mayor Daly's finest let loose with the tear gas," Hrubek was saying in his sweet gravelly voice. "Talk about environmental degradation."

Bianca laughed heartily as they emerged from one of the sleeping rooms. "Oh, Lark. Hi. I showed Frank the accommodations. He told me this great story about the crummy hotel he stayed in during the 1968 Democratic Convention. Did you come to fetch us?"

"Your mousse awaits you," I murmured, eyeing Hrubek.

He gave me a bland smile.

Bianca led the way. I trailed after Hrubek, hoping for a quiet word—to no avail. He was moving at a brisker clip than at the airport, hardly using the cane, and he stayed close to Bianca. She had invigorated him.

Everyone, notably Hrubek, laced into the mousse. Between listening for the patrol car and worrying that Hrubek would let something slip about Mary, I scarcely tasted mine. My stomach burned. I was standing by the fireplace. I set my sherbet glass, half full, on the mantel and leaned against the wall, trying to ease the tension in my shoulders.

Marianne went back to the kitchen with the coffeemaker— to brew another pot, she said. Keith had drifted toward us from the window, Del from the booze trolley. Mike spooned the last of his pudding, set the glass on one of the end tables, and excused himself. He had homework, he said, and went off. Bianca and Hrubek were exchanging hotel stories near the fireplace, Hrubek on the couch and Bianca on the hassock at his feet like a good acolyte. It was an affecting picture.

Out in the hall, the phone rang. Angie jumped up.

"Let Marianne get it in the kitchen," Bianca said lazily and Angie sank back on her chair. "Probably one of the conference participants looking for directions to the farm."

"What time do you want me this evening?" I asked.

"Six forty-five."

"Okay."

Bianca turned back to Hrubek and checked the workshop agenda with him. He was nibbling on a biscuit and didn't comment. Angie picked up a teak tray and began loading it with dishes. Del gave her his mug and sherbet glass. Keith went back to the windows. He seemed to be brooding.

I half-listened to Bianca charming her guest and wondered about the phone call. I would have to leave soon to change clothes and organize myself for the reception.

Marianne entered from the hall. "That was Dale." She glanced at Angie. "You're clearing up. Good. Let me get the other tray, too. I want to vacuum in here pretty soon."

Bianca stood and stretched. She wore one of her bright tunics over stirrup pants. Silver bracelets clanked when she raised her arms. "What did Dale want?"

"To interview us again." Marianne turned to go back to the kitchen. "He asked who was here."

Keith took a step toward her. "Did he say anything about a warrant?"

Angie plunked Mike's mug and dishes on the tray. "A warrant? What would he be searching for at this point?"

I glanced at Bianca. She had gone pale.

Del snorted. "Man needs a search warrant to find his own dick."

Nobody laughed. Hrubek was frowning. Keith moved in behind Hrubek's chair.

Marianne shrugged. "Dale said not to leave. He'll be right out. Do you want Mike to set up the chairs, Bianca?"

"Uh, no. Better wait till after Dale has come and gone. What a damned nuisance."

I was studying Bianca, trying not to be obvious about it, looking for signs of guilt. I didn't see any. She chewed her lip and looked irresolute.

Marianne glided away.

Angie confiscated my mug and my unfinished mousse. I supposed I should help her. Marianne came back with the other teak tray and took Del's whiskey glass from him. He surrendered it without a fight.

Keith said, "Let me carry that for you, Angie."

Angie had retrieved Hrubek's dishes and Bianca's. She looked startled at Keith's offer but handed him the loaded tray. "Thanks."

Keith walked off toward the kitchen. At the carpeted step up to the hall he stumbled a little and the dishes rattled on the tray, but he righted himself without dropping it and went in through the dining room. Marianne bunched a couple of paper napkins, set a mug onto her tray, and peered around. Vacuuming seemed redundant. The room looked good, almost ready for company.

When Keith came back, he was moving stiffly, hands at his sides.

"I should show you to your room, Frank." Bianca helped Hrubek to his feet and retrieved his cane for him. "The deputy will want to talk to the rest of us, so you might as well use the time to get settled. There's nothing you need to do. Why don't you take a little nap?"

Hrubek laughed. "Lark will tell you I slept halfway here in the car. . . ." He moved toward the door with Bianca following. He was so tiny she masked him from my view.

Bianca stopped short. "What the hell? Keith!"

"Sorry," Keith said.

Bianca's voice rose to a squeak. "Is that a knife?"

Beside me, I heard Angie gasp. I took a step forward, the better to see.

"Go easy, Bee." Keith had twisted Hrubek around and was holding a long thin knife, a boning knife, at the older man's collar. His left arm pinned Hrubek to him. "Back off."

Bianca didn't move.

"I said back off," Keith shouted. "Back off or I slit Hrubek's throat."

Bianca took a step to the side. I couldn't see her face and Hrubek's was blank with astonishment, but Keith snarled like a cornered cougar.

"What the shit . . ." Del levered himself to his feet, hands on the arms of his customary drinking chair.

"You, too, Del. I want you over by the fireplace. And Marianne."

Nobody moved.

"I mean it." A note of hysteria shook Keith's voice. He cleared his throat. "Dale may have a warrant for my arrest, but he's not going to take me."

Bianca said flatly, "I don't know what you're talking about."

200

Del and Marianne edged toward the fireplace. At any other time I would have found Del's pop-eyed expression funny.

Angie held out a hand. "You can't . . ."

"Don't tell me what I can't do, bitch." Keith dragged Hrubek back a step. Hrubek blinked. The knife gleamed at the knot of his necktie. "He's my hostage. Famous Frank. I'm taking him with me."

I swallowed hard. "Where?"

"What's it to you? I'm not going to stick around waiting to be arrested, that's for sure."

Bianca said, "You can't mean you killed Hugo."

I heard someone near me draw a sharp breath.

Keith gave a Jack Nicholson laugh. "You better believe it, sweetheart. I killed once and I don't mind doing it again." He sounded as if he were playing a new role and hadn't quite got the lines memorized.

"It's not like you, Keith. You wouldn't harm a fly." Bianca sounded tearful. "Put the knife down, please. You'll hurt him."

Keith was panting a little. "I don't want to. But I will if I have to. I called the hospital while Angie was clearing lunch away. Jason regained consciousness this morning, and Dale interviewed him."

"I don't understand," Bianca moaned.

"Dale put two and two together."

Hrubek cleared his throat.

The noise seemed to startle Keith. For a moment the knife wobbled closer to Hrubek's neck, then it steadied. Hrubek closed his eyes. Bianca gave a sob.

At that moment my brain stirred to life. There was a knife at Francis Hrubek's throat. Keith had destroyed one good man. He was not going to destroy another, not if I could help it.

Bianca pleaded with her husband, pulling out all the stops. He wasn't looking at her. He may even not have heard her. His blue gaze roamed the room and his eyes met mine.

No, I thought. No.

His gaze shifted.

I had to do something. But what? I am a physical person, an athlete by training, impulsive and impatient by nature, as American as cherry pie. Every squirt of adrenaline was demanding action. But I knew better. I knew if I made a dive for the knife Keith would slit Hrubek's throat without compunction.

My father's family background is Quaker. Not for the first time in my life, I wished he had raised me in that tradition. What Keith needed was friendly persuasion.

A car wheeled up, crunching gravel. All of us froze. I could hear Angie breathing. Keith's hand trembled on the knife.

The doorbell chimed.

Silence.

"Tell them . . ." Keith's voice was tight.

"It's the *front* door." I made my voice softer. "Front door, Keith. Dale always uses the back."

"A fucking Jehovah's Witness." Keith gave a wild laugh. "Go answer it. Tell them to leave. If it's the cops . . ."

"I'll get rid of them." I eased past Angie and walked slowly to the door. The bell chimed again.

My feet made no noise on the Berber carpet, but I was walking so lightly I would have made no sound on polished parquet. I eased the door open.

"Meadowlark Farm? You ordered flowers." The kid wore a single earring and had dyed his hair Shinola black. He thrust a big formal arrangement toward me. Daffodils and forced tulips, I thought. The flowers were bright under the film of translucent green paper. Wasn't Angie supposed to supply flowers for the reception? I wondered, with monumental irrelevance, if the daffodils were organic.

"Uh, thanks. I'll take them." I grabbed the box from him and set it on the hall floor. I started to close the door.

"You gotta sign, lady."

He took a pad from his jacket pocket and handed me a ball-point pen. I scrawled my name on the order with shaking fingers.

"Okay. Have a nice day." He turned and slouched down off the porch.

I closed the door with extreme care.

When I returned to the archway that led down to the living room no one had moved. Outside, the florist's truck started up and crunched away. The engine needed tuning.

"Who was it?" Bianca, her voice high with strain.

"Flowers for the reception," I said.

Keith gave a snort, half laugh, half sob. "All right. Now I'm going to take Hrubek out to the Cherokee."

Bianca began to plead with him. Her technique sounded automatic, as if she had used similar persuasion before in less harrowing circumstances. The rest of us listened and gaped. Keith's eyes kept shifting.

"How can you do this to me?" Bianca wailed at last. The clincher.

"Bianca," I heard myself say, "shut up."

"But . . ."

"Hush. Be still."

There was a moment of silence, then Keith laughed again, a high cackle. He must have watched a lot of horror flicks. I could see the knife trembling at Hrubek's throat. He was gray with fright. I probably was, too.

I stepped down into the living room very slowly. As I moved, Keith wheeled Hrubek to face me. "No farther. Stop right there."

"All right." I took three long slow breaths, in and out. The room was large and well-lit and there were other people in it, but my vision was so focused on Keith and Hrubek they might as well have been spotlighted on a darkened stage. "I don't understand why you need a hostage, Keith."

"I killed Hugo, you dumb cunt."

Angie drew a harsh breath.

Let it go, Angie, I thought. Let it go. Maybe she read my mind.

One of Jay's jobs when he was with the Los Angeles department was hostage negotiation. Difficult work, but interesting, he'd said. The hardest part was putting yourself into the perpetrator's viewpoint. The second hardest was listening.

Keith was still cursing—laying into Hugo, Angie, me, Bianca. I let the words roll past me.

When the torrent dried up, I said, very gentle, "You killed Hugo, but you didn't murder him, did you?"

Keith gaped.

I met his eyes and forced a conciliatory smile. "I'll bet it was just an accident. The two of you quarreled, and he fought with you and hit his head. You didn't mean to kill him."

"How did you know that?" The once-mellifluous baritone rang hoarse.

"A guess," I admitted. We stared at each other. As I looked into Keith McDonald's frightened eyes, I tried to think the way he thought. "Hugo hit his head on something . . ."

"The crates . . ."

"And he didn't get up."

"I tried to wake him." Keith drew an uneven breath. "I thought I'd just knocked him out, but he wasn't breathing and I couldn't find a pulse. It was raining. I didn't know what to do."

You could have called an ambulance, my analytical self said sternly. You could have tried CPR. I shoved Reason back into its cave.

"He was dead!" Keith sounded almost indignant. At least I could imagine Keith's shock.

"What happened then?"

"It was time for lunch."

He lost me. I blinked, groping for words.

"Lunch!" Angie exploded. "You left Hugo's dead body in the rain and came in for a little chicken fricassee? Christ, Keith, that's the coldest thing I've ever heard."

Oh, please, I thought.

Keith's voice took on a defensive whine. "I came back to the house and ate. If I hadn't, Marianne would've sent out a goddamn posse. I almost threw up at the table."

"Upsetting," I murmured.

He shot me a grateful look. "Afterward, I said I was going for a long walk, did anybody want to come. I didn't think they would. It was raining and the wind was blowing hard." The knife sagged. "I went back to Hugo."

Angie made a disgusted noise but didn't say anything, thank God.

"I hid the bike behind that stack of crates, and I used your cart to wheel him to the ice house, Angie." Keith's voice choked.

I thought of Hugo's mutilated corpse and clenched my teeth. I had to think like Keith. What did he want me to say? "It was clever of you to use the ice bin." I didn't look at Angie. Marianne gasped and began to sob.

Keith's eyes shifted. "I just . . . at first, I was stalling for time. Then I remembered the harvest schedule. I knew it would be a while before Bianca needed to use the ice house. I could move the body later."

"But you didn't go back?"

"N-no. I couldn't make myself go out there." He drew another ragged breath. "And what the hell does it matter? I'm getting away from here, and Hrubek's going with me. It'll take Dale a while to drive out. We'll be long gone by the time he reaches the farm."

"You mean you've been planning your getaway?" Del rumbled.

The right question.

"You're damn right. I had it all figured out. I was going to slip away during the fucking reception." Keith sounded proud of himself. His mouth tightened. "I figured nobody'd miss me."

Poor baby. Bianca should have asked him to sing. I swallowed my revulsion.

"I kept calling the hospital." Keith shifted the arm across Hrubek's chest. Hrubek's eyes were closed. "When they said Jason had developed pneumonia, I thought I'd have time to make a smooth exit. He wasn't supposed to regain consciousness." He cursed comprehensively.

I was thinking about the escape plan. The Cherokee had four-wheel drive. An all-terrain vehicle. On the other hand, it was bright red. Also, driving with one hand and holding a knife on an unbound prisoner was not a very practical proposition. Of course, Hrubek wasn't part of the original plan. He was, so to speak, a bonus.

I said, "About the Cherokee, won't it be difficult . . . ."

"There's a gun in the glove compartment." Keith's voice hardened. "There's a rope. I know what I'm doing. I'll tie Hrubek up in the back seat. I know a guy with a plane." There were half a dozen small landing strips in the area. "If there's no pursuit, I'll leave Hrubek in the car at the airfield. Otherwise . . ." He made the clicking sound associated with a throat-cutting gesture. "Tell Dale . . ."

I said slowly, "It won't work, Keith. Maybe Dale will hold off for now, but you can't count on it. My husband used to negotiate with hostage takers, persuade them to surrender peacefully. The last time he tried it, the lieutenant in charge called in the SWAT team while Jay was still talking. The man who was holding the hostages was shot to doll ribbons." And Jay was caught in the cross fire. What was likely to happen here was that Dale would pull in as Keith was leaving, give chase, shoot out the tires or some damned thing, and Keith would panic. He would kill Hrubek and be killed himself. Everybody would lose.

"I don't think it will work," I repeated. "Look, they can't charge you with first-degree murder if you turn yourself in. It was manslaughter, maybe even self defense—a fight that got out of control. That happens. People will understand. Hugo provoked you, didn't he?"

"He saw me with . . ." Keith glanced at his rigid wife. "He saw something and he misinterpreted. He was going to report it."

Mary. I hesitated, threw the dice. "There's something you should know before you make any decisions. I found Mary Sadat today. At the airport."

Bianca wheeled. Keith said something.

"She's alive?" Angie squeaked.

I nodded.

"Oh, thank God." Angie began to cry.

I kept my eyes on Keith. The knife in his right hand didn't waver, but the left clenched on Hrubek's jacket. I stopped breathing.

17 ～

WHAT I'D DONE was not very wise, because I didn't know for sure how Keith had interpreted Mary's disappearance. I hoped he hadn't been playacting the day we searched the farm for her. He had seemed genuinely distressed.

That Mary might have disappeared voluntarily had occurred to no one, certainly not to me. The police had been looking for a body, and the assumption was that whoever killed Hugo had also done away with Mary. When Mary disappeared, Keith must have been baffled, even terrified. Perhaps he even thought someone was framing him.

Keith's silence lengthened. I licked my dry lips. "Were you afraid the police would charge you with Mary's abduction?" Or Mary's murder. I didn't want to say that word.

The knife sagged again. Keith nodded and licked his lips, as if they were dry.

"Well, they won't now. All you have to contend with is a manslaughter charge." I kept my voice smooth and soft. I was lying madly, ignoring the small matter of Jason's wreck, the mutilation of Hugo's body, and the other attempts to shift the blame to innocent people. I hoped Keith wouldn't spot my omissions.

The blue stare held steady. So far so good.

"Mary will be a friendly witness, Keith. She likes you." I was tolerably sure Mary had no idea Keith had killed Hugo. Mary had been afraid of Bianca, not Keith. Understandable, given that Mary was canoodling with Bianca's husband under Bianca's nose. I thought of Mike Wallace's forlorn devotion and hoped Mary's misadventure would cure her of her taste for older men.

"You talked to Mary?" Keith was almost whispering.

"Not really, not in any detail."

He let out a long, relieved breath. Maybe, I thought, *his* misadventure would cure him of his taste for younger women. I doubted it. It was a good thing I hadn't claimed to know more of his relationship with Mary than I had.

Bianca said, "I suppose you were having an affair with her." She sounded indifferent. Her back was to the French doors, so I couldn't see her face.

Keith glanced at her and tightened his left-handed grip on Hrubek. Keith's arms must have been getting tired by then. He didn't respond to Bianca.

Angie blew her nose. The noise exploded in the silence. Keith jumped. I jumped. Hrubek winced.

"You found Mary at the *airport?*" Angie sounded wounded. "Where was she going?"

I suppose Angie imagined herself in Mary's confidence. Certainly she thought of Mary as her protégé. I could sympathize with the ego blow, but it was not the time for convoluted explanations. "She was there with her sister, Angie. Finding her was pure luck."

"Sister? I don't understand. . . ."

At that point, I made a mistake. I glanced at my watch.

Keith's right hand jerked. Hrubek made a noise halfway between a gasp and a hiss, and Keith's grip tightened. "I'm getting out of here. Now. I need to get away—now!"

The wheels of my mind spun. "Christ, Keith, think. You're a smart man, a Ph.D. If you take Hrubek off as a hostage, you not only make yourself liable to a kidnapping charge, you also lose the benefit of any doubt the prosecutor may have about Hugo's death."

He wasn't listening. He began moving sideways, toward the

archway, toward me. "Get out of the way."

I stood my ground. "Kidnapping's a federal offense. Do you want the FBI on your tail? I don't know what arrangements you've made with your pilot, but I'll bet you didn't tell him you were a fugitive from justice." That was shaky. If, as I had begun to suspect, the friend was some kind of drug runner, he wouldn't care that Keith was fleeing to avoid prosecution.

"Besides," I added, inspired, "he won't be waiting for you. He's expecting you after dark. You'll have to hang around some dinky airstrip for hours, Keith. By that time, Dale will have all the cops in the county hunting for you, or hunting for your landing field, which will be duck soup for those guys. They know every cranny of the Peninsula."

Keith hauled Hrubek another step in my direction but he was listening. I could tell because the blue eyes darkened. His pupils dilated, I guess. I kept watching his eyes.

I softened my voice. "They'll throw the book at you if you harm Hrubek. Honest, Keith. If you cooperate, though, if you let Frank go and wait for the police peacefully, Bianca will have time to call your lawyer."

"Mayer? That pompous jerk couldn't settle a speeding ticket."

I said, soothing, "He's probably not a criminal lawyer, but he'll know the right people to call. Come on, think about it. A really big-shot criminal lawyer like F. Lee Bailey. You can afford the best in the country. Think what a guy like that could do to the Shoalwater County prosecutor."

He was thinking. He didn't say anything, but he frowned, he hesitated. I held my breath. I'd wondered what he'd planned to do for money. Bianca was the one with deep pockets. I had taken another risk. My luck would run out sooner or later.

Bianca came through. "Keith, honey," she said in a voice so throaty it would have done one of her father's leading ladies proud, "I'll call Paul, and I'll call Brevart in San Francisco, too. Mama's lawyer. He'll know what to do."

"Hell," Keith said. "Hell."

"The best defense money can buy, Keith. Come on, babe. Let us help you."

I took up the choral manipulation. "Where were you going, Keith? Mexico? That's a long flight in a light plane. The pilot will have to refuel a couple of times. Each time you land, you'll risk finding the police waiting for you. You'll have to pay the pilot for all that extra fuel, too, and you won't be able to use credit cards. Do you have enough money? Mexico is hard on people without money." I was hoping he didn't have a secret cache of negotiable bonds. "Or was the guy just going to fly you to Portland? Believe me, by the time you get to Portland they'll be watching every ticket counter and departure gate. Dale's already in touch with the Portland police because of Mary."

"Hell," Keith repeated. "Oh, all right."

And it was over, just like that. He released Hrubek, who crumpled to the floor. Keith looked at the boning knife in his right hand as if he weren't sure how it had got there.

I was breathing like a runner. I held out my own hand, raising it very slowly, palm up. Our eyes locked again. Then he gave me the knife, reversing it and laying the hilt on my palm.

I edged sideways, out of his range, and walked to the fireplace. Angie, Del, and Marianne were staring at me. Marianne's mouth compressed in a tight line.

"It's your knife," I croaked. "Put it back where it belongs."

"I'd rather stick it in the bastard's guts." Her eyes, swollen with weeping, were hostile.

"Marianne . . ."

She gave a sniffle, took the knife from me, and half ran from the room.

Bianca was bending over Hrubek with Keith at her elbow. Keith looked dazed. I couldn't see Hrubek's face. To be truthful, I was more concerned about Keith. He would start thinking again at any moment.

211

I strode over to them. "Bianca, the lawyer."

"But Frank . . ."

"Angie can help him. Come on, Keith." When I touched his tweedy jacket, he shied like a spooked horse. I patted his arm. "Come and sit down."

"I . . . uh, okay." He followed where I led him, docile, but for how long? Never mind that Marianne was right, it was not the time for forthright expressions of opinion. Not yet. We had to keep Keith calm until Dale arrived, and God knew how long that would take. Keith could still panic.

Throughout the interminable scene, I had been listening for the patrol car, hoping it wouldn't roar up and impel Keith into murderous action. Now I wanted it to sweep up, lights, siren, and all. Not to mention Jay.

I led Keith over to the comfortable armchair Del used for serious drinking and got him to sit. I perched on the arm and kept my hand on Keith's sleeve. I wasn't going to let him out of touching distance until I saw him in handcuffs.

From the hallway, Bianca's voice rang clear and loud. She had a great many faults but dumb she was not. I heard her, Keith heard her. She was calling in the lawyers.

Angie had regained her composure and common sense. She knelt by Hrubek, talking to him in a low voice. When he stirred, she helped him sit up. I suppose he had fainted from the strain, as who shall blame him? I had feared a heart attack. I hoped he hadn't injured himself falling.

Angie said something and Hrubek's voice rumbled a reply.

"Del," she called over her shoulder, "he wants a drink."

Keith shifted in the armchair.

I said, "That's a good idea, Del. Fix Keith a whiskey, too, will you?"

Del cleared his throat. "Yeah. Sure, right away." He sounded as meek as one of his unshorn lambs. He poured Hrubek a jolt of neat scotch, then measured out two shots over ice cubes with a spritz of soda. He brought that glass to me.

When he saw my expression, he said, "He don't like it plain." Del didn't look at Keith.

Keith was not taking in the subtleties of the situation. He gulped his drink, ice clacking on his teeth, and gulped again. His hands were shaking.

I could sympathize with that. As the adrenaline ebbed, I had begun to tremble, too. I hoped Keith wouldn't notice. All I wanted to do was curl up somewhere and go to sleep, but that natural impulse was just going to have to wait.

Nobody was saying anything, nobody was looking at Keith. That was dangerous. Keith was a boy who liked the limelight. I tried to think of a distraction. Ideas popped up like crocuses in January and withered on the brainstem—the weather, politics, the baseball strike. I even considered mentioning the great folksongs that had come out of American jails. Fortunately I thought better of the Midnight Special.

We waited. In the hallway, Bianca talked. She was on to a different lawyer now, her voice still calm and clear. Marianne came back with a glass of ice water for Hrubek, and between the two women they got Hrubek to his feet. He announced with dignity that he had to use the bathroom and Angie took him off to the residential wing. He leaned on her.

I watched them out of sight. If Keith had hurt Hrubek I would never have forgiven myself—or Bianca. Maybe I wouldn't forgive Bianca anyway. It was her fault that Hrubek was there at all. At least she wasn't a murderer.

Suddenly I remember the blasted reception. I did not look at my watch again, but I was sure hours had passed. At any moment half a dozen slavering journalists would start circling the farm like jackals. I did not doubt I would be the rawʳ meat Bianca would toss to them.

Marianne said something to Del. He shook his head no. They glared at each other, and Del went back to the fireplace. He sat incongruously on Bianca's hassock. I could feel him watching Keith, keeping his distance, but Marianne walked over to me.

"Is there anything I can do, Lark?" She still avoided looking at Keith.

I suppressed a wild impulse to tell her to whip up a coffee cake. "You could help Angie with Frank Hrubek. See if he wants a doctor."

The lines of her face eased. She nodded and glided off, once again a woman with an understandable purpose in life.

Keith had finished his whiskey and was staring at the ice cubes. I thought of the ice house the day Marianne and I found Hugo and my gorge rose. How could Keith have done that? I had called him clever. I despised myself.

In the hallway, Bianca fell silent. I heard the phone click as she hung up the receiver. Keith's head turned. He watched his wife reenter the living room, walking slow and careful. I thought she might ignore him and go over to the sunlit window again, but she turned and came to us.

She faced Keith without expression. "I left an urgent message for Paul Mayer."

Keith jerked up straight in the armchair. "Message!"

Her mouth tightened. "He wasn't in, Keith. It's Sunday. I'm sure he'll come right out as soon as he listens to his tape. Brevart is flying up tomorrow morning to coordinate your defense."

Keith's shoulders eased back against the chair.

"I left word for the twins to call, too."

He stiffened again. "No! Don't tell them yet."

Bianca's intense brown eyes were bleak as winter. "They have to know what's going on."

"I can't talk to the boys." I could feel Keith's agitation.

It was unlikely that he'd be free to talk to his sons anytime soon, but Bianca refrained from saying so. She turned to me instead. "What time is it in Italy?"

After a blank moment, I cast my mind back to my last trip to Europe. "Uh, nine or ten hours' difference, I think."

"Too late, then. I'll call Mama and Fee in the morning."

"I need another drink." Keith's voice held a tight edge of hysteria.

Del stirred on the hassock, but Bianca took the empty glass and strode to the drinks trolley. She splashed scotch over the half-melted ice cubes and brought the glass back. No seltzer.

Keith took it from her, swallowed, grimaced.

Bianca rubbed her hands on her tunic, as if the brief contact with her husband had been physically soiling. "About the reception tonight, Lark, I've been thinking...."

Thinking? When had she had time to think? I tried to frame a diplomatic response.

"Hi, guys."

Our heads jerked.

Mike Wallace bounced into the room from the conference wing. He must have come down the spiral staircase from the computer room. "Hi! What's happening?"

All of us gaped at him. After a moment, Del stood up. "Come out to the kitchen with me, son."

"Hey . . ."

Del took Mike's arm and led him away.

So there we were, Bianca, Keith, and I, all set for a tête-à-tête. Keith stirred.

At random, I said, "That song you played at Hugo's memorial service, Keith, the Scottish song . . ."

"The 'Lament for Charles Stuart.'"

"You sounded so sad. That was why I decided you hadn't killed Hugo deliberately." I was just trying to make conversation, but I realised with a small jolt that I had stumbled on the truth. Of course, I hadn't known at the time what had really happened. In fact, the song had misled me into thinking Keith was innocent. He was not innocent, just not guilty of murder.

Keith began to cry. I took the glass from him and handed it to the still-expressionless Bianca. Then I patted his shoulders. *Will ye no' come back again?* Not if you're dead. Keith buried his face in his hands and wept. I patted. I was damned if I was going to hug him.

Bianca placed the whiskey glass on the trolley and walked to the French doors. She stood there, staring out at the brilliant afternoon with her back to us. Thinking again, no doubt.

Keith sobbed. I soothed. Off in the kitchen, I heard Mike's high excited voice asking questions. There were a lot of questions to ask.

When Dale finally arrived, he came to the front door, just like the florist. Del let him in. Jay was with him, and Lisa Colman and another deputy. They forged right in after the briefest of exchanges, so it was clear that Del hadn't tried to explain anything.

When the doorbell rang, Keith grabbed my hand. His was hot and damp. I didn't try to pull away.

Lisa marched right up to us. "Keith McDonald, I'm arresting you for the attempted murder of William Johnson and Jason Thirkell. I should warn you that other charges are pending. You have the right to remain silent. . . ." She had the Miranda warning letter perfect.

As she recited the familiar words Jay caught my eye. Keith was still holding my hand in a desperate grip. Jay raised an eyebrow. I grimaced and sat still.

I did see Keith McDonald in handcuffs, though there were preliminaries. Bianca told the detectives she had called the family lawyer. Lisa asked her to call again. Keith stayed silent. It was all very proper.

The Wallaces and Angie filtered back into the living room, drawn by the anticlimactic drama of the arrest, and eventually Lisa, Dale, and the anonymous deputy went off with Keith. Somebody rescued the hothouse flowers from the front hall. The phone rang—one of Bianca's sons. She withdrew to her suite to talk in private. I had no idea what she was thinking and I didn't want to know.

Jay had stayed behind when the police left. "So what happened?" he asked. "Obviously something did." The question—Mike's question, too—triggered a babble of explanation. Everybody talked including Mike. Everybody except me. I just sat there on my perch and shook.

Jay came over and stood behind me. He rubbed the back of my neck with a warm hand. It felt good but didn't stop the shaking. After a few minutes, he walked around and sat where Keith had. Then he pulled me down onto his lap and wrapped both arms around me. That did help. I burrowed in his chest.

"My wife needs something hot to drink," he said. "Hot and sweet."

Marianne broke off an indignant comment on Keith's character. "I'll fix tea." I thought I might be forgiven, eventually.

The explanations went on. I burrowed and shook. I suppose I looked foolish. Jay and I are the same height, so my knees and elbow were sticking out at odd angles. I didn't care. I kept my eyes shut tight and thought about all the awful things that could have gone wrong.

But nothing had. Keith was in custody.

Marianne brought the sweet tea, which I dutifully drank, and I finally stopped shaking. By that time, as they say, Jay was in possession of the facts. When I had stopped jittering, he boosted me up and stood beside me, arm around my shoulders.

"I'm going to take Lark home now." He fished in his pocket. "Mike, here are the keys to the Toyota—that crummy car parked in the front drive. Will you move it out of the way? I can get it later." He tossed the keys and Mike fielded them.

"The reception," I mumbled.

"Home," Jay said firmly.

"I'm coming back."

He gave me a squeeze. "I can't stop you, if you insist, but you're coming home now."

"There's no time!"

"Nonsense. It's only three."

I couldn't believe it. I checked my watch. He was right.

Jay looked around. "Coat? Purse?"

Angie went off to find my things. When she returned, she helped me into my jacket and draped my handbag over my shoulder by the long strap. "I have a message for you from Frank Hrubek."

"Oh, God—Frank. I should have asked . . ."

"He'll be fine, Lark. He's a tough old bird."

I heaved a sigh. "That's a relief. I was so scared. . . ."

"All of us were. Anyway, Frank said to tell you thanks."

"That's the message?"

"No. The message is 'Plan B.' He said you'd know what he meant."

I gave a shaky laugh. Our contingency planning was going to pay off.

18 ~

FOR REASONS BEST known to himself, Jay didn't take the faster Ridge Road home. Perhaps he wanted to talk. If so, he must have found my dazed silence annoying. We were entering Kayport before I came out of my preoccupation sufficiently to ask about Jason and Bill.

Jay geared down at the first stoplight. "Bill's a little better. The doctors think he'll be partially paralyzed, though."

I swallowed nausea. Bill was the classic innocent bystander.

The light changed and Jay eased down Main Street past my darkened bookstore. "Jason regained consciousness right after you called me from Clatskanie, and he was able to give Dale a fairly coherent statement."

"And?"

He grimaced. "He and Bill saw McDonald with Mary."

"In Seaside?"

"Yes. They also saw Hugo speak to McDonald outside the candy shop. They weren't close enough to hear what was said, but Jason says Groth was angry."

"Wow! Why didn't they say something sooner?"

"Jason claims he didn't think much about it until Mary disappeared. McDonald was always fooling around with women students. And Jason didn't like Groth."

I digested that. "But Bill and Jason told the police they hadn't seen Hugo at all the day he was killed. Why did they lie? Was Jason blackmailing Keith?"

We rolled past the hospital and out onto Highway 101. "Jason insists he just talked to McDonald. The kid's smart. He isn't admitting anything, and maybe he didn't ask for money, but I suspect McDonald interpreted what Jason said as blackmail."

"Was that enough to charge Keith . . . ?"

"Enough to suggest he tampered with the pickup, anyway. We found a witness at the college. She saw McDonald hanging around Jason's rig Friday afternoon. She took the ballad class last term, so she's sure of the identification."

"Student or staff?" Staff members often took classes.

"Student. Another groupie," Jay said wryly. "Still, she thought McDonald's behavior was odd. There have been car burglaries, most of the faculty are long gone by four on Friday, and it was a student lot. If she hadn't recognized McDonald, she would have called security."

We were both silent, I thinking about the difference that call might have made.

"A damned shame she didn't call it in." Jay shook his head sadly. "Dale got a preliminary report on the pickup. The lab says the line that carries fluid to the power steering was cut."

"But Jason drove all the way home and a long distance on that back road before the wreck."

He shrugged against the shoulder harness. "It was cold out. The line wasn't severed, just slit. The fluid dripped out slowly."

"But wouldn't he lose his steering?" I'm a willful car moron. I don't want to know what goes on under the hood.

"No, darling, he wouldn't," Jay said with elaborate masculine patience. "Just the *power* steering. It was probably sluggish well before they reached the worst of the curves, but Jason might have made it off the mountain if he hadn't been speeding. And if the road surface had been dry."

"Then the wreck wasn't inevitable."

"No."

"Keith was just hoping?"

"I don't pretend to understand McDonald's mental processes."

I had spent some effort that afternoon trying to understand Keith's mental processes. "It sounds half-assed to me."

Jay passed a dawdling senior in a long Lincoln. The needle dropped back to fifty-five. "Keith *is* half-assed."

"Of course, it would have worked if you hadn't insisted on searching for the pickup."

"True."

"Keith is capable of forethought. He planned a quiet escape from the farm for this evening. He had it all set up. Then he saw Hrubek and heard Dale was coming, and he took Hrubek hostage."

Jay made a clucking sound. "English majors—creatures of impulse."

"Cut it out." I brooded. "I told him I thought they'd just charge him with manslaughter if he surrendered peacefully. He believed me, I think. Did I . . ." I started to ask whether I had lied to Keith and discovered I didn't care. I groped for words. "I didn't jeopardize anything, did I?"

Jay glanced over at me. "Only your life, my sweet. I wish you'd stop doing that."

"He was going to slit Frank Hrubek's throat!"

He said gently, "You did what had to be done, Lark. Don't worry about it. Let the lawyers figure out what the charges should be."

"Mary . . ."

"Mary can probably give Dale some idea of McDonald's frame of mind the day Groth was killed."

"And Hugo's, too. Mary wouldn't talk to me at all." I twisted sideways, the better to see his face. "What do you think happened?"

Jay slowed as the camper in front of him signaled a left turn. "I didn't know Groth, so your guess is as good as mine. Better, probably." The camper turned off and the Honda picked up speed. We were almost at the village of Shoalwater. Jay said, with diffidence, "I got the impression Groth had strong principles."

"He wasn't a fanatic!" Even as I protested, I wondered. Fanatic was Angie's word for Hugo. Fanatical and rigid.

"How do you think Groth would have reacted, if he thought McDonald was hitting on one of the female students?"

I closed my eyes and tried to visualize Hugo's face. It was already fading, a sad ghost. "He wouldn't have liked it, but I think he would have talked to Keith before he reported anything to Bianca."

"Or to the Dean."

That was a possibility I hadn't considered. "But Bianca was Hugo's employer, and they had a lot of history."

Jay stopped at the only stop sign in Shoalwater. There was no traffic at all, but I spotted a patrol car at the Grub 'n Stuff Drive-in. "Does she care about Lover Boy's infidelities?"

I thought about it. "I don't know. Today she seemed indifferent, but I've heard her say some pretty bitter things about Keith."

Jay chuckled. "You ought to hear the Dean on that subject."

"All the same . . ."

"She hasn't divorced the sucker yet, and God knows she's had grounds."

"True."

"I think Groth threatened to report McDonald to the college. He must have known McDonald was already on shaky ground because of the earlier harassment charges." He headed out of town on the country road that leads to our house. "Since Groth was technically also a faculty member, in the sense that he was supervising our students, the Dean would have had to take his evidence seriously."

"He'd listen to Hugo, but not to someone like Carol—is that what you're saying?"

"Not exactly." He topped the ridge and began to wind down the steep hill that leads to the Shoalwater Approach and home. "A lot of women on campus believe a male administrator won't take their word against a male faculty member. That's not quite what happens. At least with the Dean."

"Then what does happen?"

"He doesn't want to believe anything negative. Typically he postpones action until something forces him to take steps. Then he overreacts. He forced McDonald to resign as department head, for example, instead of instituting a process of counseling and observation. Seemed to think he'd solved the problem."

"Clearly not."

Jay sighed. "My point exactly. So McDonald stepped down, bellyaching."

"I suppose he thought he was the aggrieved party."

"Yeah. Sexual harassment is a touchy subject."

I glanced at him, wondering whether he was touchy about it, too.

His mouth twitched in a grin. "And he went right on acting like a bird in mating season."

I flashed on a TV special I'd seen on avian courtship and had to suppress a smile, too. Good old Keith, flicking his tailfeathers and warbling sweet songs. My amusement faded. "He's an idiot."

"He's not real sharp."

"What I don't understand is why it would matter so much to him to keep the teaching job. Bianca has more money than the GNP of Paraguay. Keith doesn't have to work."

Jay swerved around a pothole. "Come on, Lark, it's his identity. He revels in it. Bianca is an overwhelming personality. She was probably overwhelming as a twenty-year-old hippy. Now she has big money, too. She'd *erase* the guy if he was dependent on her."

I rubbed my forehead. "I don't think she means to overwhelm people." Why was I defending Bianca? I changed the subject. "Why did Hugo go out to the greenhouses to talk to Keith?"

"Instead of to the farmhouse? So Bianca wouldn't overhear."

"I thought you said she wouldn't care. Be consistent."

He slowed the car for a sharp curve. "It's all speculation. You knew Groth. How would you explain it?"

"I don't think Hugo would have wanted to hurt Bianca unnecessarily. Maybe he thought he could reason with Keith. So Hugo met Keith at the greenhouses, and they fought." And Hugo hit his head and died.

Jay pulled into the driveway and set the brake. "Groth was smaller and lighter than McDonald. I think McDonald attacked. There's more than one head wound. He may even have meant to kill Groth, but it's hard to prove intent."

I thought about Keith's behavior that afternoon. "More likely he just panicked. But he did mutilate the body . . ."

"And leave it where he thought it would incriminate the Vietnamese crew. That stinks."

"Will it make a difference?"

"To the charges? Maybe. A good defense lawyer might get around it. It *will* matter when it comes to sentencing."

We got out and went into the house through the back door. My kitchen looked bright and welcoming. I didn't want to leave it. I made a pot of coffee.

Jay watched me. "Why don't you go for a run?"

I pressed the button that turns the coffeemaker on. The device cleared its throat. "I don't have time."

"You have two hours, sweetheart. Go for a run and take a long hot shower afterward. I'll fix us something to eat."

I gave him a hug. "You're terrific."

He kissed me. "You, too. Go on, Lark. Scoot."

What he didn't tell me was that Dale would be waiting in my nice bright kitchen when I came down from my shower—waiting and wanting another statement.

I dashed into the kitchen and slid to a halt.

"Hi, Lark." Dale raised his coffee mug in salute. He looked exhausted but content.

"Jeez, can't it wait until tomorrow?" I had known he would want a statement sooner or later.

"Is tomorrow better?" It wasn't. Dale didn't wait for a reply. "The prosecutor has to know what happened this afternoon. May affect the amended charges."

"Okay." I glanced at Jay. He was making toast and sautéing something. All of a sudden I felt ravenously hungry. "Omelets?"

"With mushrooms and goat cheese."

"Hotsy-totsy."

He grinned and spooned the mushrooms into a dish. "Neither of us has done any grocery shopping lately. That's the cheese you bought at Christmas." He ducked down so he could see Dale through the pass-through. "Want an omelet?"

"Uh, sure. Thanks."

So we ate omelets and I filled Dale in on the events of the afternoon. He recorded a lot of chewing and slurping. As he turned the machine off and stowed it in its leather case, he said, "Good thing you talked McDonald out of it before we got there. I hate a hostage situation."

"Bianca talked him out of it." I finished my third cup of coffee. I was going to be wired. "She promised him F. Lee Bailey."

Dale snorted. "That'll make the prosecutor's day."

"*You* talked him out of it, Lark." Jay's voice was warm with approbation. So I didn't argue.

He took me out to the farm but said I'd have to drive myself home in the Toyota.

I got out and faced him over the roof of the Accord. "You could come back and get me."

He smiled. "Not on your life. I'm going straight to bed. I got about two hours' sleep on that damned hospital cot last night."

"I'll tell you all about the workshop over breakfast."

He mimed a kiss and got back in the car. I watched him drive off and wished I could go with him.

Frank Hrubek was sitting at the butcher-block table in the farmhouse kitchen, eating an enormous sandwich and eyeing Marianne's canapés. He greeted me cheerfully.

I divested myself of coat and purse. "Are you okay?"

"Never better. Thanks to you, my dear."

Marianne took something from the oven, set it on the tiled counter with a thump, and said Bianca wanted to see me. Somebody didn't think I was wonderful.

I wasn't up to pacifying Marianne, and I didn't want to see Bianca, either.

Marianne said her employer was off in the conference wing showing the last of the journalists to their quarters. I took that as a hint to leave Marianne's domain. Frank smiled at me around a bite of sandwich.

Two strangers—one male, one female—fell silent as I entered the living room. I gave them a distracted greeting. They told me their names and I forgot them immediately. The flowers were in place, someone had built a fire, and the room looked like an upscale hotel lobby—in other words, Keith's melodrama might as well not have happened. Whatever her opinion of me, Marianne's price was above rubies. I checked to make sure someone had photocopied Frank's handouts and the participants' schedules. Then Bianca entered from the conference wing.

When she saw me, she walked over, her face as blank as it had been for Keith that afternoon. There were no effusions of greeting. She was pale but composed. "I'm going to make a statement at eight. I'll leave everything else to you and Frank."

Thanks a lot. I made no comment. She nodded and went over to talk to one of the writers.

Plan B got off to a fair start. Frank's charm and Marianne's goodies kept the journalists happy for an hour. Del and Angie circulated. All of us except Bianca trouped down to the seminar room and the reporters admired the amenities. When we climbed up to the computer room, they went into a feeding frenzy. They accessed the Internet, scanned data bases, dived into the library. Two of them started playing games, and one, a woman with frizzy red hair, borrowed a laptop. The others had brought their own. Angie and Del conferred in a far corner. At least they were speaking to each other.

Frank and I stood back against the French windows and watched the writers mill, Frank smiling to himself, I listening. It was safe to assume they hadn't heard of Keith's arrest yet. Bianca was going to create a sensation.

When Frank and I finally herded the participants back to the living room, she was waiting by the fireplace. She was all but tapping her foot.

Bianca had a lot of presence and she looked great for a woman whose husband had just been arrested. She was wearing one of her tunic outfits, but that night the colors inclined toward melancholy—blues and muted greens. She climbed up on the ledge of the fireplace and launched into speech.

She identified herself with charming modesty, thanked the writers for coming, said she was sure they'd learn a great deal about sustainable agriculture, and pointed out that the first session, preceded by coffee and muffins, would begin at nine A.M. by which time the broccoli harvest would be well underway. I had forgotten the broccoli.

One of the writers, a grizzled veteran of newsrooms from L.A. to Vancouver BC, said, "What about this killing, Ms. Fiedler?"

She gave him a melancholy smile calculated to freeze him with guilt. "Your curiosity is understandable. I have some information for you. This afternoon my husband, Keith McDonald, was arrested."

That got their attention. The redhead with the laptop plumped down on the nearest chair, flipped the computer open, and thumbed it on. The others began fumbling in purses and jacket pockets for notebooks.

Bianca told them the charges and explained briefly about Jason's wreck. She waited for them to quiet down. "As you may imagine, I and my staff are devastated. I would have cancelled the workshop, but it was too late."

Liar, I thought without heat. If she had given me a single reproachful glance, though, I would have walked out.

She touched her eyes with an honest-to-god lace handkerchief. "Keith's lawyer has advised us not to comment on the case. It is, as it were, *sub judice,* and I'm sure you won't want to jeopardize Keith's defense. My staff . . ." She looked around—at Del, at Angie, at Marianne, who was bringing on a fresh tray of crudites, at me. "My staff have agreed not to give interviews."

That was news to me. I glanced at Frank. He winked.

Rumbles of protest from the journalists.

Bianca smiled another brave, guilt-making smile. "I do understand that you'll want color stories, however, and of course you may photograph the farm. Lieutenant Colman of the Shoalwater County Sheriff's Department will be holding a press conference at one tomorrow afternoon at the courthouse."

That was going to screw up the workshop schedule. I began mentally rearranging the first field trip—a tour of Angie's greenhouses. Fortunately, we had set the Shoalwater Bay expedition for Tuesday afternoon. I wondered how much science writing the journalists would do, given the temptation to file fiction with the *National Enquirer.*

Bianca gave the reporters nothing more. They tried, of course. For ten minutes, they battered her with provocative, leading, and occasionally stupid questions. She just stood there, smiling her guilt-inducing smile, and shook her head. Then it occurred to a couple of them that the bare fact of Keith's arrest was a story they'd better sell while the market was hot. The frizzy redhead made for the kitchen phone and the grizzled veteran for the hall. The others soon dispersed in search of other telephones. I think the phones in the conference wing were extensions, but perhaps not. The reporters didn't return.

Bianca sent Del and Angie off, and Marianne began clearing away the food debris. Frank Hrubek stuck around the living room long enough to make it clear to Bianca that, arrest or no arrest, the workshop was going to continue under his eagle eye. He wanted no more interruptions of the schedule. She agreed meekly. He shook her hand, grasped mine, stood on his tiptoes, and kissed my cheek. Then he shuffled off to bed. We watched him go. What a man.

"Lark . . ."

I turned.

Bianca's face was again without expression. "Keith wants to see you."

"No," I said politely.

"He's very depressed. He wants to talk to you."

I looked deep into her intense brown eyes and lost my temper. "I do not want to talk to Keith. Ever."

She blinked.

In case she had not grasped my point, I added, "I despise Keith. I loathe what he did to Hugo." I'm afraid my voice was rather loud, but I had had this small problem of getting a negative through to Bianca.

She glanced toward the conference wing. "The journalists . . ."

"The hell with them," I howled. "Do you know that Bill Johnson is paralyzed? Do you care?"

Her eyes brimmed tears. "But you sounded so understanding. . . ."

"I was lying through my teeth, Bianca. I just wanted Keith to hand over that knife. I will not, repeat, *not,* go to see him in jail or anywhere else. Tell him that."

"Okay." Her voice was mild. She looked ruffled, even embarrassed.

It was not the response I expected. I probably gaped like a fish.

"Then you didn't mean what you said about F. Lee Bailey?"

"That was the inspiration of the moment."

She looked at the carpet. "I don't intend to squander my, er, patrimony on Keith's defense lawyers. He's guilty. If the charge is manslaughter, I think he should plead guilty. If it's murder, I'll pay for a decent Seattle lawyer, for the kids' sake. But I won't waste Eli Fiedler's fortune defending the indefensible. Hugo was a good friend to me. A better friend than Keith." She frowned at the floor. "Besides, I have other uses for the money."

"The study center?"

She nodded, still not looking at me. "And the minute the verdict is in, one way or another, I'm filing for divorce."

"Well," I said. "Good."

She looked at me finally. Her brown eyes were soulful. "I couldn't get through to Keith this afternoon. Thank God you did."

Considering I had told her to shut up, I thought that was pretty generous. I said goodnight and went home.

I suppose the workshop was a success. It produced three published articles on sustainable agriculture, a tribute to Frank's ingenuity, knowledge, and charm. He worked those writers hard. They barely had time to file six news stories, three color pieces, and an interview with Carol Bascombe.

Bianca had forgotten to warn the interns not to speak to reporters and Carol obliged them. She was very colorful. The broccoli harvest went on all week, though Bianca had to hire Mei Phuoc's youngest son as interpreter. Frank left early Thursday morning, but not before he signed my stock. I was sorry to see him go.

By Saturday, when the other workshop leader, Eric Spielman, left in a rental car with the last of the reporters, I was near collapse, Keith had been charged with second degree murder, and Trish Groth had given birth to a healthy baby girl.

An eventful week.

I had recuperated sufficiently by Wednesday to leave Bonnie in charge of the store. It was Jay's spring vacation, so he took me to Raymond in the Accord. I brought a bouquet of Angie's certified organic daffodils and my favorite edition of *A Child's Garden of Verses.* Jay dropped me at the door of Trish's small, trim house, and told me he'd be back in half an hour. Tactful. I thought that might be about twenty-five minutes more than I could bear, but I didn't protest.

Trish answered the door herself. I had phoned, so she was expecting me. It is a cliché that new mothers look radiant. Some, I am told, look like death warmed over, but Trish shone—her hair gleamed, her complexion glowed, and her smile beamed like a spring morning. She also looked about fifty pounds lighter. "Come in, come in. The baby's asleep but we can take a peek. What lovely flowers!"

I won't say I was instantly at ease, but I felt more cheerful. Trish's mother, a slim woman with a champagne rinse and a fashionable pantsuit, shook hands, smiling, and effaced herself. Clearly she had no reservations about grandmotherhood.

Trish led me back to her bedroom. The baby was sleeping in a bassinet by her mother's bed. "I'm nursing her," she murmured, running a finger along the baby's rose-petal cheek. The baby, who was wearing a lace cap, yawned and gave a tiny snort.

"What did you call her?" I whispered.

"Jane Christine. Jane for Jane Austen, Christine for Christine de Pisan, the medieval writer." Trish caught my expression and laughed aloud. "Hey, I'm a librarian! I promise to call her Jenny." She ushered me back to the living room. "That's what Jane Austen's brothers always called her."

I had to smile. In the lace cap, the baby looked a bit like the only extant portrait of Jane Austen.

Trish pulled me down beside her onto a comfortable sofa and unwrapped the book. "I love it. Look at the photographs."

I had found the 1940s edition my mother read to me. The photos are black and white, and pure magic.

Trish turned the pages slowly, savoring. "I've already started reading to her. You can't begin too soon."

"I know."

"Listen!" She began to read. She had a great voice and she didn't sing-song the verses.

> When I was down beside the sea
> A wooden spade they gave me
> To dig the sandy shore.
> My holes were empty, like a cup.
> In every hole, the sea came up,
> Till it could come no more.

She choked on the last line. "Oh, God, I miss Hugo."

I hugged her and said nothing.

She sniffed and gave a watery laugh. "Though why that poem should remind me of him . . ."

"Well, there's an emptiness." I swallowed. "But life is filling it. Maybe that's why." I thought about Hugo. He hadn't approved of Trish's pregnancy, but he had approved of life.

We were both crying by then. Fortunately, Trish's mother came in with tea and cookies, and the baby started howling, so it was all right.

Jay was waiting for me when I made my exit.